PRAISE FOR THE SILVER MYSTERY SERIES

"The main characters are compelling. Foiled Silver has everything: humor, mystery, even a little romance. You keep reading as the excitement builds to a smashing and surprising conclusion!"

—Dana Newman, Executive Director,
Talbot County Free Library

"Susan Reiss captures the magic, mystery and charm of that quintessential Eastern Shore town – St. Michaels. Secrets lay hidden for generations among the stunningly beautiful estates along the Miles River. Can't wait for her next 'silver' adventure."

—Kathy Harig, Proprietor,
Mystery Loves Company Bookstore

"*Tarnished Silver* is a fabulous debut novel! Abby Strickland is someone I can relate to, my kind of heroine. I admire the way she rises to the challenges thrown in her path. She's a brave and loyal person whom I would love to call a friend (if she were real, of course). Susan Reiss is a great storyteller, and I'm really looking forward to more stories in the Silver Mystery Series.

—Kassandra Lamb, author,
Kate Huntington Mystery Series

"Silver, art and murder lead to an exciting read!"

—S. Jennifer Sugarman, artist

"This series will transport you to the Eastern Shore of Maryland, but will remind you of whatever town has a special place in your heart—hopefully without murder. It leaves me wondering what other secrets this quaint little Eastern Shore town is hiding and I'm waiting for Susan Reiss to tell us."

—Barbara Viniar, Retired President
Chesapeake College, Wye Mills, Maryland

"This is a series that captures the local flavor of our area – St. Michaels, the food and the quirky characters who live here and visit. The descriptions of all the real places make me feel like I'm there. The mystery kept me turning the page. This is a series I recommend to my library patrons… and to you.

—Shauna Beulah, Branch Manager,
St. Michaels Library

SILVER MYSTERY SERIES BOOKS

Tarnished Silver
Sacred Silver
Painted Silver
Hammered Silver
Foiled Silver

TARNISHED SILVER

SUSAN REISS

Ink & Imagination

Published by Ink & Imagination Press
ISBN: 978-0-9893607-1-5

This work of fiction was inspired by the Plein Air Easton Art Festival. Any resemblance to a person, living or dead, is unintentional and accidental.

Cover Design by Damon Freeman
Interior Design by Jennifer Jensen
Author Photo by Bob Bader

Website: www.SusanReiss.com
Facebook: Susan Reiss
Twitter: @Susan Reiss
Goodreads.com: Susan Reiss, Goodreads Author

For Joey
Then, Now and Always

CHAPTER ONE

Silver: a soft, gray-white element mixed with other metals to craft table utensils, serving pieces and hollowware used for fine dining and entertaining. The metal becomes hot easily. Be careful not to burn one's skin. Properly maintained, it reflects light beautifully.

—"The Butler's Guide to Fine Silver" Mr. Hollister, 1898

The ocean waves lapped at my toes. Their warmth caressed my foot then tickled my ankle. I pulled my leg away but the wet strokes continued up my leg. I pried open one eye and a furry black head with floppy ears popped up, tail wagging. I squeezed my eye shut and silently begged, *Oh, please let me back into my dream on the sandy beach by the blue water.*

No such luck. Simon, a solid Labrador retriever puppy, jumped on my body with a thud, so happy that I was awake. He pranced around the bed, triumphant that he had escaped the kitchen once again. Only a temporary guest, he was certainly making himself at home.

That's when all hell broke loose.

The ding-dong of the doorbell cut right through my brain and sent Simon flying off the bed and downstairs. I pulled the pillow tight over my ears, willing the person to go away. But the doorbell chimed again and again as someone held a finger on the button. Simon scampered back into the room, threw back his head and howled.

No fair. It's Saturday morning. A glance at the clock confirmed it was too early for a visitor. I groaned when I realized it must be Christine, my next-door neighbor. Anytime she could get her husband to watch the baby, she'd zip over to my place and paw through the boxes of antique silver. They'd arrived unexpectedly as part of my great aunt's estate. For the past several weeks, Christine was helping me unpack the pieces so they could go up for auction on eBay. I should say, I organized them, she oohed and aahed, then I organized them again.

The doorbell stopped ringing. Maybe she gave up. No, she'd switched to rapping her knuckles on the door. Simon flew down the steps again while I silently prayed that he didn't fall and break his neck. The sound of sharp claws scraping at the front door propelled me to my feet and into a pair of sweatpants and a sweater. I didn't need to pay my landlord to repair the damage made by a puppy that wasn't mine.

"I'm coming!" *As if anyone could hear me over all the barking.*

Simon returned and scampered around my feet as I carefully navigated my way down the stairs. There ought to be a law against determined neighbors and energetic puppies so early in the morning. From force of habit, I glanced at the mirror in the hall. I tried to smooth down my reddish-brown curls and wiped a mascara smudge from under my green eyes. My skin looked a little pale, nothing that a little sun couldn't fix though I'd have to use blush more often now that I was approaching thirty and didn't want a face full of lines and wrinkles. At least the freckles were pale too. Good enough for the next-door neighbor.

I turned and what I saw through the little windows by the door stopped me in my tracks.

It wasn't Christine outside.

There was a man wearing a dark business suit looking back at me. Slowly, he placed a badge against the glass. The police? I grabbed Simon by the collar and pulled him close to me.

"Shhh, that's enough. Be quiet." I whispered. I wanted to tiptoe back upstairs and hide. But the police knocked on the door again, watching me. I shook off that strange feeling. *Why should I hide? I haven't done anything wrong.*

I straightened up and deposited Simon back in the kitchen behind the gate. I opened the door with the chain in place. After all, you can never be too careful when you live alone.

"Yes, can I help you?"

"Good morning, I'm Detective Collins with the Virginia State Police," he announced in a cold, no-nonsense voice that matched his icy blue eyes. Tall and lean, his carefully pressed suit, white shirt and blue striped tie underscored his authority. "Miss Strickland, this is my partner Detective Granger. You are Abigail Adeline Strickland, aren't you?"

"Y-yes." My voice quavered when it should have sounded firm and innocent.

"May we come in, Miss Strickland? We need to ask you some questions."

After I looked at his identification, I released the chain and the two men squeezed into the hallway of my cozy townhouse.

Automatically, I led them to the living room, which was a mistake. The chairs and sofa, even the tables were covered with stuff. Both detectives eyed the mounds of silver along with the cartons and packing material cluttering the floor. They didn't touch anything but they seemed to inventory everything.

"Are you moving, Miss Strickland? May I call you Abby?" asked Collins, trying to be friendly now that he was inside my house.

"No, I inherited all these pieces and now I'm selling them bit by bit on eBay." I looked around the room with a sigh. "I don't have room for it all as you can see. Go on in the kitchen while I put the dog outside."

Simon was reluctant to be banished to the backyard. By the time I got back to the kitchen, the men had sat down at the table. The dirty dishes in the sink were a little embarrassing but what could I do? I wasn't expecting company this morning.

"Sit down and I'll put on some coffee."

"We don't need coffee, ma'am," announced Collins.

"Maybe you don't, but I do." As I started my coffee-brewing ritual, my hands were shaking. *Get hold of yourself.* I stole a look at the two men. They might be partners but they were mismatched. Detective Granger, with a Marine buzz-cut, wasn't much taller than my 5'8" and his jacket seemed a little strained by the effects of a few too many doughnuts. *Stop it,* I told myself. *This is no time for jokes.* It was the other man, Detective Collins, who sent a cold shiver through me. He sat up straight in the chair without touching his back to the chair. He opened a file folder. No time for chit-chat. He'd come to investigate a crime but I couldn't figure out what would bring them to my door.

Calm down. You haven't done anything wrong. To be honest, I hadn't done much of anything... right or wrong... for weeks but unpack silver and list it on eBay. Except for that quick trip to Annapolis yesterday. I started filling my mug before the brewing cycle was done.

"Sorry to bother you so early but we need to ask you a few questions," he said. "Abby, do you know a woman named Lorraine Andrews?" he asked.

I sloshed coffee on the counter. So, this was about my quick trip. "Yes, sir. I met her in Annapolis yesterday." His eyes narrowed as he waited for more of an explanation. I was starting to feel like a bug under a microscope. "She bought a silver cake breaker from me on eBay night before last. Right after the auction closed, she sent me an email asking me to meet her, to deliver it. So, I did."

"Why did she want a cake breaker?" He stumbled a little over the name of the serving piece. He was probably more comfortable talking about guns than antique silver.

"She said she was giving a dinner party – tonight, actually –

and she needed to serve a special dessert called the Fair Winds Torte. I recognized the name of the cake because it keeps popping up in the food pages of the paper."

"I bet the recipe would be worth some money to a fancy cooking magazine," Granger said.

"I have no idea." My head was turning back and forth as each man spoke, making me a little dizzy.

"Why did she want that cake breaker?" asked Collins.

"She said it matched her silver pattern and she wanted to serve the governor a slice of his favorite cake without the filling squirting all over the place."

"So, she told you the governor was coming to dinner?" Collins asked.

I nodded and Granger made a note in his little spiral book then he looked around my kitchen. It didn't take him long to focus on the hanging rack loaded with pots, a large colander, a variety of whisks and a soup ladle. "Looks like you're serious about cooking."

Not sure where this was going, I played along. "I like to experiment with soufflés and stews. They make a good dinner for one person."

Collins joined in. "Do you like to bake?"

"No, not really. It usually means cooking with chocolate and I don't need the calories." I sat down, wrapped my hands around the coffee mug. "Look, you didn't come here to talk about soufflés or cakes. Why don't you tell me why you're really here?"

Detective Collins glanced at his partner, pulled a photograph out of his file and handed it to me. "Is this the cake breaker you sold to Lorraine Andrews?"

It took only a moment for me to answer. "Absolutely not. The one I sold Lorraine was in pristine condition. This piece is so mangled I can barely identify it as a cake breaker. What happened to it and how did it get red paint all over it?"

Collins ignored my questions. "Abby, how do you know Evelyn Truitt?

"Who?"

"You don't know the name Evelyn Truitt?' asked Granger.

I shook my head and started to suspect they were playing some cop game with me.

Collins pointed at the picture. "That's not red paint, Abby. It's blood. Your cake breaker was used to murder a woman last night."

I let go of the picture and it fluttered to the table. "M-m-murder?"

"Yes, ma'am."

I couldn't get my breath, thinking about the bright, energetic woman I'd met the day before. "Lorraine?" I asked softly, not wanting to hear the answer.

"No, ma'am. Evelyn Truitt was murdered in Lorraine Andrews' house on the Maryland Eastern Shore. The victim was Mrs. Andrews' housekeeper," Collins reported.

My voice squeaked as I asked. "The lady who was making the cake for the party?"

"What?" Both policemen asked at the same time.

"Lorraine said her housekeeper was making the cake. Is that the woman who was killed?" Collins nodded. "How sad." A sigh escaped my quivering lips. "Lorraine was so excited about the cake."

Collins was watching me closely. "So, you did know Evelyn Truitt."

"No." I couldn't believe the police were grilling me about a murder committed many miles away while I sat in my own kitchen. As the reality of the situation started to sink in, I felt I had to defend myself. "I didn't know Evelyn Truitt. I've never even been to the Eastern Shore." Then a thought struck me. "How does a person kill somebody with a cake breaker?"

Detective Granger rubbed his chubby hands together. "We figure he grabbed the handle, swung the thing hard, right into the victim's neck and yanked—"

"Detective!" snapped Collins.

My coffee turned to acid in my stomach at the vivid description.

In a calm, almost friendly voice, Collins said, "I don't think it was premeditated. It sounds more like a spur-of-the-moment reaction, a violent response to someone or something."

Was he trying to get me to confess?

Granger added, "Yeah, who plans a murder with a cake server?"

"Cake breaker!" I said and looked away, embarrassed by my spontaneous reaction.

Detective Collins looked at me closely. "Abby, where were you last night after nine o'clock?'

My breath caught. He was asking if I killed somebody. "I-I was..." I forced myself to breathe and began again. "I was here at home working on the silver, identifying pieces, setting prices and opening auctions." I rubbed the knot of nerves in the back of my neck. "I don't know what's going on, but there's one thing I know for sure. I didn't kill anybody – with a cake breaker or anything else. And I certainly didn't kill somebody for a cake recipe!"

The men studied me, waiting. The only sound was Simon clawing at the door. He started yipping.

"You'd better let your puppy in before he destroys your door," said Detective Collins softly.

Numb, I went and opened the door. Simon tumbled in and charged the two men. While he nuzzled and wrestled, I said a silent thank-you for distracting them so I could get myself together. *Murder. Selling silver was supposed to be an adventure, but not this, not murder.*

"You might want to get a crate for the dog," suggested Collins, holding on to Simon's collar.

How typical of a policeman to come up with a jail cell for a puppy. "I don't think that's necessary—"

He interrupted me. "Lab puppies are very active and love to chew until they're about two years old."

I shook my head. "It's not necessary." He started to press his point, but I plowed ahead. "He's not my dog. I'm only puppy-sitting."

Collins closed his mouth, released Simon and looked at his folder again. It felt good to score a point against these men who had disrupted my morning though I filed away the idea of a crate, just in case. I gave Simon a dog cookie as a reward while Collins read an incoming text on his cell phone.

He nodded at Granger and closed his file. "Well, Abby, thanks for your time. We appreciate all the information." They got up to leave.

As Collins went out the door, he turned and said, "Abby, I wouldn't contact Lorraine Andrews right now. You don't want to be involved any more than you are already."

"I told you, I did nothing but sell a nice lady a silver cake breaker. Nothing." I insisted.

"I guess that was enough," he said as he turned and walked away.

CHAPTER TWO

Tarnish: that which dulls or discolors the luster of a shiny surface; to stain, soil or destroy the purity of something or someone.
—"The Butler's Guide to Fine Silver" Mr. Hollister, 1898

Simon clawed at my leg. He didn't care that the police had questioned me about a murder. He wanted his breakfast. Now.

Just as I filled Simon's bowl and put it on the floor, there was a knock on the door again. Were the police back before I could eat some toast to settle my stomach? Annoyed, I pulled open the door and Christine breezed past me, her shoulder-length blonde hair bouncing in a perfect flip.

"Abby, I had no idea you were entertaining guests so early in the morning. It's so unlike you." Her Southern-belle accent was thick as molasses on a cold day. "If I'd known, I'd have brought over some of my banana bread. Oh, well." She shrugged as she turned and headed toward the living room, a woman on a mission. "My Marvin will take care of Baby John for awhile so I can help you work on this lovely silver. Now, where did I leave off?"

Left standing alone by the door, I groaned. One cup of coffee was not enough to fortify me for a visit from Christine. My cell phone chimed from the kitchen. When did I get so popular?

The caller ID flashed the name of a once-close friend. "Morning, Reg. You're up early."

"Abby, I'm glad I caught you." He was a little out of breath. "I need a favor."

I was surprised. This man wanted a favor from *me*, the person who handled the technology for his new software startup, the person who was now unemployed because he had closed the company a month ago. Only the thought of our friendship over the past five years kept me from punching End Call.

"What's up?" I said, hoping my impatience didn't show.

"Something's happened down at my aunt's place in St. Michaels on the Eastern Shore. I heard about it on the news. I keep calling but she's not answering the phone at Fair Winds or her cell. I have a bad feeling about this. I need to go down there. I want you to go with me."

Bells were going off in my head. *Eastern Shore? Fair Winds?* Could it be that Reg's aunt was Lorraine, the silver collector? No, that would be too much of a coincidence.

"Abby, Abby," Christine rushed into the kitchen. "You have to see what I found in Box #4." She grabbed my arm and pulled. "You have to come."

"Abby? Are you there?" demanded Reg.

"I'm here." I held up a finger and pointed to the phone so Christine would wait quietly. Instead, she left the kitchen with a little pout.

"Reg, I know this is going to sound strange…" I felt like I was about to step off a cliff. "Is your aunt's name Lorraine Andrews?" I held my breath hoping he would say no.

"Yes, how did you know?"

"And her home, is it called Fair Winds?" I asked, my voice just above a whisper.

"Y-yes. Abby…"

I shut my eyes tight and asked one more question. "And does Evelyn Truitt work for her?"

"Abby," His voice was laced with fear. "What's going on?"

"Reg, I can tell you that your aunt is okay."

"Thank the ... How you know?" he sputtered.

"I know because the police told me when they questioned me this morning. They said Evelyn Truitt was murdered last night, but your aunt is okay. Since I don't have a job…" I couldn't keep myself from making the dig. "I'm selling sterling silver on eBay to pay my bills. Your Aunt Lorraine bought a cake server from me. It was the murder weapon."

Silence on the phone. I didn't know what to say either.

I looked around and Christine was in the doorway, tapping her foot.

"Abby," Reg said in a whisper. "We have to go down to the Shore. You have to come with me."

"Reg, I—"

"Abby, I need you."

Everything seemed to get so complicated when Reg was involved, but now he needed a friend. With a sigh, I agreed to go to his place that was on the way to Route 50 and Fair Winds.

Christine wasn't pleased when I hustled her out of my house. I had to promise we'd work on the silver together later.

With the front door closed and locked, I leaned against it and wondered what I'd done to deserve all this commotion. When I moved to Washington, D. C. from Seattle five years earlier, I wanted a fresh start with things neat and organized like the symmetry of computer code. It was what I needed after Gran was diagnosed with cancer and died just before I graduated from college. I cancelled the trip to Europe that we'd planned so carefully. Instead, I spent the time going through all the belongings in the old house, selling bits of my childhood. Then, I moved to get away from the sad reminders and to live a simple life. What I got was excitement, career challenges and success… until Reg upset everything.

Simon pawed my leg with an urgency that made me sprint to the back door to let him out again. I looked around at the jumbled warehouse that was once my tidy living room. Growing up in the old Victorian house, I'd lived with antiques, patterned wallpaper and colorful Oriental rugs. Now, living alone, I preferred simple lines and neutral colors. A group of family photos hanging in the dining room was the only echo of my past. I picked up the letter from the family attorney that had arrived with the boxes.

> "I was surprised to receive an annual bill in your aunt's name for a rental storage unit. I investigated immediately and discovered the items packaged in these boxes. I assumed you would want to look at the contents so I've taken the liberty of forwarding them. It seems your Aunt Agnes was an active, successful dealer in sterling silver flatware and hollowware."

I didn't know which surprised me more: the vast collection of silver or the news that my Aunt Agnes was a silver dealer. She'd lived with Gran and me in the big old house since I could remember. I knew she dabbled in sterling, but I had no idea she was doing business in a serious way.

I put the letter down on the dining table stacked with silver teapots, gravy boats and a collection of serving pieces in the Chantilly pattern by Gorham, the one Gran loved the best. Tears pricked at my eyes. Silver and tea parties were just part of the loving home she'd given me after my mother died. Only she didn't prepare me for the big hole she left in my heart when she died. Aunt Agnes survived only another six months, lost without her little sister. Too many memories, too much pain stirred up by these boxes. My life was messy enough without them.

In just a matter of weeks, I'd gone from creating software code to looking for a new job. Why did all the people act so superior when interviewing me? Did they have to rub it in that they had a job and I didn't?

I shoved a box. *Take that for saying I wouldn't fit in with their operation. How could you tell after talking to me for five whole minutes?* I elbowed a small box. *I deserve better… better treatment, better opportunities, better chances to work where I'm want.* I planted my feet and pushed against a really big box with all my strength. *And that's for the cheery job counselor who thinks hunting for a job is fun and easy.* My foot slipped and my knee cracked against the hardwood floor. OUCH.

My joint hurt, but it felt good to take out my frustration on the boxes instead of my psyche. I'd tortured myself over the past few weeks. I should have seen it coming. Were there signs that people and circumstances at the office were conspiring to pull the rug out from under my life?

Enough already! It doesn't matter. You have to deal with what is *right now.*

At this moment, I needed some ice for my throbbing knee. I hobbled to the kitchen, made an ice pack and pulled a chair over to the fridge. I needed to follow my morning ritual. I called it *Plan for the Day,* a game using refrigerator magnets. It helped me concentrate just on the day's events instead of drowning under thoughts about everything going on in my life. Gran started it when I was a little kid and it helped me recover from the trauma of my mother's death. I always found comfort in the game's simplicity and logic. Let's say I had to work on finding a job: I'd pull a magnet with a little telephone on it along with a computer magnet and a dollar sign to the center of the refrigerator door. Seeing them every time I was in the kitchen kept me focused on what I had to do. I'd planned to spend my Saturday organizing the house and setting up more silver auctions on eBay. I should have pulled the magnets of a little house and a silver spoon. Instead, the murder committed with my cake breaker had changed my plans. From my vast collection of magnets, I picked a car, a sailboat and a tombstone to represent my trip down to St. Michaels.

My cell phone beeped with an incoming text.

ARE YOU COMING?

Reg was impatient as usual. Whenever he got something in his head – whether it was a new idea for software functionality or a place to go – it had to happen right away. But this time was different. Something terrible had happened and he needed to go to the place where he grew up.

I quickly typed:

GETTING DRESSED. LEAVING SOON.

I hit send, retrieved Simon from the backyard and raced him up the stairs.

CHAPTER THREE

A well-fashioned serving piece combines the beauty of silver and the craftsmanship of the silversmith. Nothing detracts from its look more than tarnish, for which there is no excuse.

—"The Butler's Guide to Fine Silver" Mr. Hollister, 1898

All dressed and ready, I called out, "Simon, how would you like to go for a ride in the car?" He dashed to the hall closet door, pulled his leash off the knob and paraded around with it clasped in his teeth, taking himself for a walk. Smart dog. Very cute. And a new game of Keep Away was born.

"Okay, okay." I grabbed the leash and attached it to his collar. Armed with bottles of water, food bowls and his cookies, along with my purse and computer tablet that went everywhere with me, we worked our way out the front door. He jerked the leash as a cluster of mommies led by Christine rounded the corner pushing strollers, retrieving pacifiers and chatting. It was a *play date*. How my life had changed. One minute, I was a software guru and the next, the only adults I saw were cops or play-daters.

Somehow, I managed to hold on to everything and get to my

Saab. It was a teal convertible, the same blue color that sparkles in an Australian opal. When Gran ordered the car, she paid extra to have it painted her favorite color. I loved putting the top down on a cool, sunny day like this, but with Simon riding shotgun, I was content to open all the windows. It took fifteen minutes for me to get to Reg's condo building overlooking the Potomac River. He was pacing the sidewalk. When I pulled up, he opened the door and started to get in.

"Took you long enough. We'll put your car in my parking space and..." He scowled. "What is that dog doing here?"

"I figured we'd be gone all day and I can't leave him home alone that long." My voice sounded apologetic which irritated me. Sure, Reg was upset but I didn't have to let him intimidate me. I cleared my throat. "Don't worry. He won't be a problem. I'll take care of him."

"And who is going to protect the leather seats of my new car, huh?" His lips stretched into a thin line. Usually, Reg commanded attention wherever he went. I didn't know if it was his good looks – tall with broad shoulders and thick black hair – or the confident way he moved. Just being with him could make you feel good about yourself, but today, he wasn't his usual well-groomed, put-together self. The label of his fisherman's sweater stuck out at the back of the neckline. His hair was messy from running his fingers through it, a nervous habit.

"Abby, this isn't going to work. We'll take your car. I'll drive," he announced and moved around to open my door.

"But I—"

"Don't worry, I know how to drive a stick shift." He extended his hand to help me out of the car. "And I'll give you money for gas."

I sprinted around to the passenger side, almost afraid he'd take off without me.

"And keep that dog under control, okay?" he said. "Things are crazy enough without dealing with a puppy."

And with that, we were off.

In minutes, we were dodging crazy drivers on the Capital Beltway around Washington, where the traffic was heavy every day of the week. The cars to avoid had diplomatic license plates from who-knew-where. Bored with the endless crowd of cars surrounding us, Simon curled up on the back seat and went to sleep. His snoring competed with my thoughts about the murder. Diplomats and politicians gave lavish parties. Lorraine said the governor loved to have the Fair Winds Torte served at his official dinners and the cake was famous now. Did someone break into Fair Winds to steal Evelyn's cookbook? Did she surprise the thief who lashed out and killed the baker?

When we stopped to pay the toll for the Chesapeake Bay Bridge just beyond Annapolis, Simon woke up, stretched and yawned as we made our way across the almost five-mile long bridge high above the Bay. Simon's nose twitched madly at the tangy smell of salt.

"Relax," said Reg. I didn't realize that my hand had curled into a fist. "I've driven this bridge thousands of times. I could do it in my sleep."

"Oh, please don't." I cringed as the concrete barriers along the edge of the lane whizzed by. Forcing myself to relax, I kept my eyes on the white sailboats gliding across the water far below. A container ship riding high moved over the surface like a giant water strider.

Not long after we reached the Eastern Shore, Simon started wiggling around in his harness, making little puppy sounds. Warning signs. I promised Reg it would take only a minute so we stopped by the Easton airport for a quick walk. On the tarmac, there were small single-prop planes, several private jets and a Gulf-stream jet capable of international travel. Anybody could have zipped in, killed Lorraine's housekeeper then disappeared into the night by car, plane or boat. I didn't envy the cops. It wasn't as easy to find a murderer as it seemed on TV.

Back in the car, I took the wheel in case Reg had to get out fast when we got to Fair Winds. Following the signs pointing to St.

Michaels, we crossed a little two-lane bridge where I was captivated by a panoramic view of the blue-gray Miles River. Flaming red maples and buttery yellow birch trees lined the shore. Here and there, massive estate homes peeked out through the changing leaves. I wondered what could happen inside such a house that could lead to murder.

"We're here, finally. That fence marks our property," Reg said as he sat up in his seat.

I wanted to get a good look at Fair Winds, but I had to keep my eyes on the road. The cars ahead had slowed to a crawl. It seemed that murder had drawn a crowd. In addition to the nosy neighbors, cars were parked on the shoulder and the grass, all marked with a hodge-podge of insignias representing law enforcement – Maryland State Police, Talbot County Sheriff and

St. Michaels Police. Leaning on the vehicles were people in uniforms and business suits, all looking very official. I kept a sharp eye on the car in front of me as it crept forward. This was no place for a bumper-crusher, in front of all those cops.

We inched along toward the main entrance and the two stonewalls flanking the driveway. Chiseled into a flat stone panel were the words *Fair Winds*. The leafy branches of old majestic oak trees formed a coppery canopy over the long drive, almost the color of my curly hair. Yellow crime scene tape strung across the asphalt driveway flapped in the wind.

Reg leaned forward against his seatbelt. "That's the main entrance to Fair Winds. Who are all these people?"

"The murder must have drawn every police officer for miles. This would be a good time to pull off a robbery or something." I was trying to lighten the mood, but all I got was a groan.

"Pull off, Abby," Reg ordered. "Turn into the drive,"

"But—"

"Just do it."

The turn signal clicked and I nudged the car into a right turn.

RAP, RAP, RAP. An officer in a drab beige and olive-green uniform knocked on the hood of my car. His substantial hat held in place by a thin leather strap rested so far down his forehead that his eyebrows disappeared. Intimidation must have been the idea and it was working.

His commanding voice nailed my attention. "STOP! You can't come in here. This driveway is closed. There's nothing here for you."

Oh, if you only knew that the murder weapon was my silver cake breaker.

I powered my window down ready to explain, but Reg yelled at him.

"Officer, this is my home and—"

"You need to get back on the main road. Now. This is a crime scene." The officer took two steps back to give me room to turn the car and motioned me back to the road.

Reg erupted. "Abby, stop! For the love of..." He snapped off his seat belt and started to open the passenger door, but he wasn't fast enough.

Another officer laid his hands on the door and muscled it closed. "Stay in the car, sir," he ordered.

The commotion attracted attention and other troopers moved into position around the car. One raised his hand toward his gun.

"Reg," I began quietly. "Maybe we should—"

"No, stay here." He lowered his window and started to explain. "Officer, I'm Reginald Lambert and this is my home. My aunt—"

The trooper cut him off. "Driver's license... please."

Moving slowly, Reg reached for his wallet and showed the officer his identification.

"I understand someone died here," Reg continued, trying to mask his irritation. "But I'm trying to find my aunt, Mrs. Lorraine Andrews. I..."

"All right, all right. Let me through, please." A tall man with glistening skin the color of mahogany worked his way through the crowd of law enforcement. His starched white police uniform shirt outlined the contours of well-developed muscles. The gold badge on his chest glinted in the sunlight. He leaned down to the open window and said, "Mr. Reg, what are you doing here, getting everybody riled up? We've got enough trouble going on."

The trooper by the door asked, "Chief, do you know this man?"

"Yes, yes, I'll take care of this." He raised his right hand waving away the crowd and leaned down. "The man is right. You can't go down the drive. This is an active crime scene."

"Okay, we'll use the service road," Reg shot back.

The chief lowered his head and shook it slowly. "With all due respect, what part of *active crime scene* don't you understand? Only official investigating personnel are allowed on the property or inside the house." He raised his head and eyed me closely. "And you are…" he paused almost hiding a chuckle. "One of Mr. Reg's girlfriends?"

"Well, I—"

"I'm Chief Douglass Luken, chief of police in St. Michaels." Done with me, he turned back to Reg. "You and your girlfriend need to move on down the road before these boys from State get antsy."

"Not before I find Aunt Lorraine," insisted Reg.

"Oh, that's easy. They packed her off to the hotel early this morning, the one on the harbor. Now, you move yourselves along. You'll find her at the hotel." He stepped back from the car and, in a loud voice, directed the officers out of the way so I could move safely back on the road to St. Michaels.

CHAPTER FOUR

As Butler of the House, you must keep an accurate inventory of the sterling silver. Many pieces have been handed down and all are very expensive. Treat each one with the utmost care.

—"The Butler's Guide to Fine Silver" Mr. Hollister, 1898

While we drove in silence, I thought about the elegant entrance to Lorraine's home and her story about the selection of her wedding silver pattern. When we met in Annapolis—was it only yesterday—she told me about the serious decision she'd made so many years ago. She was descended from two old Maryland families and all the women had chosen an ornate silver pattern made in Baltimore called Kirk Rose Stieff. Lorraine's desire for something simpler caused a scandal in the family. Her momma was so upset she didn't know what to do and her grandmother took to her bed. Lorraine talked about doing her research before doing battle with her family matrons. The Chantilly pattern she wanted dated back to 1895 and was made by Gorham, the company that made the White House silver for Presidents Lincoln and Grant and created the America's Cup yachting trophy. History and prestige overcame their objections. That's why Lorraine was so excited to find a Chantilly cake breaker nearby so she could have it for the governor's dinner.

Soon, the speed limit on the St. Michaels Road dropped from 50 MPH to 35. I figured we'd arrived, but I was not impressed. I expected to see a charming village, not warehouses, landscape machinery and a hardware store with inventory all over its front lawn. When the speed limit dropped to 25 MPH, everything changed. Old trees with fluttering red and gold leaves towered over small charming houses, many with porches and rocking chairs. A large sign with a bright gold sailboat on it announced, "Welcome to St. Michaels."

"This is more like it," I whispered.

"Abby, take your next right. When we get to the water, turn left toward the hotel," Reg directed.

I followed his instructions and stopped by the hotel's front door.

"Park here while I see if she's here."

As soon as Reg got out of the car, Simon pulled against his seat harness, trying to get close to me. I was rubbing his ears and slipping him a cookie when Reg burst through the hotel door and got back in the car.

"She's not here!"

"Where would she go?" His intense reaction surprised me. "At least we know that she's okay."

"Yeah, okay enough to go into town for lunch. Drive."

I put the car in gear and drove through the rows of cars in the parking lot. "All we have to do is check the restaurants and..." Reg sighed. "What?" I asked.

"Obviously, you haven't been to St. Michaels before. You have no idea how many restaurants there are in this town."

"Well, does she have a favorite?"

The strain on his face relaxed away. "Yes, yes she does. She likes to go to the Crab Claw. Not the fanciest food in town, but she knows the people there really well. She grew up with the owner."

He directed me through the main part of town crammed with cars and tourists. In the midst of all the activity, I turned right and found a shady parking space right next to the car that Reg confirmed belonged to his Aunt Lorraine.

"Why don't I give you some time alone with her? Simon needs a walk so I'll..." but Reg was already sprinting up the outside stairway of the restaurant, taking the steps two at a time.

Left alone, Simon and I looked at each other, then he cocked his head to the side in that cute puppy way.

"Don't look at me. I don't understand men either. Come on, let's go for a walk."

Holding Simon tight to his leash, we followed along a brick sidewalk under tall shade trees and old homes. The quaint feeling was a lot like Alexandria, Virginia where I lived, but there was one big difference: the people. At home, they were consumed with getting *the* right invitation, *the* new car, *the* bigger house – things that shouted success. Here, I saw a homeowner wearing a battered straw hat puttering in her yard. Couples walked arm-in-arm, quietly chatting. On the main street, Simon was busy avoiding passing feet and strollers. The shops offered antiques, fashions, yarns and more.

Scarecrows were everywhere, part of the fall festival decorations. By the Carpenter Street Saloon, a scarecrow witch had ridden her broom into a telephone pole. A "good ole boy" scarecrow smoked a corncob pipe while sitting on a bench by the bank. In a chic clothing store window, a lady scarecrow with long eyelashes and luscious naughty-girl lips was reading Poe's poem, "The Raven." Something about her was familiar. It took me a minute to make the connection that the scarecrow looked like Angela, the hotshot sales maven Reg had hired to pump up the company's sagging income. Within months of her arrival, our doors closed and my professional dreams shattered. Simon tugged on his leash, reminding me it was time to move on, in more ways than one.

Hearing the sounds of live music, we strolled down a side street. Just beyond an old stone church, there was a park with an old-fashioned bandstand overlooking the harbor. People—parents, children, seniors, lovers—wandered around the wide grassy area rimmed with flower beds lush with lilies, roses and ornamental grasses swaying in the breeze. The Crab Claw Restaurant stood across the water and I remembered why I'd come. I guess it didn't matter if it was a big city or a quiet village, violence could touch you anytime, anywhere. I looked around at the people again with a suspicious eye. Was the killer posing as a tourist? Was it someone who lived in town? A chill rippled over my skin. Could it be someone walking through the park right now?

I jumped when my phone announced an incoming text:

JOIN US FOR LUNCH.

That's what I needed, something to eat to calm my nerves. Simon and I scurried back to the car. I hadn't realized how hungry I was until I read *lunch.* The air was cool so I opened the car windows for ventilation and left a tired puppy snoring in the back seat.

As I walked toward the restaurant, I felt a little awkward about seeing Lorraine again. If she hadn't bought the cake breaker from me, maybe her friend would still be alive.

Don't be ridiculous! She wasn't shopping for a murder weapon. She wanted a beautiful serving piece for her dessert. If she hadn't bought it from me, she'd have found one somewhere else. Even though the logic made sense, I was glad Reg would be at the table, too.

I climbed the stairs and entered the restaurant on the second floor. Inside, the décor was pretty much what you'd expect in a waterside restaurant: prints of sailing ships, local water charts and huge stuffed fish hanging on pine-paneled walls. The hostess led me to the main dining room with a panoramic view of the harbor. Red-and-white checked plastic tablecloths and simple wood furniture suggested that the owner preferred to focus on the food and let the view of sailboats, flags and sunlight glinting off the water create the atmosphere.

Reg and Lorraine were sitting at a prime table by the windows. When she saw me, she held out her arms in welcome. "Abby! I'm so glad to see you."

We hugged and I sat in a flurry of questions about what I'd like to drink, what did I like to eat, was I hungry? A young waitress dressed in short shorts and a colorful T-shirt advertising the restaurant delivered a cold bottle of beer to Reg. She oozed the sensuality of Daisy on the old TV show, *The Dukes of Hazzard.* Her tanned skin was loaded with freckles and it was clear that she wasn't pleased to see me with Reg. She stood with her feet planted and a hip cocked at an angle.

"My name's Jackie. I'm your waitress. Know what you're gonna have?"

Lorraine jumped in. "Abby, have you ever picked blue crabs?"

I shook my head. I wouldn't know how to select one crab over another. And, for that matter, I thought crabs were red.

Lorraine went on. "Then Jackie, I don't think we should give her steamed crabs on her first visit to St. Michaels."

"Nope, she wouldn't know how to eat 'em. Probably cut up her hands on the shells." Jackie mumbled. "And starve to death."

Falling into her normal role of gracious hostess, Lorraine suggested Crab Imperial. "The large chunks of fresh crabmeat are drenched in a buttery white sauce and covered with crunchy seasoned breadcrumbs... or maybe a simple crabmeat salad, if you aren't too hungry?"

"I'm starved!" I blurted out, glad Lorraine had taken charge. I wasn't sure I had the wits to spar with Jackie.

"Crab Imperial it is! Jackie, make sure she gets the appropriate side dishes, too. Thank you, dear."

"Yes, ma'am." Jackie wrote down the order and sashayed away.

"This is a lovely surprise," Lorraine said. Sadness shaded her eyes, red from crying. Dressed in black, her face, so animated when we met in Annapolis, was weighed down by grief. "I'm glad you're here, both of you." She patted Reg's arm. "I'm glad you brought along your friend …and mine. I can really use the company." She raised her hands and covered her face for a moment, then dropped them in her lap. She straightened up in her chair in an effort to stay in control of her emotions. "This is a ghastly business, someone breaking into my home and… and hurting Evie." Her voice wilted with the weight of words. "I can't believe what's happened."

"I told Aunt Lorraine about the police visit you got this morning," Reg said.

I hazarded a question, THE question. "Do you have any idea who…" My voice trailed off. I didn't want to say *murdered your friend.*

Lorraine shook her head and lowered her gaze to the table. Jackie, the waitress, chose that the moment to descend on us to rearrange the table, moving the salt and pepper shakers, forks and knives, glasses and napkins so she could lay down a white paper table cover.

"I'm having my favorite comfort food, steamed crabs," A little smile came to Lorraine's lips. "My old and dear friend Sylvia has owned this place for years. The people here know and care about me."

"We don't use newspaper anymore when we serve crabs," Jackie announced to me, the tourist, who had no idea what she was talking about. "We don't use dishes neither. You get 'em right on the table when they come hot out of the pot." She put down a stack of napkins, a small wooden mallet and other accessories for a crab feast.

Lorraine tied a large plastic bib around her neck. "This building used to be a crab cannery, but my friend turned it into a successful restaurant. People from up and down the East Coast come by car, bus and boat." She straightened the napkins and moved them away from the bubbling cup of melted butter perched above a small lit candle. "Eating here is like having lunch with friends in my own kitchen." Her voice broke. "That's where it happened, you know, in my kitchen."

Jackie reappeared with a basket of tiny muffins and biscuits still hot from the oven. We grabbed our favorites, slathered butter on them and devoured the goodies. I guess murder makes a person hungry. Jackie poured iced tea while her eyes moved between us trying to figure out what was going on. After fussing as much as she could, Jackie went back to the kitchen unsatisfied.

Reg cleared his throat. "This morning, when I heard the news on the radio…" His words hung in the air full of awful possibilities. "I thought, I thought it was you." He gave Lorraine's hand a gentle squeeze. "I mean, they didn't identify the victim or anything. When you didn't answer my calls…" He picked up the cold bottle and held it against his face. "I pulled on some clothes and called Abby."

"I'm glad you did. If you'd driven down here by yourself, you would have gotten a ticket for sure since it's a holiday weekend. You got enough speeding tickets when you were a teenager, thank you very much. I thought you were going to bankrupt us with all those fines." She patted his hand. "I'm sorry you were frightened, but, as you can see, I'm all right, dear. You're very sweet."

Reg clasped his hands under his chin and pulled his eyebrows together. "What I don't understand is why the State Police are at Fair Winds? You said our police chief thinks Evelyn walked in on a robbery. Surely they can handle the investigation."

"It must be procedure when there's…" I lowered my voice. "A murder."

"But she was just an employee," countered Reg.

Lorraine looked stricken by the word, *employee.*

"She was Lorraine's friend," I added with a meaningful look to encourage a little sensitivity.

He ignored it. "Okay, she was a friend, but nobody special enough to get the attention of the State Police."

"Who knows what is proper procedure and what is posturing?" said Lorraine with heat in her words. "Those cops threw me out of my own house. 'It's a crime scene,' they said. After they questioned me for hours, they gave me only a few minutes to gather some things before I was *escorted* from my home. A stranger fingered the contents of my tote and my purse. Maybe they thought I'd make off with vital evidence. Maybe they think I'm the murderer." She tightened her lips into a thin line as her anger rose. "As if I would hurt my oldest, dearest friend."

I wasn't sure if she was insulted, furious or both.

"I checked into the hotel there." She pointed to a large gray building on the other side of the harbor. The balcony railings shone bright white in the sun. "I could have called any one of my friends, but they'd make a fuss."

"Maybe the police procedure has something to do with the governor?" I suggested.

Reg clenched his teeth. "I get so sick of those adrenaline junkies overreacting to everything. They don't care who they walk on."

Jackie put down another tall bottle of beer with ice crystals melting down the side. "What else can I get for you?" Her voice chirped with sweetness as she looked at Reg.

"Nothing," he said, waving her away.

Jackie's bright smile melted as fast as the ice. She turned and dragged herself back to the bar. It wasn't like my friend to bark at a server.

A shrill voice split the air. "Lorraine! Lorraine!" An old woman with tightly curled white hair rushed up to our table. "Oh, my dear!" She leaned over to deliver an air kiss. "I heard the awful news this morning. Millicent called me, you know. Well, Benjamin said – that's my husband, you know." She gestured toward a man with thick white hair being seated with another couple on the other side of the room. "Benjamin says, 'Harriet, if you are a real friend, you'd call Lorraine.' So, I dialed the number at Fair Winds but only got the answering machine."

Reg mumbled, "Join the club." Then, he focused on draining his beer bottle.

Lorraine jumped in. "Harriet, I don't believe you know my nephew Reg Lambert." She pronounced his last name in the French style, with the T silent.

Reg held up his empty beer bottle, waggled it in the air and Jackie jumped into action.

But Harriet would not be derailed from her story by a simple introduction. "I do hate answering machines so I hung up." The woman gushed. "You'll know that blank message was me because here you are… of all places… after such a terrible event. We're here only because our friends are visiting from Philadelphia." She took a much-needed breath.

I bet good ole Benjamin didn't get too many words into a conversation.

"Harriet, I…" began Lorraine.

"Oh Lorraine, I know how devastated you must be. To lose your valuable housekeeper. Murder. How dreadful. And at Fair Winds, in your very own home." Harriet oozed plastic concern all over the table. "You just don't know who those people will bring into your house or what goes on while you're asleep."

Lorraine shot back, "Evelyn was my friend as well as a trusted employee."

Harriet was taken aback but only for a moment. "I understand." She nodded knowingly, but I suspected she didn't know a thing. She leaned closer and dropped her voice. "Do they know who did it?"

"No, Harriet, they don't." Her words were brittle. "But, thank you for asking."

"Oh, my dear, you know I'm here for you. Why, just this morning I was saying to…"

"Oh, for heaven's sake!" Reg slammed his fresh beer bottle down on the table sending a shower of beer into the air. "Can we have a little privacy?" Harriet's eyes opened so wide I thought they would fall out and roll around on the floor. I used my napkin to cover my giggle. "Forget it." He leaned over and gave Lorraine a kiss on the cheek. "I'll see you at the hotel." He marched across the wood floor and out of the restaurant.

CHAPTER FIVE

A silver piece may have a soft bluish color or patina. It is a sign that the silver has mellowed over the years. The patina comes from frequent cleaning and use but truly, only age and maturity can give it a lustrous patina.

—"The Butler's Guide to Fine Silver" Mr. Hollister, 1898

"Well, I…" huffed Harriet, as her eyes followed him.

"You'll have to forgive him." She played the false concern to her advantage. "He's very upset about what happened. We all are. I'm sure you can understand. He grew up with Miss Evelyn in our house."

Harriet frowned and shifted her attention back to Lorraine. "Well, I suppose… since…"

Lorraine cut in. "It was very nice of you to say hello." She gestured toward Benjamin. "Oh, I think your husband is looking for you. Enjoy your lunch."

"Yes, well, if you need anything. I must…." Harriet toddled back to her party.

Lorraine let out a deep breath in relief.

I whispered across the table. "Who was that woman?"

"That was Harriet, a transplant from Philadelphia or someplace like that. She's as harmless as a hungry blue fish with a school of minnows in its sights. She serves on all the *right* committees, goes to the *right* church, tries very hard to know all the *right* people. With friends like that—"

Jackie interrupted. "That was exciting. 'Bout time somebody…" She saw the look on Lorraine's face and cleared her throat of the words caught there. "Ready for your crabs?" She was carrying a tray loaded with a mound of bright red crabs with pale white underbellies. She slid them into a neat pile on the table in front of Lorraine. The sight of her favorite comfort food brought a small smile to her face.

The mass of red shells and black beady eyes hypnotized me.

"Abby?" Lorraine's voice broke the spell. The strain of murder and loss was getting to me. "Abby?"

"I'm sorry, did you say something?"

"I was asking you if you'd like to try eating one of the crabs," said Lorraine.

I tried to hide my shudder just thinking about touching those shells and sharp claws. "Ah, no, not right now." I pointed to the pile. "Um, they seem to have a lot of dirt from the Bay on their shells. Don't they wash them first?"

It was good to hear her laugh a little. She looked at the crabs and nodded. "I guess that gritty stuff looks like dirt, but it's Old Bay Seasoning. It gives them a kick."

She sat up straight and pushed things around on the table: melted butter on the right, coleslaw to the left, tiny fork, small knife and metal claw cracker within easy reach. She slipped a ring set with a huge diamond from her left hand and put it on a small paper plate to the side. "If the spice gets under my ring, it irritates my skin. My dear Thomas, gone so many years now, gave me this ring for our engagement." Then she slipped a small circle of diamonds from her right pinky finger. "This was Momma's wedding band. I can't believe how little she was. Wearing them brings me joy every day. I never go without them."

Lorraine reminded me of my grandmother. She too was widowed fairly young, but wore her diamond engagement ring until she died. She said a person should enjoy beautiful things, not hide them away in a drawer or safe. It seemed that the two women had something in common.

It was time to get down to the business of eating lunch. Lorraine straightened her bib, selected a large bright red crab covered with the gritty seasoning, twisted off the large claws and, with experienced fingers, dove inside for the succulent white meat. She moaned with the first bite, dripping with melted butter. "Ah, so sweet.

Something didn't make sense to me. "Why are they called blue crabs when they're fiery red?"

"They're blue when they come out of the water, but they turn red when steamed just like lobsters do. You're not the first to be confused. There's a story the watermen love to tell about some tourists crabbing off a public dock with a net and a chicken neck tied to a piece of string as bait. A waterman – the guy who catches crabs – saw them pulling up blue crabs then throwing them back. He had to go over and ask why they weren't keeping the big ones. They said they'd gone to a crab feast the night before and found out how to catch their own. They wanted the red ones, but only the blue crabs were biting. The story goes that the waterman went back to his boat, brought them a bushel basket and volunteered to take the blue crabs off their hands. After a while, the family gave him a basket full of blue crabs and went away disappointed that they hadn't caught a single red one."

Laughing, I almost choked on my sip of tea. "Come on, Lorraine. That can't be a true story."

She shrugged dramatically. "You didn't know the difference." She gave me a mischievous smile.

Jackie appeared at our table again and, with a grand gesture, put a shell-shaped dish of bubbling Crab Imperial in front of me. The steam rising from it was thick with a fresh seafood aroma.

Lorraine smiled knowingly. "There's nothing liking eating seafood here on the Shore because it's fresh. Look." She pointed at a long, thin boat pulling up to the bulkhead below us. "That's a waterman bringing in his catch for this restaurant. He probably pulled some of those crabs less than an hour ago. A waterman leaves the dock between four and five in the morning then lays out his lines and bait in time to put crab on our table by mid-afternoon."

When it was cool enough to eat, I savored the delicious taste of the Chesapeake Bay blue crab. We sat together quietly enjoying our lunch and building up our strength.

After a while, Lorraine put down the mallet and wiped her hands on a fresh napkin. "I guess I'm not as hungry as I thought." With a sigh, she asked me, "Do you want to know what happened?"

Glad my curiosity would be satisfied, I nodded.

"You have a right to know since the police got you involved." She bit her lip white to keep from crying. After a few moments, she steadied herself and launched into the story.

"As you know, I was going to host a dinner for the governor tonight. Daddy started the tradition years ago. He said you could get more done over excellent food in an elegant atmosphere than in hours of meetings at the State House. We were going to serve a seven- course meal using the good china, crystal and, of course, the silver."

She massaged her forehead. "After I left you in Annapolis yesterday, I came straight home to Fair Winds. The kitchen was busy, just like the old days when I entertained all the time. Evelyn and the staff were chopping and peeling, simmering and sautéing. The smells in the kitchen were heaven. Evie is – was – a master planner. She had staff setting the table, polishing the silver, doing all those little things that are so important." She looked at her watch. "The guests would have been arriving right about now in time for a little fishing before dinner." A sigh escaped as she straightened her bib. "Evie was putting the finishing touches to The Cake. It was a work of art sitting on its crystal cake pedestal. I gave her your cake breaker. She was thrilled. We spent the evening in the kitchen and dining room doing things together, making sure everything was just right." A smile crept across her face, a quiet smile of memory that soon dissolved.

"We worked until after eleven o'clock. I was exhausted, more than ready to go to bed. I told her to do the same. If she had, maybe…" Lorraine paused but only for a moment. "She said there was something else she had to do. She promised she'd go to bed soon. We said goodnight." Lorraine bit her lip. "To think that…"

I reached out and touched her hand. "You couldn't have known. You never know when it's your last chance to say good-bye. I lost my mother in a car crash where she died instantly."

Lorraine put her hand over top mine and found the strength to continue. "I went upstairs, took a long hot shower and got into bed. It was just after midnight when a woman screamed." Slowly her face cringed as if she heard the awful sound again in the quiet of the restaurant.

"What did you do?" I asked softly.

"I ran downstairs in my bare feet to find Staci, one of the maids, in the foyer just screaming her head off. I tried to get her to tell me what was wrong, but all she could do was point down the hall toward the kitchen." Lorraine took a drink of water and continued in a monotone voice.

"When I walked into the kitchen, I almost slipped. There was blood on the floor, blood everywhere. Bright red. Shiny." Lorraine cocked her head a little to the side. "You know, I never realized there was so much orange in the red floor tiles. They clashed with the blood." She brushed imaginary crumbs off the paper tablecloth and raised her eyes to the view outside. I suspected she wasn't seeing the sailboats, only the horror she'd found in her kitchen the night before.

"That's when I saw her. She was on the floor by the counter, on her back. Her mouth was wide open in a silent scream. Her throat…her throat was in shreds. Blood soaked into her white apron. Evie always insisted on a white apron in the kitchen." She ran her tongue over her lips. "Her beautiful cake was smashed on the floor, bits of frosting spattered on her face." Lorraine turned her head away from the harbor, her hand squeezed in a tight fist, struggling for control.

After a few moments, she looked at me. "You know, it's ironic that Evelyn should… that her life should end in the kitchen." Lorraine's voice was steady. "We shared so much there, drinking coffee – sometimes with a little brandy in it – talking about everything. We've been together since we were little." Her eyes filled with tears. "Why?"

She seemed to search my face for an answer. I couldn't think of a thing to say.

She broke the silence. "Did you know that Evelyn and I met because of blue crabs?"

"Tell me," I said gently.

"I grew up at Harraway Hall, Daddy's farm on the Tred Avon River, not far from here." She sat up in her chair, prim and proper. "Momma dressed me in white summer pinafores and sent me to private schools." She relaxed and smiled. "Evelyn grew up on Tilghman Island where many make their living from the water and family means everything. The spring before we met, her mother died trying to give birth to her baby brother. She lost them both. One day, Evie was on her father's boat when he brought some crabs up to the house for one of Momma's parties. We've been friends ever since, growing old together." She pushed her hair behind an ear. "Don't get me wrong. I'm still very busy with two working farms to manage. Dealing with no-till, pesticide-free agriculture to protect the Bay is a challenge. I still entertain, but not like I used to." She gently laid a fist on the table. "I'll soon turn sixty, but I'm not ready to curl up like a slug and die. Neither was Evie." She drooped in her chair. "What's happened shows you shouldn't postpone something you want to do. We planned to go to Europe again…"

In a moment, Jackie was at her side. "You all right, Miss Lorraine?"

"We were just talking. Really, I'm fine," Lorraine assured her.

"Okay, if you're sure." Jackie said reluctantly. Then, she perked up. "How about some dessert?"

I piped up with the obvious question. "What do you have?" What a mistake. I got lost as Jackie recited a long list of cheesecakes, ice cream flavors and homemade pies.

Lorraine held up her hand. "Bring us both a piece of your Key Lime pie." She announced to me. "It's the best north of Florida."

"And I'm brewing a fresh pot of coffee. I'll bring some as soon as it's ready." Jackie hustled off to fill the order. A young busboy wandered over to clear away the broken crab shells and used paper napkins. Distracted by the music blasting through his iPod, he grabbed the little paper plate holding Lorraine's diamond rings and started to tip it into the trash.

CHAPTER SIX

Be ever vigilant. If a silver utensil is misused under most normal conditions, it can be damaged almost beyond repair. For example, a raw or undercooked egg yolk can turn a silver spoon black.

—"The Butler's Guide to Fine Silver" Mr. Hollister, 1898

"STOP!" The order pierced the air and the boy froze. "Give that to me!" She reached out for the paper plate. "Careful, careful." The boy slowly moved it toward her.

"Got it." Lorraine took the plate holding the diamonds in her two hands and placed it back on the table. "I'd be devastated if I didn't have my diamonds." She smiled as she slid the rings back on her fingers. "Now, they're back where they belong."

And I started breathing again. What just happened reinforced my idea of living simply. If you had things you cared about, you had things you could lose. And what I'd lost already still hurt too much.

People started filling the tables in the Crab Claw's main dining room. The tourists not lucky enough to snag a table by the windows wiggled their way close to the glass to ooh and aah at the view. The regulars clustered close to the bar and each other. Lorraine watched the people, occasionally acknowledging a nod or discreet wave.

She gave a warm smile to two young men as they seated their lady friends. Leaning close to me, she murmured, "Those two boys grew up with Reg. I'm sorry he left. He would have liked seeing them."

She took off her bib, folded it and, with a sigh, put it on the table. "It's been quite a time. I can't imagine what it was like for Reg this morning. He is usually such a sweet boy."

"I didn't realize you two were related," I confessed.

Her lips drew tight into a thin line and the words squeezed out. "Yes, he's my sister's child. She and her husband were killed in a ferry accident in the Irish Sea shortly after he was born. They'd left him with a nurse in London while they took a little weekend trip to Ireland. Momma and I went over and brought him home. My daddy kept him close and spoiled him something fierce." She smiled as she visited her memories. "I guess he was the son Daddy never had." Then, her eyes fell to the tabletop. "Daddy dropped dead of a heart attack when Reg was eleven. We were all upset, but Reg was like a boat without a tiller and so angry. Almost overnight, a sweet boy turned into a first-class hellion. He got to be too much for Momma and me to handle and my husband couldn't devote time to him like Daddy did. I guess Reg resented that, too. Desperate, we enrolled him in a good prep school in Western Pennsylvania." She folded her napkin carefully. "I don't think anything could have filled the hole Daddy left in his life. I'm not sure we did the best thing by sending him away, but it was the best choice at the time."

Funny, after all the time we'd spent together, he'd never mentioned such a life-changing event.

Lorraine asked, "So, tell me how you know Reg."

Suddenly uncomfortable, I kept it simple. "I've known Reg for several years now. He brought me into his software company as the head of technology."

I thought about all the nights and weekends we'd spent talking over cold pizza about his vision for the software and how I was making it a reality, how we hammered out details of what our future clients would need and how we'd make it all happen, together. That's why it was so hard to understand why he'd closed the company without warning and wouldn't return my calls. I felt like I'd lost more than a job. I'd lost my friend. But that wasn't what Lorraine needed to hear.

"He's a good man," I said.

"That's nice. Were you two ever...?"

Her question hung in the air, hungry for a good answer, the kind that would lead to an announcement that her nephew had met a wonderful girl and was going to settle down to raise a family.

"If you're asking if we ever dated, the answer is yes." I had to hide a giggle, because of the naughty smile that blossomed on her face. "Unfortunately, it didn't take long for us to discover we were better friends than we could ever be as..." I paused, not sure if I should use the word and was surprised when she did.

"Lovers. You were better friends than lovers, right?" I nodded. "That's too bad. I suspect you are very good for him. And now?"

I shifted in my chair. This was the tough part. "We worked together until he closed the company." I looked down at the table afraid that her careful attention might detect the bad feelings I was trying to hide. "I'm sorry about what happened to it. When it comes to software development, it always takes longer and costs more. I think all the worry took a toll on him. I just wish --"

"Here we go," Jackie interrupted, swinging two huge slices of creamy Key Lime pie down in front of us.

"Now, for a little bit of heaven," Lorraine said as she picked up a fork.

The taste and texture of the pie lived up to the hype. As we relaxed over our coffee and two empty dessert plates, a man in a suit came up to our table.

"Mrs. Andrews?" He asked, addressing Lorraine.

"Yes?" She grimaced as she craned her neck to look up at him. He must have been six foot six.

"I need to talk to you, ma'am."

"And you are…?"

The man shot me a sideways glance and lowered his voice. "I'm Officer Bell from the Maryland State Police."

She held up her hand to him. "Stop right there. If you want to talk to me, I must ask you to sit down. You're breaking my neck." She glanced around the restaurant. "And you're really attracting a lot of attention. Only out-of-towners and wedding guests wear suits in St. Michaels."

"Ma'am, I was hoping we could—"

She pointed to an empty chair. "Sit." He paused for a moment, smoothed his tie and sat in the chair next to her. "Yes, ma'am." He looked over at me again.

Lorraine jumped into the awkward silence. "This is Abby Strickland. You may say anything you wish in front of her. She's already been questioned by the police."

The agent raised his eyebrows and looked at me with more than casual interest. "And why is that?"

Lorraine said, "She sold me the cake breaker that was used…" She bit her lip then went on. "That was used as the weapon last night. Now, what is it you want?"

"I was wondering if you could tell me if you've seen anyone around your estate in the past few weeks—"

"Farm," said Lorraine.

"I beg your pardon, ma'am?"

"Farm. Fair Winds is a working farm. You might as well get your facts straight. Fair Winds is a farm that has a great big main house and gardens."

"Yes, ma'am. Have you seen anybody around the farm looking for a job or a handout?"

"No, and why would I have that information? You need to check with the St. Michaels Police Chief. I suspect he has talked to my farm manager. He would know." She tilted her head and frowned. "Why is this important?"

"We're looking at all angles, especially because of the dinner guest scheduled to visit your home today."

"Oh, you mean the Governor," Lorraine said.

The officer cringed a little and glanced around, hoping no one had overheard.

She continued. "You think this has something to do with him?"

"The governor has received some threatening letters during the past month. We've been keeping an eye out for a stalker. There was another article in the *Baltimore Sun* about a week ago talking about the governor and the cake made at Fair Winds. A few days ago, another threatening letter came in. It compared the governor to Marie Antoinette who said, 'Let them eat cake'."

A little laugh escaped Lorraine's lips. "Sounds like your stalker is well-versed in French Revolutionary history. What does that have to do with Evelyn?"

"People are having trouble with unemployment, mortgages and all. We think the letter writer has probably been hit hard and planned to break into Fair Winds to do some damage or harm someone there."

Lorraine paused to take in this new information. "And you think Evelyn surprised the person?"

"It's possible," he said softly.

A lone tear trembled on her eyelashes. "What a waste."

He said, "I'm sorry about what happened, ma'am. I understand the victim was a friend. I do need to ask you these questions to track down the person who did this. We have to explore all possibilities. You never know if it was a random act of violence or terrorism."

"Oh!" Lorraine took a sip of water and closed her eyes trying to get control of herself. After a moment, she responded. "Ask your questions. I just hope I have the answers you need."

The officer leaned on the table. "If it was the letter writer who broke into Fair Winds, he may have tried to poison the famous cake in the kitchen."

"Poison the cake?" Her voice rose. "Oh, dear."

"The cake has been sent to the crime lab in Baltimore for testing."

Lorraine's shoulders slowly sagged. "Of course, it was. And we won't get a taste of her last cake." Her face lit up with sudden interest. "Maybe it wasn't about the cake. How do the diamonds play into all this?"

"We're still working out different possible scenarios, ma'am."

She looked him in the eye. "You really think it was your stalker lashing out?"

"Yes, we do."

"I think you're wrong," declared Lorraine. "Our police chief thinks that Evelyn walked in on a robbery in progress and the thief or thieves panicked. It will be hard enough finding whoever did this without you people seeing stalkers and terrorists in every corner."

"But..."

She caught her breath. "Alright, alright, it's a possibility. Just don't forget that my personal safe was wide open. Some cash in it was gone and we found one of my diamond earrings and some loose stones on the floor." The officer tried to protest again, but Lorraine wouldn't allow it. "Really, what self-respecting threatening letter writer would walk away from diamonds, especially in these economic times?" She shook her head. "That's my opinion. You're free to disagree."

"You're entitled, ma'am." He rose and pushed the chair under the table. "I'll be talking to your farm manager." His manner was very stiff. "Thank you for your time, ma'am." He turned and walked out of the dining room.

"I swear those people see plots and conspiracies everywhere," Lorraine said in a clipped tone. "I wonder if they sleep with one eye open."

"I guess it's the nature of the job," I offered.

"I suppose, but it's… it's…." She sighed. "I just want them to find the person who hurt Evelyn."

I lowered my voice. "Do you have any idea who it might be?"

She shook her head slowly. "It almost hurts too much to think that I might know someone who killed another human being, let alone a friend." She looked around the room.

Across the room, Harriet's eyes shifted from the officer and bore right into us.

"Our visit from the officer has made us the center of attention," Lorraine whispered.

I followed her gaze and hoped Harriet couldn't read lips. People at other tables were sneaking peeks at us.

Lorraine straightened up in her chair. "I think it might be time to leave. Let the police do their job while I take care of the arrangements. I have to put some notes together for the obituary. I'd like it to be nice. Think you might be willing to help me since you're a writer?"

It didn't seem like the right time to point out the difference between writing software and writing an obituary. And I was qualified since I'd worked on two not so long ago.

"Anything I can do to help," I said while putting my napkin on the table.

She tilted her head to the side. "Thank you. Since I can't go home, we can go to my little office at Harraway Hall, Daddy's farm."

"Ready when you are." Then, I remembered. "Oh no, I can't. Simon is in the car."

"You left your friend in the car while we sat here jabbering?" She was appalled.

"No. I mean, yes. Simon is a Labrador retriever I'm puppy-sitting for a friend. The weather's cool so I parked in the shade and left the windows open for ventilation. After all the running around he did in the park, I'm sure he's still napping."

Lorraine laughed, a much-needed release of nerves and

tension. "Simon is a dog? I thought…oh, never mind what I thought."

"Would you like to meet him?"

"I'd love to and I bet he'd enjoy a romp on the lawn at the Hall."

As Jackie came to the table, I reached for my wallet, but Lorraine insisted it was her treat. "Jackie, would you put it on my tab, please?"

"No, ma'am. Miss Sylvia told me it's on the house and to give you condolences from all of us."

Tears filled Lorraine's eyes as she looked at the servers, bartender and cook standing by the door to the kitchen. They nodded and somehow, she forced a smile, in thanks. We scooted out of the restaurant just as Harriet was making a move toward us. I figured she wanted to know about our visitor in the suit. I was relieved to see Jackie run interference for us.

Walking to my car, I made excuses every step of the way. "I'm afraid the car is a mess. Who knows what we'll find? Simon shreds every piece of paper and tissue he finds."

"I'm sure he's a love," said Lorraine. "I can't wait to meet him. I love dogs." She hurried ahead of me to the parking lot and I had to scurry to catch up.

She stopped by my mud-splattered, dead-insect-dotted Saab. "Is this your car?" asked Lorraine.

"Yes, um, how did you know?"

"It looks like something you'd drive," she said as she admired the lines of the convertible. "And it has a Virginia license plate."

Maybe the police should listen to this sharp, very observant woman.

I hit the remote and she opened the passenger door. All thirty pounds of puppy were launched at the poor woman. I rushed around to grab Simon, apologizing profusely.

"I'm so sorry. Simon! Down!" I grabbed for his collar but he wiggled out of my grasp, preferring to wash Lorraine's face with lots of slobbery licks.

"He's fine," she said, trying to control the exuberant welcoming committee. "You must be Simon." His tail was wagging so fast that I thought it might fly off. "Okay, okay, get in the back seat so I can get in the car." Without a moment's hesitation, he jumped in back and sat down, panting with excitement.

I looked at the dog, then at Lorraine, then back at Simon in disbelief. "How did you do that? I can barely get him to sit."

Lorraine smiled. "It's all in knowing how to talk to your dog." She turned to Simon, still sitting primly in place. "Isn't that right, Simon?"

He barked. She laughed and I just shook my head.

CHAPTER SEVEN

Fine sterling silver speaks of the simplicity of elegance. It is the mark of good taste and carries a tradition from the maker who created each piece and the people who used and maintained it over the years. If one learns the history of the use and design of each piece, one's appreciation will grow.

—"The Butler's Guide to Fine Silver" Mr. Hollister, 1898

Following Lorraine's directions, we left St. Michaels and, in a few minutes, turned on a tree-shaded road lined with deep ditches that left no room for driver error. When we came around a bend, Lorraine announced we were in Royal Oak. All I saw were a few small buildings and an old church now used as an antique store. She pointed to a building on the corner surrounded by a hodgepodge of rusty garden seats, a trellis and other oddities.

"That must be the junk shop," I said with a laugh.

"Don't let looks deceive you. An old Royal Oak family has run it for years. That's where I found an antique Davenport desk designed to fit in the captain's cabin of old sailing ships. Now, I have a perfect place for my personal correspondence and yes, I still write letters." We both laughed. "Turn here, Abby."

"When Gran and I went antiquing, we loved finding old family photo albums from the 1800's, everybody standing so rigid and staring into the camera. We thought it was sad that they ended up in an antique store, their names and special events lost to time. Sometimes, we'd make up stories. That's when I think I fell in love with history, not the part about dates and battles. I love to hear people's stories. When you look at an old sterling silver carving knife or soup ladle, do you ever wonder about the people who owned it, their family celebrations or disasters? If only those silver pieces could tell stories of where they've been…"

"Then we'd know who killed Evie." Lorraine's comment was on the mark. "Bear right here then take your third left."

I followed her instructions, afraid to fantasize anymore. Soon, the car was crunching along a gravel drive, tall pines towering overhead.

"The entrance to Harraway Hall is a little different from Fair Winds," Lorraine said as she cast an eye over the empty fields at rest for the winter. "Daddy built it into a working farm. Everybody knew him and Momma. He didn't need to impress anybody. It wasn't like it is today with people from the Western Shore – Washington, Baltimore, and Philadelphia, even New York – buying up property and building entrances to impress." She pointed. "Turn right here." We veered onto another gravel drive that led into a thick wood of pine trees.

"Don't get me wrong. Daddy wasn't the type to be 'up with the chickens.' His farm manager oversaw operations, but Daddy was an active landlord. He studied crop rotation, worked with the companies to develop better seed and took care of the people."

"It has a different feel from Fair Winds," I suggested.

Lorraine chuckled. "Fair Winds is different. My father-in-law gave it to us as a wedding present. He wanted us to have..." She lowered her voice took on a pompous tone. "…an estate on the

Eastern Shore befitting Thomas 's Philadelphia Main Line family roots and his position in the investment banking world."

"Please tell me he didn't talk like that," I said, stifling a giggle.

"Oh yes, he did. The first time we saw Fair Winds, we were speechless. All we wanted was a little place down here where we could spend weekends without moving in with my parents. He thought it was the perfect gift so we made it as cozy as possible and put the acres of grass to work. Now, the farms are a source of jobs and income so it all works."

We drove toward the water glinting just beyond a line of heavy rocks along the shoreline. A small one-story building appeared as we came around a bend.

"Here we are. This was Daddy's farm office with a view of both the fields and the river."

I stopped the car and sat for a minute to take in the beauty of the water that looked like a river of sparkling diamonds.

Lorraine opened her door. "Come on, I'll show you where I grew up."

Without warning, Simon scampered out the door.

"Simon!" I yanked open my door and started to sprint after him. On his own and free, there was no telling where he'd go and how I'd get him back.

"Abby, don't worry. He's safe here and won't go very far, will you?" Simon came back and sat at her feet. She scratched the puppy behind his ears and he wagged his tail so hard, his whole body shimmied. A chilly blew off the water as Lorraine led me to a path through the trees with Simon at her heel.

"Let's walk over to the main house before we go to work."

Lorraine was stalling, but she'd piqued my curiosity. "Sure," I said. "Lead on." Simon started to dash off. "Simon! Come here and stay close."

"He seems to know his way around. He's leading us in the right direction," she said. "The house is on the other side of these trees. It's rented to a CEO from New York who does something with the media. He spends a lot of time in Washington and entertains here on weekends. I won't go into the house without an invitation, but we can walk around the grounds. There is a hut on the property that's haunted," Lorraine said in a hushed voice.

I stopped in mid-step. "Haunted?"

"Not to worry," she said. "It's deep in the woods near the north boundary. There really is a ghost, you know," she said with a little smile playing on her lips. "Momma would visit him when she needed help."

I coughed. "She conspired with a ghost?"

Lorraine shook her head. "No, when a clock needed repair, she'd put on her galoshes and take it to the hut for Choffee to fix."

"Choffee?" The story was getting stranger by the minute.

"Here's a historical story for you. It seems Mr. Choffee was a watchmaker. During the Revolutionary War, he was assigned as an aide to the Marquis de Lafayette. They toured the Eastern Shore and the clockmaker fell in love with the area. After the war, he built himself a little place in the woods. And some say, he's still there fixing clocks."

"Lorraine, that's not history, that's superstition, a fairy tale," I insisted.

Lorraine shrugged. "We never had a broken clock in the house. I'm just saying..." She continued down the path ahead of me.

I've always believed there's a strong connection between mothers, daughters and, in my case, granddaughters. Lorraine had her mother's ghost story. I had the watch on my wrist, a gift from my grandmother who raised and loved me like a daughter.

I wasn't sure why, but I didn't want to be caught alone near the woods so I scurried to catch up with Lorraine as she stepped on the sunlit lawn ahead. I wanted to take off my shoes and wiggle my toes into the thick grass.

"Daddy was born on Tilghman Island, just a few miles from here by boat. When he was young, he traveled to the Western Shore for school and a lot of parties. That's how he met Momma. Mary Margaret Murray was the belle of the ball from a fine old

Baltimore family. The story goes that she had her pick of the eligible young men, but the night she danced with Daddy, she fell in love. When he proposed, I suspect she already had her bags packed. There was a big wedding in Baltimore, but once they settled here, she never looked back. You know, Abby, with your interest in silver, you should see the Murray Silver Collection at the Baltimore Museum of Art. Maybe we'll go together sometime."

"I'd like that."

The main house of Harraway Hall was large and rambling. Its red brick walls looked solid enough to stand for yet another century. We walked around to the back, past flowerbeds filled with roses, to a huge patio with old-style wooden rocking chairs that seemed to call out, *Come, sit awhile and enjoy the view.*

Lorraine stopped and stared at a little building down on the dock.

"Who lives there?" I asked.

"No one. Daddy used to have a Chris-Craft launch, a beautiful wood boat. He built that little boat house to protect it from the elements. A wooden boat really should stay in the water, but the sun and rain beating down on it really takes a toll." Lorraine got a faraway look, remembering.

"What are you seeing?" I asked.

She took a moment before she answered. "I'm remembering the night of my 18th birthday party and my sweet friend, Evie. My parents loved to throw parties and that was one of their biggest. People came from everywhere and brought their friends. The boys looked so handsome in their white dinner jackets. All the girls wore long fancy dresses. We danced out here on the patio to a live band. There was every kind of food you can imagine. The pink punch for the girls and boys was more potent than Daddy would have allowed, thanks to the boys and their flasks.

"Evie worked the big parties for some extra money after she graduated from high school. She didn't want to come as a guest, said she'd feel out of place with all the *fancy people.* Before the party, she came up to my room and said I looked beautiful."

Lorraine laughed at the memory. "My little sister was the pretty one, not me. But that night, I was."

"The party sounds like it was right out of a storybook."

"It was, until it turned into a nightmare." Lorraine drew in a long breath. "There was an older boy from New York, a friend of a friend. He was handsome and charming in every way. He danced like the prince in Cinderella, holding me like a precious doll as we glided round and round. I was thrilled when he suggested a walk in the moonlight down by the water. On that dock, he put his arms around me and I thought he was going to kiss me. Instead, he slammed me against the boat house. His hands were everywhere. I begged him to stop. He ordered me to stop squirming. I tried to scream. He put his hand over my mouth. He pressed his body against me.

"Then we heard someone running down the dock. He looked up to see who it was. Next thing I knew, he was flying through the air into the river."

"Was it your father?" I asked.

"No, it was Evie. She rammed into him like a football player. She held me while I cried, then she fixed my hair and straightened my dress." Lorraine chuckled with a soft smile as she remembered her friend. "She said she didn't like the way he was sniffing around me and when we disappeared from the party, she came to track us down. She had to make sure I was all right.

"When we started back up to the house, we heard the drenched prince yelling, 'Hey, what about me?' I'll never forget what Evie said to him." Lorraine added a little southern twang to her words. "'Swim back to the Western Shore where you belong, for all I care!' That night she said she'd stay close to watch out for me, always. She kept her promise all these years."

Lorraine put her trembling hand on her chest, looked back at the boat house and whispered, "Oh, Evie."

Tears spilled out of Lorraine's eyes and rolled down her face, past the traces of past smiles and disappointments left by life. She turned her back to me as if embarrassed when the tears didn't stop.

I stood quietly and stared out at the water, trying not to intrude on her grief, but it seemed to reach out and wrap its tentacles around me as well.

I felt the lonely memory of losing a beloved someone and the hole it left. After my mother's funeral when I was five, I was moved into Gran's house. People whispered that my father couldn't bear to look at me, because I was a miniature version of my mother. They said he was overwhelmed with guilt, because he was driving when the accident happened. I remember spending hours looking at her picture and staring at my face in the mirror. Dad focused on his naval career and lived on the edge of my life. Gran and Aunt Agnes filled in gaps with love.

With no warning, Simon charged out of the trees, streaked across the lawn and slammed into me. He was turning into a loyal little friend who seemed to sense when I was feeling sorry for myself and ready to jar me out of it. Thank goodness.

As fast as Simon appeared, he was off again, jumping at the geese honking overhead. Maybe he thought he would sprout wings and fly after them. *Ah, the eternal optimism of dogs.*

The bells in the little town of Oxford across the water chimed the hour.

"Oh," said Lorraine in surprise. "Is that the time? We'd better get to work on the obituary." We called Simon and retraced our steps through the woods.

"How did Evelyn end up at Fair Winds?" I asked.

"That was Momma's doing, like so many other things. When I accepted Thomas's marriage proposal, my life turned into a whirlwind of wedding plans and housekeeping details for our new homes in Baltimore and at Fair Winds. It was too much for me but Momma knew what to do. We asked Evelyn to take care of Fair Winds." She tucked her hair behind one ear. "She didn't want the job, said she didn't know how to run a big place like that. You know what she was worried about?" I shook my head. "She said she wouldn't know how many pounds of flour to keep in the pantry. Momma and Miss Dorothy, Momma's housekeeper, trained her into a magician. Evie handled everything from endless food for a weekend fishing party to the ticklish situation of a guest passed out on the lawn. She also handled the more mundane things like a leaky roof or staff upsets. Don't know what I'll do now."

We returned to the car and the farm office. It was a quaint little building with weathered cedar shingles. Inside, it was geared for efficient, modern operation. A massive mahogany desk was organized with standing files, a multi-line telephone and a computer setup. She motioned me to sit at the keyboard as she settled into a chair on the other side of the desk.

She asked, "Where should we start?"

"We could start with the basics like where she was born and raised, her education, that kind of thing."

"All right, Evie was born and raised on Tilghman Island and graduated from St. Michaels High School."

I started typing. "Was she ever married?"

Lorraine's right hand curled into a fist on the arm of the chair. "Do we have to mention that horrible man?" She looked away when she saw my shocked expression. "He's dead and he wasn't from around here, so it doesn't matter." She went on quickly. "Put in there that her daddy's name was…" I typed in Eastern Shore names and places.

"Did she have any children?" I asked.

In the silence, I turned to find her staring out the window but I didn't think she was seeing the river. "Lorraine?"

She gave her head a quick shake. "What did you say?"

"I asked if Evelyn had any children so we could list them."

She paused. "No, no children." She got up and started to pace.

I kept my eyes on the screen and hoped my face didn't betray my hunch that there was more to Evie's story than she was saying.

"Let's talk about her work with the women's shelter, Naomi's House. She was a big supporter, volunteering time and giving money, clothes and toys for the children, whatever the women needed to help them start again."

My fingers flew over the keyboard as she filled in details. When she was done, she leaned back in the chair exhausted and looked at me.

"She would have liked you, Abby. She liked your cake breaker and couldn't wait to try it." I could see a little shudder go through Lorraine's body. I could feel it too as I remembered how someone had used it to end her friend's life.

I should have said something comforting. Instead, I blurted out, "It doesn't make sense." I was mad at myself for talking about the 800-pound gorilla in the room: murder. I couldn't ignore it now. "It doesn't make sense that somebody would murder a valued friend and important member of the community who should have died peacefully in her bed at a ripe old age." I opened the barrette holding my curly hair and gathered up the stray strands. "I'm sorry but it's bugging me. Who would want to hurt your friend?"

Lorraine sat perfectly still.

With a snap, the barrette was back in place. "Are you okay?"

"I was just watching you. You have great hair, young lady."

Her comment surprised me. People talk about the strangest things when they're stressed or want to avoid a topic.

She went on. "When I was your age, I wanted curly hair. In two seconds, you fixed your hair and it looks adorable."

"Well, thank you. I'm surprised it hasn't turned to frizz being so close to the water." I wanted to let her escape the painful topic but she could be holding the answer and not realize it. "But we're getting away from the big question: Who could hurt Miss Evelyn? Any ideas?"

Lorraine sagged against the back of her chair and said in a small voice, "I haven't a clue." She looked up at me. "You must have an analytical mind with all of your computer work. What do you think?"

"Maybe the real target was the governor like the officer said at lunch," I suggested. "She surprised him and…"

"The State Police are investigating that possibility." Her dull tone dismissed that line of inquiry.

I thought for a moment then came up with a new idea. "What about the governor's cake?"

"The Fair Winds Torte?"

"Yes, it's been in the media. Maybe somebody wanted the recipe and was willing to do anything to get it. Special dishes – especially desserts – can make a restaurant famous. If a food company produced the cake for grocery store freezers, we could be talking about millions."

Lorraine's eyebrows shot up in surprise. "I never thought about it that way."

Thinking we were off to a good start, I continued. "Okay, what else?"

Fictional detectives always said that if they could figure out the motive, they could find the killer. They were my only reference point since I'd never met a real detective until this morning.

"There's something we must not forget: the open safe in my study. The money was gone and there were diamonds on the floor of the study and in the kitchen. That says robbery to me. Chief thinks Evie was in the wrong place at the wrong time. If it was someone off the street, he's long gone."

"Or it could have been someone local who knew about the safe," I said.

Lorraine considered the possibility for a moment. "Maybe, I don't know." She looked down at her hands and spoke just above a whisper, "If she surprised somebody, it makes sense that he'd grab the nearest 'weapon' and use it."

I continued her line of reasoning. "The cake breaker is a wicked-looking thing. Wield it with enough strength and it could do some damage."

"It did," Lorraine said quietly.

"Maybe it was kids looking for money for drugs," I suggested.

Lorraine shook her head gently. "I think you're reaching."

"There are drug-related crimes all the time."

"In the cities, yes, but out here in the country, it not that easy to get to the main house on a farm or estate. It's too obvious if someone comes up the driveway and it's hard to cross the fields in the dark. It can even be dangerous. You can walk into barbed wire or step in a hole and break an ankle. Come up with something else," she suggested.

I stared out the window, trying to meet the challenge. "There's the possibility that Evelyn was the real target. Maybe someone had a grudge."

"Impossible. Everyone loved her," Lorraine declared.

"Did she fire someone recently? Maybe she caught a maid stealing and …"

Lorraine shook her head. "No, and no. Abby, you're concocting quite a mystery story," she interrupted. "But there's no basis in reality. Come up with something else."

"Could someone have been after you?"

"Me?" She bolted upright. "Whatever for? I'm nobody."

"Lorraine, you're Somebody here on the Eastern Shore. Maybe someone felt slighted or was angry or… I just want to raise the possibility that the murderer may come back."

Lorraine turned her head slowly toward me and swallowed. "I don't think it's anything like that, but you've given me an idea."

My eyes followed as she moved around the room, straightening papers, brushing away some dust. She wasn't going to tell me.

She said in a calm voice, "There's only one more thing we need to add to the obituary – the time and place for the service. Save the file on a memory stick and we'll take it with us."

While I went through the process, she glanced outside then opened the door as Simon started barking. A gust of wind blew the door out of her hand. I pulled the memory stick and followed her outside. Simon was jumping on Lorraine, then running around in circles.

I chuckled. "He probably saw a bunny rabbit."

"I don't think so. He knows." She knelt down and scratched him behind the ears. "You know, don't you boy? Weather's coming in. We need to leave now."

As she locked the door, I scanned the sky above us. "A storm?"

"Look over toward the west." She pointed. "The Bay area is fickle. Weather can change quickly, especially in the afternoon." I turned, squinting against the freshening wind, and saw a line of deep gray clouds bearing down on us.

"That's a squall coming in," she said, leading the way to the car. "Can't tell what's behind it."

The wind tried to knock us off our feet. Fat raindrops slapped the windshield just as we got in the car. Driving down the gravel road through the open fields, I had to grip the steering wheel while the wind rocked the car. Water was pooling on the paved road.

"Should we pull over?" I asked, concerned about the weather and the big ditches lining the road up ahead.

"Oh no, you're doing fine."

That was when the storm hit full force. Whimpering, Simon crawled into Lorraine's lap.

She looked at the rough weather then looked at me. "I don't think you want to drive back to Washington tonight in this storm. It's Saturday night of a holiday weekend. You should stay over."

I shrugged while keeping my eyes glued to the road. "What does Saturday have to do with it?"

"It's a dangerous time to drive on the Shore. People drink all day and, no matter how hard you try, you can't protect yourself from a drunk driver. That's what happened to my Thomas. A guy passed out at the wheel, totaled my husband's vintage Thunderbird and took his life. The guy walked away with a few scratches. Please stay, Abby. I don't need something else to worry about."

"Nobody has a room for a woman with a puppy. I'll drop you off. We'll be fine." Out of the corner of my eyes, I saw Simon snuggle against Lorraine. Traitor.

"I'm sure Miss Constance will have a room for you at the hotel, and you'll be my guest."

"I can't let you do that. Besides, they won't allow the dog."

"Nonsense. This hotel caters to people who love boats and dogs. Miss Constance makes accommodations all the time." She chuckled. "No pun intended."

I started to protest, but she rolled right over me. "Having your company today has been a godsend to me. You saved me from wallowing in my thoughts or listening to empty platitudes from people like Harriet. I'm not ready for my time with you to end."

She nuzzled Simon who turned toward me and whined. What could I say?

Lightning flashed in the gloom. Thunder cracked right over our heads. Simon buried his head under Lorraine's arm.

"Then it's settled," she announced. You just have to get us to the hotel safely."

CHAPTER EIGHT

If any drop of water or food chances to fall upon the exterior of silver hollowware, it should be carefully mopped off at once. Nothing can change the silver's appearance more than moisture.

—"The Butler's Guide to Fine Silver" Mr. Hollister, 1898

Huge raindrops pounded the car. After dropping Lorraine at the hotel's front door, Simon and I sat huddled under the convertible top quietly hoping it wouldn't leak.

"What do you think, Simon? Should we wait or make a run for it?"

Lightning flashed. Bone-rattling thunder exploded around us. Simon clambered into my lap squeezing his body between the steering wheel and my chest. I gasped for air.

"It's okay, it's okay." I tried to move him so I could breathe. No luck so I moved the seat. He whined and cuddled closer. "Okay, we'll go!" He clung to me with his paws on my shoulders, the whites of his eyes showing in terror. "Easy, big fellow. I can't carry you." He whined again. "You're going to have to get down. It'll be fun running through all those puddles." I tried to sound brave for him.

KER-RACK! He clawed my shoulder. I grabbed the key and the end of his leash and threw open the door. Simon launched himself and dragged me through the downpour. The wind grabbed the lobby door of beveled glass and Lorraine had to help me pull it closed. It was a relief to enter an elegant lobby filled with calming music, quite a contrast to the violence outside.

"Oh dear, you're soaked," said a small woman with smooth, rich skin the color of café au lait. A small brass badge on her chest winked in the light, Constance, Hotel Manager.

My clothes stuck to my skin and water dripped off the tip of my nose onto an Oriental rug. I hopped over to the tiled floor. "I'm sorry, I'm sorry."

Simon danced in circles on the end of the leash. "Simon, settle down," I begged.

He froze in place and braced his legs.

"Noooo…" Lorraine and I both cried.

Too late. Simon swung his head from side to side, ears flapping. The shaking traveled all the way down his body until the tip of his tail flicked away the last drop. Proudly, he sat down in the pool of water, panting.

I looked at the manager. "I'm so sorry. I'll get some paper towels and…"

"Don't move, please," she said. Her arms reached out to keep me where I was.

I looked down at the floor around my water-logged shoes and saw I was standing in a pool of my own.

"Now, don't you worry about a thing," said the manager. "Miss Lorraine, we have to get this girl out of those clothes before she catches cold."

"Oh, I agree, Miss Constance. It would be a crime if she got sick." Lorraine winked at me.

A teenager in a maid's uniform rushed up with a tall stack of towels and put them on a table. She sopped up the water on the floor while her boss offered me a towel.

"Start at the top," she ordered. She handed a towel to Lorraine, then knelt down and wrapped one around Simon as he wagged his tail, throwing more droplets everywhere. He loved the new game of Wiggle-out-of-the-Towel until Constance said, "Stay!" in a voice that even made me freeze. These two women – Lorraine and Constance – knew how to get what they wanted with a single word or a look. I felt like a little girl again… and safe with these strangers even though there was a murderer out there somewhere.

"Here, let me have that wet towel." Constance handed me another dry one.

I rubbed my skin that was bumpy from the chilly air. My curly hair kept channeling water down my back.

Lorraine handed me another dry towel. "Wrap this around your head to dry out those pretty curls."

"My hair is a disaster." I groaned. "It'll be one massive tangle."

"We'll see about that," said Miss Constance as she walked behind the hotel desk.

In a few minutes, the floor was just damp and the maid carried off the tall stack of soggy towels. I stood in the middle of the room shivering.

"Miss Constance, could you arrange a room for my friend?" Lorraine asked.

"Of course, let me see what we have," she said as she put down the phone. In a flash, she was tapping on a computer keyboard. "I have a nice room on the same floor as the spa. I'll have Housekeeping make sure the room is ready," reported Constance, picking up the phone.

"Thank you, Lorraine, but…" I looked at the drowned-looking puppy at my feet. "Um, what about Simon?" I asked in a weak voice, hoping they had a good answer for my canine situation.

Constance declared that he would be a welcome guest, too.

"So, you see, there's no problem," said Lorraine.

The manager laughed with a gentle shake of her head. "Miss Lorraine, you're always taking care of everybody else. Now, I've taken care of you both."

"You always do, Miss Constance." Then, she crouched down to give Simon a good rub behind the ears. "You're a good boy, even if you did try to give the hotel an indoor swimming pool." His tongue shot out and licked her chin. She smiled, "Yes, you are a good boy."

Constance came around the desk and gave Lorraine a no-nonsense look. "It's all arranged. The spa will take care of your friend while you're having a massage." Lorraine started to protest. "I don't want to hear it." She softened her voice. "I can't imagine what you're feeling in your heart, but your muscles must be tight and achy. I can't do anything for Miss Evelyn. Please, let me do this for you."

Lorraine opened her mouth to argue then nodded silently in acceptance.

"Alright then, up you go to the third floor. They're waiting for you in the spa." She went to the elevator door and pushed the UP button. "I'll get a key ready for Abby and she'll be right along."

Lorraine entered the elevator and said, "She'll need some dry clothes."

"Don't worry, I'll take care of everything. You go on now." The elevator door slipped closed.

"And Simon?" I asked.

"Leave him with me," she said, gingerly touching his damp coat. "He'll be just fine." Then, she shot me a quick look. "He is house-broken, isn't he?"

"Oh, yes!" Mostly, I added to myself along with a silent prayer. Simon would get more walks tonight than he'd ever had before.

"Wait right there for a moment." She took Simon's leash and led him through a door to the back office. I felt my cheeks get hot with embarrassment when a distinguished man walked through the lobby with his well-manicured wife. Her eyes ran up and down my soaked clothes and the towel turban on my head. Did I hear her sniff as she turned and led her husband up the staircase? I guess some people are just rude. I was relieved when Miss Constance came back, handed me a room key card and guided me to the gift shop off the lobby. In minutes, I was holding a new pair of black slacks along with a blue cotton sweatshirt that she said would look great with my copper-colored hair.

I rode the elevator up to the spa floor where the staff showed me straight to the showers. The hot water felt so good and, I must admit, the attention of the bustling spa staff made me feel special. Somehow a stylist tamed my curls into shiny spirals, then I was settled into a deep, overstuffed chair and put my feet in a soaking tub of warm water. With a cup of coffee in one hand and a glossy fashion magazine in the other, I let the mechanical fingers of the massaging system in the chair deal with my tense back muscles.

"Hi, I'm Cindy." A woman with kaleidoscope hair in shades of red and blonde sat down on the other side of the tub of swirling water. "Let's see what we have here." She picked up my right foot out of the water and frowned.

I was mortified. I never thought there was anything wrong with my feet but, looking at them through the eyes of a professional, I saw a jagged toenail, dry cuticle and chipped polish. I started to say that my toenails hadn't been a priority, but no explanation was necessary. Cindy was a professional and started humming as she went about doing her job. I opened the magazine and tried to relax. Soon, a woman sat in the chair next to mine and her technician turned on the hot water. She must have been a regular, because they all started gabbing. I tuned them out until I heard Miss Evelyn's name.

"Miss Evelyn was such a nice woman, but she could be tough as nails," said my chair mate.

"What do you expect after everything she went through?" remarked the other nail tech.

"That happened a long time ago."

Not to be left out, Cindy added, "It could be that her past came back to haunt her."

The client jumped on the comment. "What do you mean?"

Yes, what did she mean? I held the magazine still as their conversation went round and round. I wanted to look at them, but I was afraid they would stop talking if they saw a stranger so I stayed still and listened.

"That no-good husband of hers made enemies. Maybe they came back to get what they were owed," said Cindy.

Was that why Lorraine didn't want to mention Evelyn's husband in the obituary?

"That was years ago!" The woman squealed. "Oh, look at the time!"

"Hold still, Tiffany," said her technician. "You made me mess up."

"Sorry, Bobbie. Mom-Mom is babysitting the baby and she'll kill me if I'm late."

"Just settle yourself so I can finish. Ya know, I don't think time matters when there's money involved. If a gang is at the center of this… well, we hear about those bad boys all the time."

Their conversation opened up new possibilities that Lorraine and I hadn't considered. Evelyn's husband was dead and a good-for-nothing, but if he owed money to the wrong kind of people, they might not stop at murder to get what they wanted. I sat very still so I wouldn't miss a word.

"My cousin Staci works at Fair Winds." Cindy said. Her comment got everybody's attention. "She got me out of bed before the sun was up, banging on my door, crying and fussing. She wanted to stay at my place after what happened out there."

"Why?" someone asked.

"She's the one who found the body. She was afraid she would be next. You know how she goes on."

Her audience groaned. Then they all had an opinion.

"Staci has an overactive imagination."

"I don't know."

"Give me a break. You know she's a ditz sometimes."

"No, I meant that I don't know if this is the right color for my nails," said the client sitting next to me. "Do you think it's too bright?"

"You're the ditz!"

I had to control a giggle. This spa was true to the reputation that all salons are the best source for news and gossip.

"Really, Tiff!" Cindy insisted. "Stay with us. We're talking about important stuff."

You tell 'em, Cindy! These women could hold the key to who murdered Evelyn and not realize it. Please get back to the important stuff.

"I just can't think about it anymore," Tiffany whimpered. "It's too horrible."

"I bet the police were very interested in what Staci overheard last week," Cindy continued. There was a smirk of satisfaction in her voice now that she was the center of attention again. "Staci heard a man hassling Miss Evelyn about money. He said she *owed* him because she was a Truitt, too." She paused for dramatic effect. "And, he said that it was no way to treat her own stepson."

"Stepson?" they said in chorus.

"Her husband had a boy hidden away somewhere?" Tiffany asked in shock.

"It seems so. He's from someplace down in Virginia." Cindy's distaste for the state dripped from the word.

Oh, this could be the missing piece to the puzzle! Stay calm. There might be more. Considering how much they seem to dislike Virginia, I vowed not to volunteer where I lived while I was on the Shore.

The voice named Bobbie asked the question I wanted them to answer. "What did Miss Evelyn say?"

"Staci heard her say that he must be as rotten as his father to wait all these years to show himself and then come around for a handout. She sent him packing."

I realized with a start that there was a tickle in my nose.

"That woman was tough as nails, I'm telling you. Bobbie, aren't you done yet? I have to go," Tiffany whined.

Pressure was building.

"Maybe she was too tough. I'm thinking that maybe she got him so riled up, he came back and—"

No-o-o. I sneezed.

The women were silent. I lowered the magazine and found all three of them staring at me.

"Sorry, do you have a tissue?" I asked in a small voice.

My ill-timed sneeze ended their conversation. No one said another word. Cindy gave me a bit of a dirty look but, really, how could she forget there was a person, a stranger, attached to the toes she was polishing?

In minutes, I joined Lorraine at the front desk. Her spa treatment had smoothed away some of the worry lines. She was saying to the spa manager, "Carly, you and your staff worked wonders. My body feels much better and see how wonderful my friend Abby looks."

"It was the least we could do," Clara said, then she turned to me. "That reminds me. Miss Constance called to say that she put Simon in your room?" The statement ended like a question that invited clarification. The woman was a dry sponge, thirsty for gossip.

"Sorry, Carly," said Lorraine in a flat voice. "Nothing hot and sizzling for you today. Simon is her dog."

Carly's face fell with a thud. We said our goodbyes and scooted out the door.

As soon as we were alone, I said to Lorraine in a strained whisper, "You'll never guess what I found out. I—"

"I know exactly what you're going to say, Abby. You found out you can feel human again."

I tried again. "No, um, yes, but I—"

"Yes, we both need to thank Miss Constance. She really knows how to take care of her guests."

The elevator opened and Lorraine moved inside. I grabbed the edge of the door to keep it from closing.

"Lorraine, there's something you have to know. The—"

She shook her head lazily. "The only thing I have to know is that a warm, comfy bed is waiting for me and I could sure use some sleep."

The woman certainly deserved a good night's rest. My news could wait until morning when we both would be thinking a little clearer. I took my hand away to release the door. As it slid closed, I heard her say, "Tomorrow, we'll have pancakes at The Cove, the hotbed of news and gossip in this town."

CHAPTER NINE

A piece of silver – whether a utensil or serving piece – may be scratched by accident during normal use, but the most frequent cause of scratching is the lack of precautions. Only those members of staff with the proper training and awareness should handle the silver to avoid damage to any piece.

—"The Butler's Guide to Fine Silver" Mr. Hollister, 1898

Early the next morning, a hotel maid delivered a cable-knit cardigan sweater in forest green, my favorite color.

"Miss Lorraine said to wear it, because it's chilly. She'll meet you in the lobby in thirty minutes," she said.

I dressed quickly and the soft warmth of the sweater felt good. Simon and I went outside for a quick walk and scurried back to the lobby just as Lorraine appeared. Miss Constance materialized from her office and led the yawning puppy behind the front desk where he did his little turnaround dance and nestled into a corner for a nap. She commented on how well behaved he was. Was she talking about my Simon—I mean, my friend Gwen's dog? The

Eastern Shore certainly had a magical effect on the hyperactive puppy.

Lorraine and I left on our quest for pancakes and information. We walked along the harbor where watermen tied up their boats. She explained that their design was native to the Chesapeake Bay, long and low to the water with a little cabin on the bow. The rest of the boat was open so the waterman had easy, unobstructed access to his catch. One fellow was working on his engine.

"It sounds like a NASCAR race," I yelled to Lorraine. "His muffler must be broken."

"You have no idea how loud a race can be." She winked. "But here, most watermen don't use mufflers."

"A crab could hear him coming from miles away."

Lorraine laughed. "I don't think it bothers them."

We turned right and walked up a little street called Chew Avenue.

"That's a funny name for a street, isn't it?" I asked and hoped I hadn't insulted some time-honored tradition.

"Yes, it is if you don't know the history. This street was named in honor of Benjamin Chew, a patriot born in Maryland who worked with the Founding Fathers and became the first Chief Justice of the Pennsylvania Supreme Court." Lorraine laughed. "Somehow, he had time to father fourteen children, twelve of them girls – which would be enough to drive any man back to work."

We wandered by quaint little houses she said were more than a hundred years old. Church bells sang out the quarter-hour. "Those are the chimes of Christ Church which dates back to 1670-something. You might be interested to know that sterling silver played an important part in the history of that church."

"Did somebody in Baltimore make a silver cross or something?" I asked.

"No, Queen Anne sent a silver communion chalice engraved with the date 1710 and a matching silver paten. They're on display in the church. I'll take you to see them sometime."

All of a sudden, a dark blue SUV drove up behind us and stopped. We both turned to see the police chief of St. Michaels get out of his car. Standing by the driver's side door with the engine running, he shook his head and said in a deep voice, "Miss Lorraine, you are *the* hardest person to find in our little town. My men and I have been looking all over for you."

Lorraine put her feet together, rolled up on her toes and bounced, trying to look innocent. I suspected that she didn't want the chief to know that we were looking for clues to the murder on our own. "Well, Chief, you've found me. I dearly hope you have some good news?"

"What would you like to hear?" he asked, as he walked up to us.

"Oh," she raised her eyes to the blue sky as if searching for a good answer. "I'd like you to tell me that you found the fiend who hurt Evie." He dropped his eyes and slowly shook his head. "Then tell me I can go home."

He gave his head a little shake. "No, I'm afraid you're two for two. I'm sorry." He took in a deep breath to insert a *period, paragraph* so they could move on. "There is something I need to talk to you about..." He paused. "In private, ma'am."

"I have forgotten my manners." She turned toward me. "Abby, may I present our police chief – and my good friend, Chief Douglass Luken."

"Actually, we've already met," I said sheepishly.

He pointed at me in surprise. "Yes, at Fair Winds! Mr. Reg's girlfriend!"

I corrected him with a smile. "Friend, just a friend, Chief."

Surprised, Lorraine continued. "Then you know Abby Strickland from the Western Shore—"

"Northern Virginia, actually." I added and wanted to bite my tongue. I hoped he wasn't prejudiced about Virginia like the spa ladies were.

"That's still on the Western Shore last time I checked," he said with a crooked smile.

"Meaning?"

"Meaning you're not from here, but you are welcome." We shook hands. His grip was manly, but gentle. "Glad to meet you officially." His crooked smile broke into a wide grin, then faded away. "I'm sorry to interrupt your walk, Miss Lorraine, but seriously, I do need to talk to you, alone."

"Chief, you can talk in front of Abby."

"Ma'am, it's about…"

"Anything you want to say to me, you can say in front of Abby. She's already been interviewed as a suspect in the case by…" She turned to me for confirmation. "It was the Virginia Police, wasn't it?"

His eyebrows shot up in surprise. "You're the one?" Under his scrutiny, I had the urge to step behind Lorraine.

"The one who sold me the cake breaker? Yes." Lorraine said. "But she had nothing to do with what happened."

His brows scrunched low over his eyes, scanning me carefully. "And you're in St. Michaels now because…?"

"She came to make sure I was alright," Lorraine said quickly. "She is keeping me company until all you law enforcement people let me go home."

The Chief held up his hands in surrender. "It's not me. The State Police seem to be looking for something."

"Well, I'm sure they won't find it. You said it yourself, it was a robbery gone wrong." The Chief looked at her, all hints about what he was thinking carefully hidden. "That *is* what you said, right?" Uncertainty was creeping into her voice.

"That's what we need to talk about." He gestured to his big car. "Can I give you a ride to wherever you're going?" He continued quickly as Lorraine was starting to decline. "We need to take our conversation off the street."

We quickly got into his car, Lorraine in the front seat by the Chief. I tucked myself in the back.

"We're going to the Cove—" she started to say.

"Not yet," he interrupted, put the car in gear and drove slowly down a shaded lane. After a few turns, he pulled up close to a chain link fence next to a small skateboard park. "I don't think we'll be disturbed here. It's still too early for the kids." He shifted into park and turned to Lorraine. "I'm looking at another line of investigation."

"Something sane, I hope, not like that man looking for scary letter writers threatening our elected officials." Her little laugh at her own joke melted away when she saw the stern look on the Chief's face.

"What I'm going to tell you is in strict confidence, but I thought you should know, for your own safety."

Worried, Lorraine said, "Oh dear, tell me,"

He turned toward the back seat and his eyes bore into me.

I held up my hands in surrender. "Not a word."

He shifted his attention back to Lorraine. "Several weeks ago, we got a new case of assault. A young woman was badly beaten by her boyfriend. It wasn't the first time. She ran to the woman's shelter for protection, but, for some reason, she left and met him somewhere."

I watched the chief's expression in his rear-view mirror. The little quiver in the skin around his eyes betrayed his concern.

"Probably the same old story, the man professing his undying love, vowing that he'll change," Lorraine recited.

He nodded. "Except this time, he beat up on her again and said she'd better stop telling lies to that old lady at Fair Winds or he'd teach her a lesson, too. One of my officers remembered that's what she'd said when he talked to her at the hospital." Though I was sitting safely in the chief's car, a cold chill ran through me. "We did visit with Miss Evelyn about the matter."

"What did she say?" breathed Lorraine.

He shook his head gently. "She laughed it off. She said men like that don't have what it takes to follow through on their threats to other people. They're only man enough to beat up on their wives or girlfriends." He shook his head again. "I tried to tell her that wasn't always true. I asked her to be careful."

Lorraine gasped. “So, you think that he…”

“Yes, he may have gone to Fair Winds that night to set Miss Evelyn straight. I know this loser and he thinks the world owes him something. We’re looking for him now.”

I could barely make out what Lorraine said quietly, “Just like Clay Truitt.”

“What was that?” asked the chief.

“Oh, nothing. It’s not important.”

“At this point, anything might be important, Lorraine. Who is Clay Truitt? Is he from around here? I haven’t heard that name before.”

“I imagine not. By the time you came to St. Michaels, Clay Truitt was long dead. He was Evelyn’s husband.”

“Of course,” I murmured. They both turned to look at me. “It’s just…” I took a moment to reconstruct the conversation I’d heard during the pedicure. “Yesterday, I overheard a group of women talking about a man in town claiming to be Evelyn’s step-son. Would that make him Clay Truitt’s son?”

“And you were going to tell me about this… when?” The Chief’s voice was like a barbed hook and I felt like the squirming worm.

“Well, I…”

The Chief opened a small notepad with his pen poised to take notes. I reported what I remembered of the conversation and the names, as best I could. After he asked me some questions, wringing me dry of information, he turned to Lorraine.

“You were friends with Miss Evelyn since childhood, right?” She nodded. What do you know about this Clay Truitt’s background? Could he have a son who might be stalking her?”

Lorraine shook her head as if it would help rid her mind of the memory. “It was a painful chapter in her life, I can tell you that. I know nothing about the man before he came here.” She paused. “Except…” The chief’s eyes narrowed. “I remember he came from the Eastern Shore of Virginia. Nobody could figure out why he came up here. He must have gotten into some bad trouble down there." She looked at the chief. "You know that no self-respecting Virginia waterman would move up to Maryland unless he had to." She looked out the window at a grove of pine trees as if answers lurked in the shadows. "I knew the name of the town once…Wait, let me think. Duck?"

"That's in North Carolina on the Outer Banks," the Chief said.

"Right, but…" she struggled. "It had something to do with birds. Maybe the name of a bird or something."

"On the Eastern shore of Virginia, right?" he asked.

She nodded. He scribbled.

"Anything else?"

She shook her head. "No. Sorry."

"That's good. I can work with that. And we'll start looking for this so-called stepson." He caught me watching him in the mirror. His look pinned me to the seat like a mounted butterfly. I was sure I never wanted to get on the wrong side of this man.

He held my gaze, then said, "Good work but next time, tell me anything you find out right away. Don't wait until you're on the way to eat breakfast." I nodded so hard, my curls whipped into my eyes.

After a long moment, he turned to Lorraine and I slumped back in my seat. "Lorraine, one of these two guys may have attacked Miss Evelyn. If so, he may come back. He might want to teach you a lesson, too."

Lorraine sank back against the door, trying to take it all in.

The Chief continued. "That's why I want to assign protection to you until we find them and get everything figured out."

"A bodyguard? Her voice rose an octave. You want me to have a bodyguard?"

"I can give you one of my uniformed officers," he said.

"Absolutely not! It's a waste of your manpower and you must be stretched to the max as it is. Until I go home, I'll be perfectly fine at the hotel and today Abby will stay with me, won't you?" I nodded slowly, wondering what I would do to stop a maniac who was hell-bent on hurting her.

The Chief thought for a moment, then looked straight at me. "If there is any sign of trouble, you call 911. Don't wait, understand? I'd rather have you overreact than…" His words trailed off but left his meaning hanging boldly in the air.

"Yes sir." I had the urge to salute.

"Alright," Charming again, he asked, "Where can I drop you ladies?"

"We'll walk from here," said Lorraine.

"No, you won't." The tone of his voice was thick with exasperation. "That's what I mean. You have to be aware of your surroundings. You don't know if someone's lurking in those bushes over there or hiding behind a tree. Let's try this again, where do you want me to drop you?" He drove off slowly.

Was he being overly protective or could he be right? I peered into shadows, but saw nothing.

"Would it be acceptable to you if we walk along Talbot Street, Chief?" Lorraine's voice was haughty.

Could it be that she wasn't taking this threat seriously? I settled back against the seat to get as far away as possible from this sparring match.

The Chief caught on to her sarcastic tone and responded in a formal, respectful way. He must have remembered that Lorraine was a leading member of the community, an independent woman, used to doing things *her* way. "Yes, ma'am, a walk along the main street would be just fine and you'll take the main roads back to the hotel afterward, of course."

"Of course, but only after we've had our pancakes at the Cove, Chief." He stopped the car by a line of stores that hadn't opened yet. She tried the door handle. "If you'll release us, Sir."

He hit the button to unlock the doors. "You're not a prisoner, Miss Lorraine. You're a valued friend. I don't want to see you hurt." He gave her a bright smile that took any sting out of his words. "I'm sworn to serve and protect. I'm just doing my job."

Lorraine caved into his charm. "And doing it very well," she said with a smile. We got out of the car and he drove off.

"Which way?" I asked, trying to keep the mood light.

Lost in thought, she started to walk along the empty brick sidewalk soon to be filled with tourists again. She turned to face one of the shop windows, but she wasn't looking at the shabby-chic home accessories on display. "The more things change, the more they stay the same."

"What do you mean?" I was having trouble keeping up with everything and the mad turns my life had taken in the past 24 hours: from a murder suspect to a snoop to a guard. I was getting whiplash.

Lorraine sighed and stared at the window. "Remember when I told you not to list Evie's husband in the obituary? There was a reason. He was a no-good wife-beater, too. When they first met, everything was perfect. Evie thought she'd found the man she could make a *real home* with... that's what she called it when we were growing up... a *real home*...where there would be love and children and happiness." Her voice became caustic. "What she got was a living hell." She crossed her arms and I could see in the window's reflection, her fingers tapping out her anger. "Clay Truitt, so handsome, so charming. I tell you Abby, that's a deadly combination." She dropped her arms and moved down the sidewalk to the next shop window. "It all went wrong when Evie got pregnant. Clay wasn't the center of attention anymore and he lashed out. One night, drunk, he beat her so badly, she lost her baby right on the kitchen floor." Lorraine shuddered.

"Did she leave him? I asked.

"No, no, she stayed like many women do. She bought his sweet talk and promises. She didn't turn him in to the cops." Lorraine started walked again as if the topic was too painful to take standing still. "Then she got pregnant again."

"Did he hit her again?" Hoping the answer was no. Somehow Evie had become very real to me, someone I was starting to care about.

"Yes. We didn't know it at the time. I was away at school and she'd stopped coming to Fair Winds so Momma lost track of her.

It all came out months later when the cops found out Clay using her daddy's boat to run drugs. He got it in his head that he could do some dealing on the side and keep the money." She chuckled sadly at his stupidity. "He didn't get it. You don't cross drug dealers. One morning, they found the boat… or what was left of it… close to Bloody Point. Clay's body washed up a few days later."

Maybe the women at the spa were right. Maybe the gang tried to force Evelyn to pay her husband's debt and things went too far. Good thing I told the chief.

Lorraine looked up at the flock of geese making a racket as they flew overhead. "There she was – pregnant, no boat, no husband, empty bank accounts and her daddy dying from lung cancer."

It was hard for me to imagine how the woman in the story found the will to survive, to go on to live a good life … and die at Fair Winds. "We didn't list a child in the obituary. What happened to the baby?"

Lorraine straightened up quickly. "It died. It must have been all the stress and sadness. Come on, our pancakes await." She rushed ahead.

CHAPTER TEN

It is vitally important to select the proper serving piece for the food or confection presented. Great thought has gone into the design of the many different pieces. One must educate oneself as to what is available and confer with Cook about the menu to ensure proper presentation.

—"The Butler's Guide to Fine Silver" Mr. Hollister, 1898

Lorraine put her arm through mine and gently walked me down the street. When we reached a storefront under an overhang, she pulled open the door.

"Welcome to The Cove and a heavenly breakfast!" she announced.

And we walked into… a drug store? I was very confused as we worked our way past shelves of pain relievers, cologne and hair-color until we reached an area at the back that was partitioned off. We stepped forward, right into a 1950's-style soda shop. We slipped onto two swivel seats at the worn, but clean counter. The footrest was scuffed by generations of shoes. Only two waitresses, wearing peach-colored uniforms with little white aprons, were serving all the diners at the counter and the twelve tables beyond. They chatted with the people they knew and silently served the tourists. After they took an order, they'd stand by the pass-through window to the kitchen and bellow out the details to the invisible cook.

We sat waiting for menus, which turned out to be the right thing to do. A middle-aged couple was sitting at a table. She waved impatiently at the two servers, her hands loaded with jewelry. I suspected that *conspicuous consumption* didn't get you very far on the Shore. A quick look passed between the two women and it was clear they bumped that table to the end of the line. There was no question who was in charge in this little place.

Lynette, the younger waitress came to us and flashed a big smile. "Mornin' Miss Lorraine. What—"

The other woman in uniform zoomed in and said, "I've got them." Patti-with-an-i, according to her name badge, was the boss. "What are ya gonna have with your coffee?"

I started to ask for a menu, but Lorraine laid a hand on my arm. "We're both going to have the Sunday Special." Lorraine looked at me asking "Regular coffee?" I nodded. "…for both of us."

"I'm making a fresh pot," Patti reported.

"Perfect, we'll wait," agreed Lorraine.

When Patti smiled and walked away, I started to say something, but Lorraine caught my eye and barely shook her head. *Not here, not now.* I looked around the counter and the two tables close-by. There were many sets of eyes and ears.

Without warning, Patti set down large platters in front of us, stacked with fluffy, golden brown pancakes, so hot that the butter on top was melting fast. A separate plate held a collection of breakfast meat: thickly-cut Amish bacon cooked to perfection and little brown patties.

"Are those sausage patties?" I asked Lorraine.

"No, that's scrapple."

"Scrapple?" I nudged one with my fork.

"It's named scrapple for a reason. They take the *scraps* and make a delicious breakfast side. Don't ask what's in it. Just eat and enjoy," she declared.

I was game. How bad could it be? I picked up the little pitcher of maple syrup and was delighted to find it was warm.

"Real butter, real maple syrup" said Lorraine.

I took my first taste. Pure heaven. A meal to remember in a place where time had stopped. Finally, when I settled back in my seat, I'd eaten every morsel on my plate.

Lynnette made another pass with the coffeepot. "Miss Lorraine, I was sorry to hear about Miss Evelyn. We all were." She lowered her voice. "Do they know who did it?" Lorraine shook her head. "It's none of my business but…" Her mouth snapped shut, too late.

"Lynette, are you bothering Miss Lorraine?" demanded Patti.

"No ma'am, just refilling her coffee." Satisfied, Patti whizzed off to a table.

"Lynnette, do you know something I should know?" Lorraine asked, trying to keep her enthusiasm out of her voice.

"No… well, I'll just say what I've got to say." She looked over her shoulder to make sure Patti was busy. She leaned over the counter close to Lorraine. "Do you know Jimmy Smith from Tilghman?" Lorraine shook her head. "Well, it might interest you to know that he's been seeing Miss Evelyn these past few months?"

Lorraine sat bolt upright. "Do you mean *dating*?" She asked loud enough to turn heads at the counter.

Lynnette wiped the already dry counter. "No, don't be silly," she whispered. "He's only twenty. He's been coming up here to St. Michaels talking to her."

"About what?"

"Things. I've seen them," the waitress insisted.

Lorraine looked puzzled so she went exploring. "Miss Evelyn has… had a lot of friends."

Lynnette shook her head slowly. "It was more like he was hounding her."

"Why?" I blurted out.

Lynette looked at me, suddenly wary.

Lorraine said, "It's okay. She's with me."

The waitress gave me a suspicious look that said she wasn't so sure. She looked back to Lorraine. "Jimmy wants to work on the water by himself, not with Mr. Eddie anymore. He says the old man doesn't pay fair. Jimmy wants to buy his own boat, but doesn't have the money. I heard he wanted Miss Evelyn to loan him what he needed."

"Why would she do that? They aren't related, are they?" asked Lorraine.

"No, ma'am."

"Hey, Missy." An overweight man carefully balanced on the stool across the way waved at Lynnette. "What's a guy got to do to get some hot coffee around here?"

Lynnette moved to his place like a bullet in fear that he'd short her tip. "Yes, sir. Here you are." She filled his cup, but he didn't smile. Lorraine was right. Tourists visiting St. Michaels stood out and not in a flattering way. The man's aggressive manner might be just the ticket in a big city, but in this quaint town, it was considered rude.

When she returned, Lorraine coaxed her. "Finish your story, dear."

Lynette wiped the counter again and avoided Lorraine's eyes. "A lot of people around here think Miss Evelyn has money. Working at your big house, she don't have no expenses to speak of. She got a car and a place to live as part of her job. I guess he thought she'd be an easy touch 'cause she don't have kin to spend her money on. I heard he even showed up at Fair Winds."

Lorraine pursed her lips. "What did Miss Evelyn tell him?"

"I heard that she was real nice, but told him no." Lynette dropped her gaze. She seemed uncomfortable talking gossip with a woman like Lorraine.

"Anything else?" I prodded.

"One night when we were all at the bar, he got real upset, said he wasn't gonna be somebody's slave for the rest of his life. Seems the bank turned him down again." She raised her eyes and pleaded. "I don't want to get anybody in trouble." She looked like she was about to burst into tears.

"Not to worry. You did the right thing by telling me. Now, run along and ask Patti for our check, please." Lorraine turned to me and hid her thoughts behind a broad smile. "Did you enjoy your breakfast?"

I was mystified that she had no comment about what Lynnette had said, but she gave me that look again: *Not here, not now.*

"Y-yes, it was very good," I stammered. "Best pancakes I've ever had."

"Good! Now, I need to walk off some of those calories. Get some fresh air."

She slipped off the stool, paid the bill and was out the door before I could untangle myself from a pushy couple trying to claim our seats. On the sidewalk, I found her standing under a tree along the curb reading a printed flyer.

I walked up close to her, pretending to read the paper too and said out of the corner of my mouth, "Are you going to tell the police chief?"

"No, not yet. We don't want to get the boy in trouble if he's innocent." She squared her shoulders. "No, we're going to go the source and find out what was going on."

Suddenly, I was very nervous. "We're going to interrogate Jimmy Smith? Lorraine, I don't think—"

"No, no, we're not going to do anything like that. What do you think I am, crazy? A confrontation like that down on Tilghman Island could lead to real trouble." She turned the flyer around so I could read the headline.

TILGHMAN ISLAND DAY FESTIVAL

She made the paper dance. "It's an Eastern Shore tradition. Evie used to go every year. Standing in for her is the least I can do.

Who knows, it might help." The flyer drooped and so did her voice. "Would you and Simon like to come with me?"

The warning the police chief had given us earlier that morning echoed in my mind. Lorraine was showing no concern about her own safety. The least I could do was tag along and keep an eye on her. I felt for my cell phone in my pocket and agreed to spend the day on Tilghman Island, wherever that was.

She slipped her arm through mine again and we strolled back to the hotel. On the way, I asked about Tilghman Island Day.

"It's a fundraiser for the Fire Department. They'll have contests… races… a flea market."

"Oh, I loved going to flea markets with Gran and Aunt Agnes. Do you think I might find some interesting sterling silver?"

"Probably not." She tried to stifle a laugh. "Everything on the Island is geared to the water. There'll be *boat* races… contests involving *boats,* a flea market with things for *boats*. And mountains of food."

"Oh, after that huge breakfast, I couldn't eat another thing!" I declared.

"Just wait. The salt air will perk up your appetite. You can feast on fresh oysters, fresh crabs and fresh corn right out of the fields."

I shuffled along sure that I'd never eat again.

In no time, we were on our way out of St. Michaels with Simon safely harnessed in the back seat. Lorraine sat quietly twisting her rings on her finger and staring out the window at the rural landscape.

She jumped when I broke the silence. "I'm glad we're going to Tilghman. I've felt so helpless. It'll be good to follow up on what Lynette said."

"Yes, I feel better, too," she agreed. "The local police are working the break-in and robbery angle and the state people are looking for stalkers. I doubt anyone will consider anything else until they've exhausted those leads. By then, it may be too late."

"Too late?"

"Too late to follow clues to the real killer." She turned and stared out at the passing fields and trees again. "Somehow, this whole thing feels, I don't know, personal. It feels personal," she repeated with a growing determination.

"In what way?"

She shook her head. "I don't know. I can't imagine that Evie had any enemies –"

"Except that guy who slugs his girlfriend," I put in.

She considered that thought and nodded. "Yes, except for him. It might be something connected to that stepson people are talking about. Either Clay had a son before he came up to Maryland or somebody's lying. I don't know what to make of it," she said with a sigh.

"Maybe we'll find the stepson on Tilghman Island. He might be trolling for other members of her family," I suggested.

"If he hurt her, he'll be long gone. Besides, I'm the closest thing she had to family."

I glued my eyes to the road ahead so Lorraine couldn't read the concern on my face. If this guy was the murderer, if he'd found an easy way into the house at Fair Winds, if he knew about the diamonds, he'd be back. I'd bet money on it. He'd come back to get what he thought he was owed by the closest family Miss Evelyn had, Lorraine!

I gripped the steering wheel, worried that we might be driving straight into harm's way.

CHAPTER ELEVEN

Cleaning silver is not for the faint of heart or weak of body. In the first step of polishing silver correctly, one must use a soft, clean cloth to apply the polish compound. Rub hard with the fingers to create friction that will help smooth out tiny scratches on the surface. One should feel the heat generated through the cloth. One can remove imperfections that mar the shine only by hard work.

—"The Butler's Guide to Fine Silver" Mr. Hollister, 1898

When we left St. Michaels, the sign said it was thirteen miles to Tilghman Island, but it felt like we'd been driving for an hour. "Did I miss a turn somewhere?"

"No, just go straight." She chuckled to herself. "There's a story about a tourist who drove all the way to the end of this road and looked out over the water. A waterman came up and followed his gaze to see what he was looking at. The tourist said, 'This is the end of the world, isn't it?' 'Nope,' said the waterman, 'but you can see it from here.'"

"Lorraine! You and your stories." It was nice to see her smile.

I'm glad we brought Simon." She reached around and gave

him a scratch behind the ear. "You'll sniff new smells and won't know what to do first, will you? You are such a good boy." I could almost hear him purr or whatever dogs do.

In no time, we came around a bend in the road, paid the admission fee to the festival to the ticket sellers by the side of the road and joined the slow flow of traffic over a metal drawbridge spanning Knapps Narrows, the waterway that made Tilghman an island.

"This is like the business district for the watermen. The shoreline was once crowded with crab-picking sheds and packing houses," Lorraine explained.

I thought the area still looked busy. Gas docks and boats up on blocks competed for space with tourist restaurants. On the water, boats were tied up to one another creating a raft that narrowed the channel even more. On the island, people were walking everywhere, right next to the car, right in front of the car. It would be easy to nudge someone by accident. I jockeyed my way into the first open parking space I saw just as the low-fuel warning came on. I'd keep an eye out for a gas station so I could fill up before we left. Who knew where Lorraine would take us next?

With Simon hitched to his leash, we joined the hordes for Tilghman Island Day. Lorraine's head swiveled around as we meandered along with the crowd. "The people who live on Tilghman Island fascinate me. Some build second homes for people from the Western Shore. Many women staff the hotels and restaurants. Some leave to get college degrees then come back to work on the water. The ancient challenge of man against nature continues and all less than two hours from our nation's capital."

"I guess it isn't always about the money and prestige of working in a big city that's all about power," I said, thinking that maybe that was one thing that lured me to Washington, a busy place where I could distract myself from the fact that I was all alone.

"That's right," Lorraine agreed. "Sometimes it's about the *quality* of life. These people have good hearts. I must say they are protective and loyal to family, friends and the region. That's more than I can say about some people I've met from the Western Shore."

Good things to keep in mind as I decide what new direction to take my life.

Simon yipped. The way he was licking his tail made me suspect that one of the visitors had stepped it. I started keeping a sharp eye on what was happening around us to anticipate trouble for him and began to notice the individuals around us: One lady struggling in high heels while her boyfriend was oblivious to her pain – definitely tourists; three boys of about ten, weaving their way through the crowd, unsupervised, comfortable, at home – local boys. Simon pulled me out of the mainstream over to a tree. While he did his thing, my eye caught the bumper sticker on the back of a truck that gave me a different insight to the people living on the island.

My Eastern Shore child can beat up anybody from the Western Shore

Simon and I followed Lorraine to the firehouse where she greeted by all kinds of people.

"Why, look what the wind blew in! Miss Lorraine, it's good to see you," said an old woman with a deeply-lined face.

"Abby, this is Martha." She smiled at the grinning old woman. "She used to work for Momma."

"Sure did, for a lot of years." She moved close to Lorraine and laid a gentle hand on her arm. "We heard about the terrible time up at Fair Winds. It ain't right what happened to Miss Evelyn."

"We'll all miss her. She always worried about you. How are you doing?"

"The bunions flare up when I walk a lot like today, but I wouldn't miss the festival!" said Martha with a laugh.

Lorraine leaned down close to the old woman's ear lost in a mass of grey hair. "Martha, do you know a Jimmy Smith?"

"Smith? There're a lot of them on the Shore. Who's his daddy?"

Lorraine tried to hide her frustration at not knowing anything about the man but his name. "How about a young man up here from Virginia---"

Martha jerked away. "Virginia?"

Lorraine nodded. "Says his name is Truitt?"

Martha stared at Lorraine and said with a snarl. "Ain't heard *that* name in a long time and never in a good way."

"I know, but if you hear anything, would you let me know?" asked Lorraine.

"I'll ask around and if I hear something, I'll get up and down with you right away."

"Thank you, Martha." Lorraine patted her shoulder and we moved on.

Everyone seemed to know Lorraine and greeted her with a tip of a hat or a comment about the tragedy. I followed along behind with Simon tucked close to my leg.

"Hungry?" Lorraine drew my attention away from the crowd.

I was surprised to realize that I was, even after that huge breakfast. Appetite and salt air must go together. She made a path for us to the community center, part of the firehouse where people of all ages were going about the very serious business of eating Eastern Shore delights.

"Oyster stew, m-m-m." I read from the handwritten menu sign on the wall.

"Yes," said Lorraine quietly. "This stew is for the tourists. I'll feed you oyster stew some time that'll make you rejoice. Are you ready to try some steamed crabs?"

"No, that would be too much of a challenge for today. What about oysters?"

She declared it was a good choice. Armed with food tickets, we laid siege to the serving tables. A big man with a white apron tied over his immense stomach stopped handing out the orders and moved toward Lorraine.

"Why, Charlie," she said. "How good to see you."

He said in a low voice, "I'm sorry to hear about what happened, you know, to Miss Evelyn. You okay?"

She leaned closer to him. "Yes, Charlie, I'll be fine."

He looked her straight in the eye. "You need anything, you tell me."

"Yes, I will." She paused for a moment. "Do you know a Jimmy Smith? I don't know which family he comes from."

He looked up at the ceiling as if reading the answer off the tiles. "It might be Big Will's son or Sheldon's son. We got a lot of Jimmy's down here and more than a few Smiths."

"Thanks anyway, Charlie."

"You take care of yourself now," he said as he turned back to a group of tourists who looked very impatient. He called out, "Which one of you has the Oyster Stew?"

With our trays overflowing, we looked for a place to sit in the crowded room as Lorraine whispered to me, "I wish I'd thought to ask Lynnette which Jimmy Smith she was talking about." She gestured off to the side. "I think there're two seats together over there."

We charged through the crowd and found enough table space to enjoy our lunch. Simon tucked under the table and curled up on my feet. Lorraine had steamed crabs again. I watched with envy as she tore through them.

"You should enter the crab-picking contest. You could be a contender," I insisted.

She laughed. "Once I came in third in the non-professional class, of course. It takes a lot of fast picking to win in the three minutes they allot." She gave me a small smug smile of satisfaction.

I grinned back. "Proves you're a real Eastern Shore woman!"

She cocked her head. "You bet I am, kid," she said, broadening her accent to match what we'd heard to all morning.

We finished up and worked our way back outside.

"Miss Lorraine!" The voice of a young woman demanded attention while her straw-like blonde hair that must have come out of a drugstore bottle of haircolor attracted curiosity. Distracted by her bright blue eye shadow and penciled-on eyebrows, I had to catch up on the conversation. "I hear you're asking around about Jimmy Smith." It was an accusation, not a question.

An older woman with harsh red hair, probably courtesy of the same drugstore, stood behind the blonde and said softly, "Rita! Don't be so—"

"Quiet, Ma." Rita ordered. "Well, are you looking for Jimmy?"

Lorraine tensed, but was polite. "Yes, I've been asking about him. Do you know him?"

"Yes." It was obvious that she was going to make Lorraine work for whatever she had to give.

"Do you know where I might find him?" asked Lorraine.

"I might."

Lorraine could play her silly game and waited.

"What do you want him for?" she asked finally.

"I'd like to talk to him if it's all the same to you." Lorraine's nails were coming out and I found myself taking a step back. "Why do you care?"

"I'm his friend, that's why."

Lorraine nodded. "That why I want to talk to him, because he knows a friend of mine." Her voice cracked a little on the word, *friend* but she pushed on. "It seems he's been spending time with her."

"You mean Miss Evelyn, don't you?" She went on quickly. "He didn't do nothing to hurt her." Her bright violet lips barely moved as the words squeezed between her clenched teeth. "Jimmy is a good guy. Just because he asked her for help don't mean he hurt her."

The mother spoke up, saying each word softly and carefully. "Rita, I know you'd like to help Miss Lorraine after that awful thing that happened up at Fair Winds." She hurried on so Rita couldn't interrupt. "Don't you remember telling me about that little problem Jimmy had at the bar the other night?"

"Momma!" Rita's eyes shot red-hot daggers at her mother

causing her to draw back.

Lorraine shifted her body toward Rita. "Yes, Rita, I'd like to hear what happened." Her eyes narrowed and held the girl's gaze when she turned toward her.

Realizing that the story was out, she tossed it off as if it wasn't important. "Well, everybody's heard about it. Nothing much happened. Just because he was drunk, got mad at the world and spouted off, don't mean he's a bad person."

I stepped up. "What was he mad about?"

"Wouldn't you like to know?" she shot back. We stood there silently while she lit a cigarette and flashed her long, pointy fake nails.

"Ready to tell us now?" I asked.

Rita glanced at Lorraine and saw from her expression that she'd probably pushed it as far as she could. She blew out a stream of smoke and said, "It was about money, what else?"

I pressed her. "Why did he need money?"

"He wants his own boat. Not being from around here, you wouldn't know about that. He's got dreams," Rita snarled.

Dreams that you hope include you.

"He needs twenty thousand for a used boat. His credit's down the toilet what with the divorce and all. Darleen always thought she was better than the rest of us. She grabbed every dime she could to buy clothes and stuff then she headed to the Western Shore." She thawed for a moment. "His dad can't help and the bank said no."

"So, he talked to Miss Evelyn?" asked Lorraine.

The wall went up again and Rita made us wait again as she puffed on the cigarette, almost gagging us with the smoke. "Yeah, he asked her to help him out with a loan."

"Why would she do that?" asked Lorraine.

Rita was enjoying every moment of this confrontation, probably the only time she'd have something over someone like Lorraine. "Miss Evelyn was Island folk."

Lorraine raised her eyebrows and nodded. "That makes sense.

Island folk are tight."

"She must be rolling in it. She lived at Fair Winds for free and she didn't spend it on nothing." She paused as a thought hit her. "Who's going to get all that money now?"

Don't you wish, I almost blurted out, but swallowed the words in time. The girl's attitude and cigarette smoke were making me sick.

Lorraine said, calmly, "I don't think you have to worry about that. Tell me, did they meet up? Do you know what happened?"

Grinding out her cigarette on the pavement, she flipped her hair and said, "Nope, I don't poke my nose where it don't belong. If I hear something, I know to keep my mouth zipped, not like some people," she said with a sniff, looking at her mother. "Ask somebody else. I gotta go." She pushed her way between Lorraine and me, almost stepping on Simon.

"We just might do that little thing," I murmured as my eyes followed the girl.

Her mother stepped up to Lorraine. "I'm sorry. I tried to do my best by her, my only girl. She was a mess before, but since she got back from Virginia, she's worse." The woman shook her head, almost in despair.

"Now, don't you worry. That was good information." Lorraine glanced at me with an encouraging look.

"Yes, very good information," I joined in. "Where do you think we might find Jimmy Smith today?"

"I don't want to get anybody in trouble," said the mother.

"Of course not." Lorraine looked around at the crowd.

"We just want to talk to the guy for a minute," I added.

"I wish I was the lucky guy you two lovely ladies were looking for." The deep, resonant male voice came from behind me, but this time it wasn't Reg. When I turned around, I had to tilt my chin up so I could see his handsome face – with two small dimples, eyes so blue they reminded me of the Greek Isles, along with long dark eyelashes so often wasted on a man. His skin had a warm healthy glow set off by the white cotton Oxford shirt that covered his broad chest. The windblown hair was cocoa brown naturally highlighted by the sun. Everything I saw—his body, his face, his smile —made me swoon a little. Yes, swoon.

Lorraine's voice penetrated my brain. "… dear boy." He gave her a peck on the cheek. "Abby, this is Henry also known as Hank. Abby?"

"Yes," I offered him my hand. The press of his skin against mine sent a spark through me. "Hello, Hunk," I squeaked… and immediately wanted to die. Heat rushed up to my face. The world reeled.

He hung on to hand and chuckled. "Hey, steady there."

"I'm so sorry," I sputtered.

"Not to worry. That's a compliment." He had a nice laugh. "Lorraine is the only one who calls me Henry. But you should call me Ryan. Everybody does."

Lorraine shook her head. "Your father wouldn't have approved of you changing your name."

"Actually, Ryan is my middle name. Now that I'm all grown up, people are less likely to get me confused with my father." He winked at Lorraine. "It's better than Junior." He turned those liquid eyes on me and I almost drowned. Please call me Ryan."

"Okay." And I nodded like an idiot.

He dropped his lighthearted manner as he expressed his condolences to Lorraine. They talked like old friends, but I had no clue about their connection or his situation. I was pleased and a little bashful when he turned his attention back to me.

"And what does Abby do when she's not enjoying the Eastern Shore?" he asked.

Lorraine jumped in before I could open my mouth. "Abby used to work for my nephew's company before it closed. Now, she is a sterling silver dealer."

"Actually, I'm really a software developer. I'm selling silver until I find a new tech position," I clarified.

"Why?" he asked. His question surprised me. "Writing software can be so boring, but silver must be fascinating with all its historical connections. I suspect it's lucrative too. But now..." Putting his arms around both of us, he said, "We have something every important to do. You're just in time to join me for the boat docking contest."

As we started to walk toward the harbor, I realized that his comment validated a thought starting to take hold in my mind: Working with the silver was fun and interesting. I wasn't sure how I could make it a full-time job to support myself – or if I wanted to – but it was an option.

While he steered us through the crowd, past the oyster-shucking and crab-picking competitions, I tried to think of something to say to keep the conversation going. I was so disappointed that the cleverest thing I could come up with was a question about where I could get some gas.

"If you're almost empty, you'd better go to Fairbanks. It's a bait-and-tackle shop that sells everything. You'll find whatever you need there," he winked, "especially the gossip around the Island." He pointed at a place close to the water. "Let's go over there. It should give us a good view of the race."

While we waited for the contest to begin, Lorraine told Ryan this was my first weekend on the Shore.

"Where have you been? This is the best place on earth," he declared. "Look, they're starting. We're just in time."

I followed his gaze across the harbor to a white, long, low-slung boat with a small cabin at the bow. A waterman's boat. "In this race," he explained, "watermen – the guys who pull the crabs – race against the clock to see who can dock their boat stern first and set the lines in the fastest time. Their workboats run 35-50 feet long and aren't designed for maneuverability."

"Do you have a boat like that?" I asked.

He looked at me and smiled. "No, I'm a sailor through and through. I appreciate what these men – and some women – do on the water to make a living, but the work is harder than I want to take on. Give me a sail of canvas, a good wind and a friendly companion, that's what makes me happy on the water."

A warning whistle sounded. “Keep your eye on that slip over there.” He pointed across the water. “That’s where all the action will be. My money’s on a kid named Jimmy Smith. It’s his first race ever so he’ll be up first.”

Lorraine shot me a look with her eyebrows raised just a little. Who would have thought that this good-looking guy would lead us to the man we’d come to find?

“Is Jimmy from around here?” I asked, hoping I sounded casual, not nosy.

“Of course. He’s been on the water for several years, but he’s still a young guy. He –”

The public address system drowned out our conversation. “And here comes our first contestant.” The crowd fell silent and watched Jimmy’s boat move into position.

An air horn sounded and the announcer yelled, “He’s off.”

The boat plowed through the water at high speed, headed straight for the pilings. Closer. Closer. Suddenly, it heeled to the right and did a tight 180-degree turn kicking up a froth of white-water at the stern. A big puff of black smoke belched out of the exhaust pipe as the boat powered back into the slip. The crowd’s voice swelled in warning.

Bam! “He hit the piling,” reported the announcer. People groaned. The captain gunned the engine and the boat jumped out of the slip, costing him precious seconds. He hit reverse. White-water churned. The crowd sucked in its breath. Back, back. People started clapping. Another smoke cloud billowed. The stern dug down into the water. A man launched himself from the boat on to the dock. People yelled, “Go! Go! Go!” He ran to the bow, whipped docking lines around a piling and threw his hands in the air like a rodeo roper. An air horn blast sent the fans into a frenzy.

Could this man who was such a favorite with the crowd be a murderer?

The drama of the race wasn’t over. I could feel the tension build as the crowd quieted, but nothing was happening that I could see. The microphone clicked on. The announcer reported the elapsed time and the place went wild with screams and a few happy dances. I found myself cheering along with everyone else. I caught Ryan watching me. What was I doing, cheering for someone didn't know? Then, his burnished face split into a broad grin and he started applauding too.

"He won't win, but let's go over to Jimmy's slip and congratulate him." He led the way and we got there just as the young man pulled into his slip. Lorraine and I exchanged a meaningful look as we watched an excited Jimmy Smith jump on the dock and shake hands with Ryan, almost pulling his arm out of the socket. The young man was handsome in a rugged sort of way, medium height with arms that bulged with muscles. They must have come from working on the water, not working out at the gym. He looked strong enough to whack Evelyn with very little effort. Ryan made quick introductions and just as we moved in to talk to Jimmy, a surge of bodies engulfed us. Friends and family congratulated him and slapped him on the back.

Then we heard him say, "Wait until next year when I have my own boat. Then you'll see some real action."

The group roared while Lorraine and I looked at each other. Had he stolen the money and the diamonds and to buy himself a boat? I worked my way closer to Ryan.

I had to shout over the crowd and the announcer calling the next race. "Did Jimmy just buy a boat?"

He looked at me and yelled, "Can't hear you."

He bent closer. "Where did Jimmy get the money for the boat?" But Ryan didn't hear my question, because Jimmy had pulled him into the center of the crowd by his side.

It was useless. I'd never get close to him now. Simon yipped, his tail the victim of an old work boot. Suddenly, the crush of these people and their secrets took my breath away. I had to push hard against the tide of people to make a way out of the crowd for Simon and me. I couldn't escape to the car fast enough and felt relieved when we headed back to St. Michaels.

CHAPTER TWELVE

It is advisable to be certain that an item made of silver is of good quality. Though it meets the fineness standard for sterling, the thinness of the silver could wear just during normal maintenance of polishing and cleaning.

—"The Butler's Guide to Fine Silver" Mr. Hollister, 1898

When Lorraine, Simon and I walked into the hotel, Reg was standing in the middle of the lobby with his legs apart and fists planted on his hips.

"It's about time you showed up. You can't keep disappearing like this," he demanded.

Lorraine walked right up to her angry nephew, planted a kiss on his cheek and patted his chest with the palm of her hand. "Reg, I'm fine, as you can see." She looked him straight in the eye and continued. "I appreciate this burst of concern, but it really isn't necessary."

"I think it is, until they catch this madman running around. You know, you're making it hard for me to take care of you," he complained.

"I told you, I'm fine."

"The guy left a lot of diamonds behind," Reg insisted. "He could be back."

I piped up. "Why are you so sure it was a man? It could have been a woman."

He looked at me as if surprised I was there, then dismissed the idea with a quick shake of his head.

"Do you really think the murderer could be back?" asked Lorraine, finally taking the possibility seriously.

"Of course. Either somebody was after the diamonds... or you."

"Me?" breathed Lorraine.

"Who else? You don't think somebody came out to Fair Winds to kill your housekeeper, do you?" he said.

"It's possible." I suggested. "We—" Reg dismissed the idea with a shake of his head.

"But we found out some important things today and—" Even to my ears, I sounded a little grouchy.

"And when did you become an expert about the undercurrents and associations here on the Eastern Shore?"

"I've learned a lot this weekend," I said in self-defense.

"It takes a lifetime to learn about this place," he countered. "Believe me, I know,"

I felt a little deflated, but he was right, this was his home turf. I still felt that I could make a contribution if given a chance. "We've found some evidence that—"

He whipped around to confront me, using his body to separate me from Lorraine. "And when did you become a murder investigator as well? If I had known about your other professional skills while you were working for me, we could have made some money renting you out as a detective."

I thought his reaction was over the top. "Reg." I tried to sound calming.

He turned his back on me and appealed to Lorraine. "Don't you see? This is all a game to her. She has you traipsing all over the

Shore chasing shadows, exposing yourself to who knows what kind of danger." His hands were flying around to punctuate his points. Then he went into fantasyland. "For all you know, *she* could have been the killer."

"Me?!" I croaked.

Lorraine looked horrified.

"Yes! She started an antique silver business. She met you, found out you are wealthy and have an extensive collection. She broke into Fair Winds to steal your silver and anything else of value. The housekeeper surprised her. She panicked, took a whack to scare the poor woman, but it all went wrong. See? She could be the killer."

His words hung in the air. The only sound was his breathing, strangled with the excitement of his allegation. Then, his tense body sagged. He raised his hands and rubbed his face. "I don't know what I'm saying," groaned Reg. "I was so frightened. I thought I'd lost the only family I have." He looked up at Lorraine, his eyes wet. "I'm sorry."

Lorraine shot forward and put her arms around him. Her nephew laid his head on her shoulder and buried his face as a little tremor went through his body. I took a step back, feeling like an intruder.

I heard Lorraine say, "I think, dear, you owe Abby an apology."

She was right. He owed me an apology for those hateful words. And for all the things he'd done to our business. I had to tamp down my anger.

Slowly, he broke their embrace and he turned his boyish face toward me, all the stress drained away. I was looking at my old friend once more.

"Abby." His voice was barely a whisper. "I'm so sorry…" He held his arms out to me in a silent plea for forgiveness.

The harsh thoughts eating at me evaporated. I stepped into his embrace. With my arms around his strong shoulders, I felt a sob shake his body. "I'm so sorry, Abby. I'm not myself. Forgive me."

My concern for my old friend was little defense against the

waves of emotion rolling off him. I was almost relieved by the tap on my shoulder that broke the moment.

"Okay, you two," said Lorraine. She slipped one arm around Reg and the other around me. "Now that we're all friends again, we need a little time together to fortify that good feeling. Why don't we have dinner upstairs in the restaurant and talk? You two can tell me how you know each other and Abby and I will tell you what we've been doing today."

"Oh, no, I couldn't," I sputtered.

Reg added to my rejection of her invitation. "I'd like to spend some time with you, alone."

"No, no, I want us to all be together. It's what I need, what we need." She looked at her nephew and raised her eyebrows. I suspected it was a trademark Lorraine-look because Reg's resistance crumbled.

"Alright, I'll get a table." He sprinted up the stairs to the restaurant.

Lorraine was smiling at me as she put her hands on my arms. It made it more difficult to say what I thought was the right thing.

"I can't stay for dinner," I said. "It's been a rough weekend for you and some time with family would be good for you." My voice dropped. "I'll just get my things and …"

"As part of our little extended family, you need to stay, for my sake..." she paused, her lower lip quivering. Then she gathered herself and drew her body up to its full height. "…and yours." There was that 'Lorraine look' again. She turned me toward the elevator. "Go and freshen up. Have dinner with Reg and me. The chef does a lovely job."

I gave up. I suspected that we could debate the question for twenty minutes, but she'd still get her way. It would be dinner for three. Simon pawed my leg. He was hungry, too. We agreed to meet in the restaurant after I fed Simon. It took a little while, because he begged for more than his normal share. The fresh air and exercise must have stimulated his appetite. Simon was more than ready to curl up and nap when I left him with his babysitter at the front desk.

Within an hour, I entered an elegant but unpretentious restaurant overlooking the harbor. Gleaming white sailboats and some very big powerboats bobbed in slips down below as people relaxed or partied onboard. I had to peer through a forest of sailboat masts to see the Crab Claw Restaurant across the way. The harbor was busy with boats maneuvering for position. The long Columbus Day weekend allowed people the time to travel, even if it was just across the Chesapeake Bay to sit on a boat.

The hostess led me to a table covered with a golden-white tablecloth and set with several forks, a couple of spoons and knives. Tall, lighted candles gave off a soft glow. It would be a romantic place with the right person, but tonight, uncertainty and sadness would occupy the fourth chair at the table.

I saw Reg deep in quiet conversation with Lorraine. He seemed to take charge wherever he went. I guess that's what first drew me to him. In those early days, we'd have long conversations about every subject. When we worked together, he asked good questions, probing questions, that challenged me to come up with alternatives rather than go with a quick fix. He seemed to pulse with enthusiasm for life. Fun and good-looking. Too bad the spark just wasn't there for us. As I approached the table, the candlelight played over his face that was clouded with strain and worry. Closing the business was hard on him and I realized that up to now, he'd done a good job hiding it. I sat down quietly, not wanting to interrupt them.

As Reg rattled on, Lorraine darted her eyes across the table at me then cocked her head a little as if asking a question. I gave her a tiny smile. He caught her and blustered, "Lorraine, how can I help you if you're not listening to me?"

She turned back to him with a big sweet smile that didn't reach her eyes and she said, "You always called me *Aunt* Lorraine. Why have you stopped?"

"I'm an adult now. It's time to give up those childish things," he shot back.

"I never thought of respect as being a childish thing," she mused.

The waiter appeared and defused a potentially explosive moment. Almost immediately, a man I can only describe as roly-poly stepped up to the table. His appearance made me smile. I always heard never to trust a skinny cook and this man, in his starched white chef's jacket embroidered in cerulean blue with his name and title, *Charles Blaine, Executive Chef,* was not. He was very charming as he greeted everyone, but I noticed that he never quite made eye contact when he talked to Lorraine. It seemed strange. As he described the menu specialties, his eyes remained guarded.

"Tonight, we have for you pleasure, Miss Lorraine, the Oyster Pot Pie – local oysters, Shitake mushrooms in a Sherry broth in a puff pastry basket," he announced.

"Wonderful, you know it's my favorite," said Lorraine. "And I'll have a little champagne green salad."

He nodded. "An excellent choice." His eyes got a faraway look of delight as he described the salad. "Ah yes, one of my favorites. Baby organic greens, toasted almonds, orange, strawberries, lightly-fried goat cheese with a champagne orange vinaigrette dressing." He sighed in satisfaction. "And for you—"

Reg jumped in. "You know what I want, Chef, what I always have."

The man dressed in white paused for a moment, then his memory kicked in. "Of course, Mr. Reg. A New York Strip Steak, grilled medium rare, served with shallot and thyme jus, roasted garlic mashed potatoes and a cauliflower and broccoli gratin."

Reg nodded and handed the menu to the waiter. Then the chef who talked about food like it was an orgasmic experience turned to me. "And for you, Miss?"

"Um, the Seafood Stew sounds delicious."

"I can assure you it is. I combine shrimp, scallops, crabmeat, fresh fish, mussels and a little squid in a creamy saffron broth. It's served with a toasted baguette we bake in our own ovens."

When Lorraine had suggested dinner, I wasn't sure I could eat a thing after enjoying the goodies at the Tilghman Day Festival, but after hearing the Chef describe the various entrees, I was surprised to discover my mouth was watering.

The Chef turned to the waiter. "You will handle the other course selections and you will bring the order to me. The appetizer, that shall be my surprise." He gave us a little bow and returned to the kitchen.

The waiter looked toward Reg. "May I suggest a bottle of Bordeaux or…" His eyes lit up. "Perhaps the Standish Shiraz 2003, a fine selection for both beef and fish." He took a more deferential pose. "Unless you'd prefer a bottle of red with the steak and a bottle of white for the seafood entrees?"

"Oh, Reg. More than a glass or so would put me under the table," Lorraine moaned.

"Yes, I think one bottle for the table will suffice," Reg told the waiter.

"Then I will bring the Shiraz."

As the waiter walked away, silence settled over our table. While Reg checked his phone for emails and texts, I whispered across the table to Lorraine, "What's wrong?" She gave me a quick shake of her head and gazed at the scene outside the window. The sun was sinking low in the deepening blue sky. She pointed out a skipjack sailing on the river, a majestic sight with the sails stiff in the breeze.

"That skipjack cruises at sunset most evenings for the visitors to the Chesapeake Maritime Museum and the guests of the Inn at Perry Cabin, a very posh place. The family who owned the Triple Crown winner Secretariat once owned it then it was sold to Laura Ashley's son who redecorated every room in a cacophony of prints and chintz. She sold it to the company that also owns the Orient Express. What an experience in luxury. The Inn does a lovely tea and…"

"You don't have to entertain Abby with meaningless conversation." Reg was in no mood for polite chitchat. "You and I need to work out..."

Thankfully, the arrival of the appetizer of pan-seared sea scallops over white corn derailed their conversation. There was a flurry of activity – wine tasting, plates cleared, breadcrumbs scooped up with a nifty little device – that led to the presentation of the entrees. The chef floated by for some adoration that he richly deserved. After we finished, we sat back to let our dinners settle and commented on the finer points of the meal when the chef came up to the table followed by the dessert cart laden with an abundance of frosted cakes, flaky pies, fresh fruit, éclairs, a chocolate bombe, even crepes Suzettes.

Lorraine's face filled with anticipation. "What would you recommend, Chef?"

He glanced at her and looked away.

She leaned toward him as if to challenge him to look at her. "Anything special this evening?"

It was a challenge he declined as he looked at the dessert cart instead. "The Crème Brûlée Trio is quite delicious," he said and walked away.

Lorraine looked very surprised. "How strange. Every time I eat here, we have this little ritual. I ask for his dessert recommendation and he makes yet-another passionate plea for Evie's cake recipe. Today, nothing." She shrugged. "Maybe he's being respectful."

Or he got tired of asking for the recipe and went to Fair Winds and did what he had to do to get it. We should check to see if the recipe is still in Evelyn's kitchen because it seems to be at the center of everything.

Lorraine and I shared the Trio and followed the waiter's instructions about *how* to eat our dessert. He strongly suggested that the order we ate the three little ramekins in was very important. The first was a traditional Crème Brûlée – a light vanilla custard with a caramelized sugar topping. The second had a coffee flavor, the kind that one savors after a fine dinner. The last Crème

Brûlée was made with lemon and local honey to cleanse the palate.

After we'd scraped up every morsel, Lorraine stared out the window, lost in her own thoughts, while Reg sipped the last of his wine. My eyes wandered around the restaurant and caught a glimpse of the chef slipping down the steps to the lobby. It was an opportunity I couldn't pass up so I excused myself as if I was off to the ladies room and hoped Lorraine wouldn't follow me. I caught up with the man at the bottom of the steps.

"Chef, that was an amazing dinner."

He smiled. "I'm so glad you enjoyed it." He turned away.

"Miss Lorraine said the Fair Winds Torte would be the crowning jewel to such a dinner, don't you agree?" My question seemed to make his body stiffened so I continued. "I understand many chefs and magazines would like to get their hands on the recipe. I imagine people would pay a lot of money for it, maybe even try to steal it. You'd like it to stay in St. Michaels, wouldn't you?"

He gave me a shrug in a wooden sort of way, "Sure, it's an Eastern Shore specialty." He clutched the clipboard he was carrying to his chest.

"That makes it special."

"Of course. Now, if you'll excuse –"

"Tell me, what you'd do to have it?" I watched him closely.

"What? I don't know…" His polite expression disintegrated and his eyes grew wide as he realized what I was suggesting, murder. "I would never…" Acting insulted, he straightened his body and marched up the stairs, back to his restaurant and kitchen.

Possible suspects seemed to be piling up.

As I walked back into the restaurant, laughter drew my attention to a table in the corner. What I saw made me want to turn around and walk out again. No, not *what*, who. Sitting at a table for six, next to a beautiful woman with long platinum blonde hair, Ryan was telling a story.

I slipped back into my place at our table where Reg was whispering something to Lorraine again. I tried to act interested in what they were saying while catching quick glimpses of Ryan and his party.

I almost choked on the last of my wine when I saw Ryan walking toward our table.

CHAPTER THIRTEEN

In the finer houses, the practice of applying a thin coating to protect the silver surface is not held in high regard. This practice changes the item in a way unintended by the craftsman. It is a lazy approach to the preservation of the valued item. It is better, prudent and highly recommended to attend to preservation of silverware in a consistent and proper fashion.

—"The Butler's Guide to Fine Silver" Mr. Hollister, 1898

I managed to swallow my wine and regain my composure as Ryan the Hunk arrived at our table.

"Good evening Lorraine," Ryan nodded to her then turned those strikingly blue eyes on me. "Abby." I could only nod back. Now, words instead of wine were stuck in my throat.

Lorraine saved the day. "I don't believe you've met my nephew, Reginald," she said.

He stood and shook hands quickly with Ryan. "Actually, it's Reg."

As Ryan asked Lorraine about the Tilghman Day Festival, I noticed Reg stood between them. Was he being overprotective or was it something else? At least I wasn't the only one person that made him act like that.

"Will you join us for a drink?" she asked.

Ryan shook his head. "No, thank you. I'd better get back to my party." I followed his glance over to the blonde who looked annoyed. I couldn't see her feet, but I bet she was tapping her toe. She and Reg had a lot in common: she wanted Ryan back and Reg wanted him to leave.

"Well, good to meet you," Reg mumbled. He sat down, turning his back on Ryan and his attention toward his aunt.

Ryan didn't move. "Lorraine, I want you to know that if there's anything you need, anything at all, you just have to ask, please."

"Thank you, that's very kind," Lorraine said with a warm smile.

Reg clicked the gold signet ring on his right hand against his wine glass. It made an irritating noise that both Lorraine and Ryan noticed, but ignored.

"You have my number. I hope you'll use it. Good night everyone."

Once we were alone, Reg leaned back in his chair and said, "I don't think I've had a chance to tell you about a great honor that's come my way."

There was delight in Lorraine's voice. "Oh? Tell me, I could use some good news."

"I've been invited to go on a speaking tour," he said.

"Oh, by whom?" she asked.

It was obvious that he was enjoying our undivided attention. "The Entrepreneur's Club. They've invited me to go on a speaking tour around the country."

I thought the timing of his announcement was a little curious. *Is he competing with Ryan, like a little boy on the playground? I swear I'll never understand men.*

"And what is your topic?" Lorraine tried to stifle a yawn, exhaustion overcoming her excitement.

"They want me to talk about surviving a startup – lessons

learned and all that. They said they've picked a few outstanding entrepreneurs to meet with their members in larger cities. They think that rubbing elbows with people who have 'walked the walk', as they say, can be beneficial."

"Why would they want you?" Those words tumbled out of my mouth without thinking and I wished I could stuff them right back in again. "I mean, after all you've been through in the last six weeks, I'd think that they would want—"

"It's true that the official invitation came in while we were still fully staffed and functional, but I think they'll understand why I made the shift in operations when I explain it to them." He leaned back and played with his ring. "I think it's a good example of how an entrepreneur has to be quick on his feet, make adjustments to save an idea and the product in development. It won't be an issue with them after I sell the company and technology."

I tried to hide my surprise by gently running my finger around the rim of my wine. I hoped I sounded casual when I asked, "When do you think that will happen?"

He pursed his lips then said, "Oh, I think it will all come together very quickly now that things are moving along."

"What things—"

He snapped, "The details aren't important." He took a deep breath and exhaled slowly with a small smile playing at the corners of his mouth. "The bottom line is that everything is going to be fine and this whole startup effort will be regarded as a success."

I lifted my napkin to my lips to conceal my disbelief, then looked out the window at the boats. This wasn't the time or the place to cross-examine him, not in front of Lorraine. While they chatted quietly, I was left alone with my thoughts and they started to eat at me. I slipped my hand into my lap. It was clenched in frustration. I could help him sell the technology. A potential buyer would be suspicious if there was no consultation with the chief developer. Reg was freezing me out of everything and I didn't know why.

The hostess came up to the table and handed Lorraine a folded note. She read it and smiled.

"Yes, ask him to come in," she said.

A moment later, Chief "Lucky" Lucan walked up to our table. He wore a holstered gun and handcuffs on large black belt around a slender waist that hadn't fallen victim to the doughnuts police officers were rumored to love.

"Hello, Chief, won't you join us?" said Lorraine.

"Good evening," he said, nodding to Reg and me. "Thank you. I can only stay for a minute." He maneuvered into the chair moving the tools of his trade so he could sit comfortably. "I wanted you to know that you can go home to Fair Winds tomorrow. We should have it cleaned up and all the crime investigation stuff out there by noon."

Lorraine closed her eyes and sighed. "Thank goodness."

I imagined this was a mixed blessing for her. It would be good to be back home again, but I wondered if the memory of what had happened would haunt her? While we worked on the obituary, she'd said she'd lived at Fair Winds with her husband. After his death, Evelyn had been there to help her through that dark time. Now, she'd be alone.

Seeing everybody looking at me shook me from my thoughts. "I'm sorry, did I miss something?"

"I asked if you'd sent the obituary to the newspaper," Lorraine repeated.

I assured her that they were waiting for the funeral information to print it.

"Good," the Chief said. "They should release Miss Evelyn's body tomorrow. I assume you're planning the services?"

"Yes, yes, of course." Lorraine played with the corner of her napkin, the stress starting to show again.

"Then I thought you'd want to have this." The Chief handed Lorraine something wrapped in a white handkerchief. "It's Miss Evelyn's cross, the one she wore all the time. We had to process it for evidence, but I asked the lab to rush it in case you wanted it for the service."

Lorraine mumbled a thank-you.

"Have you found out anything about the stepson?" I hadn't meant to blurt it out, but it had been at the back of mind all day.

"Who's that?" asked Reg.

"There's a rumor that Miss Evelyn's husband had a son before he came here from Virginia and that he's in town right now," I reported. The chief's eyes stared holes in me so I carefully. "But the chief can fill you in." I hoped that redirecting attention to him, the expert, would placate him.

Reg turned to the chief. "I don't know why my aunt should know or care about her housekeeper's husband."

Lorraine looked as if she was going to explain things to her nephew, then she changed her mind. "Have you found out any information?" She asked.

As the chief answered her question, he kept his eyes on Reg. "You gave me a good lead. Seems Truitt, the husband, was from Birdnest, Virginia. I also pulled his old police file that made for some interesting reading. He was a busy guy before he came here. He saw the inside of a jail more than once, but there was nothing about a son. The investigating officer and his team will keep digging."

He got up and apologized again for barging in on our dinner. "Oh, I almost forgot," he said, reaching into the pocket of his shirt. "The lab is done with these things as well." He handed her a clear plastic evidence bag with a dangling diamond earring and some loose stones inside. "Might as well return them to you for safekeeping."

Lorraine thanked him and slipped them into her purse as he left. The waiter approached the table and Reg ordered a snifter of cognac.

"I think I'll have some Louis Treize," Reg said. The waiter nodded and went to fill the order.

"I certainly brought you up to have sophisticated tastes," she said to him with a note of irony.

He settled back in his chair and grinned. "Yes, and you did a fine job. It's all part of what makes me, me… and so lovable." He squeezed her hand. "I prefer this cognac and I can actually tell you why." He looked at me and winked. "It is one of the oldest cognacs in the world, aged in oak barrels over one hundred years old." He leaned forward, warming to his subject. "The first sip with its intense spiciness might overwhelm the more delicate palate. Once you adjust, you taste the sweetness of candied fruit, jasmine, and ginger, even nutmeg. The aroma, the taste… they're complex, but like nothing else you've ever tasted."

The waiter brought an unusual bottle to the table and extended it so Reg could approve the label.

"That's an amazing bottle," I said, truly impressed.

"Yes, it is. The decanter is Baccarat Crystal. Only the best for the best." Reg lifted the snifter to his nose to inhale the aroma, took a sip and closed his eyes in ecstasy. Gently, he set the glass back on the table. "Yes, Lorraine, you did an excellent job raising me to appreciate the finer things in life, all of what's mine."

The waiter quietly put down the check at Reg's place. Without any hesitation, he slid it over to Lorraine. She dropped her eyes and signed it. "I'm tired. It's been a long day, a long weekend. I'm going to my room." She told the waiter to leave the tab open for her nephew and charge it all to her room.

Getting up quickly, I followed her lead and said good night.

CHAPTER FOURTEEN

Silver is soft and malleable so it must be combined with other metals to give it the strength it does not have on its own.
—"The Butler's Guide to Fine Silver" Mr. Hollister, 1898

I hurried to the lobby to find Simon asleep on a blanket behind the front desk. I was grateful to replace the worries about murder and business with the important activity of walking the dog. It really didn't make sense to wake up Simon to go outside in the cool autumn air just so he could go back to sleep, but I'd learned the hard way what would happen if we skipped over this little chore.

Outside, the weather was crisp and the view above my head was impressive. In the city, light pollution overwhelmed the night sky, but here, in this village by the Chesapeake Bay, the stars shimmered in all their glory. Even the misty Milky Way was visible. We walked along the quiet streets, each lost in our own thoughts: I was mesmerized by the lights in the sky; Simon was spellbound with the scents on the ground.

When I shivered from the chill, I realized that we'd walked a lot farther from the hotel than I'd planned. The creak of tall pine trees swaying in the breeze and the rustle of dead leaves not yet fallen from the oaks gave me an eerie feeling. Normally, I wouldn't go marching off alone late at night in a strange place. True, I wasn't exactly alone, but I didn't think Simon could make a difference if somebody with bad intentions tried to ruin the evening.

A man stepped out of the shadows and I almost fainted.

Reg's white teeth flashed as he laughed at my surprise. "Nothing bad will happen to you here in St. Michaels. Nothing ever happens here." His voice was loud and his words were slurred.

Simon started to growl, then bark.

Fine watchdog you are. You wait until I almost have a heart attack before you warn me of a man in the shadows.

I put my hand over Simon's snout to stop the barking, but he kept growling deep in his throat.

"Something bad happened to Evelyn," I pointed out.

He shrugged. "It was a fluke, an exception that proves the rule." He put his hands in his pockets and looked around. "Funny I should find you out here."

"I have to walk the dog before I can go to bed."

"Whatever. It's just so you know that wherever you are, I'll always find you, even when you're somewhere you don't belong."

Confused and a little uneasy, I turned and continued Simon's walk. "Yes, you did find me." I wondered how far we were from the hotel, because I really wanted to walk into the lobby right now. After such an active and emotional roller coaster of a day, I didn't want to deal with a drunk.

"Well, the least you can do is shut up that mutt so we can talk."

He fell into step with me. I worked our way toward some bushes and almost instantly, Simon was more interested in the smells there than in Reg.

"Abby, I don't know what you're doing with my aunt, but you can go home now." He was stumbling over his feet as well as his words. "I've got this whole thing under control."

"I was trying to help her, keep her company –"

"That's what I mean." He insisted. "You don't have to do that anymore. I've got it."

"Your aunt is a nice lady. She might be in danger. Did you ever think of that? There's a murderer running around and they have no idea who it is."

"Look, Abby, you've worn out your welcome. It's time for you to go home!"

"You're not the boss of me anymore." The anger, hurt and frustration I'd suppressed bubbled to the surface. "I'll go where I want, when I want. Good night!" I looked around and saw the lights of the hotel reflected in the water. We set off in what I hoped was the right direction.

Feeling safe inside the hotel, my anger started to burn.

Men. If the men I'd met lately were any indication, they all had a problem.

I stopped to think of one man – tall, handsome, so polite. Should Ryan be lumped into this group? As Reg said, an exception can prove the rule.

Forget it. Tomorrow I'm going home, hours away from the Eastern Shore. And with that leggy blonde around, Ryan probably won't even notice. Nope, that's one I won't see again.

With a sigh, I walked by the front desk and noticed that a different clerk was on duty. I said hello and explained I was a guest of Miss Lorraine. Then, as casually as I could, I asked if he had heard of someone visiting St. Michaels named Truitt. I shrugged, "Maybe someone from Virginia who was visiting relatives locally?"

The clerk gave me a blank look. Miss Constance appeared by her office door. Did the woman never go home?

"Why, Miss Abby, our guest information is confidential." Her words sounded gentle but there was iron underneath.

"Yes, I'm sure," I stammered. "It's just that —"

"Confidential," she repeated.

I wished them both a good night and slipped into the elevator to go up to my room. Investigating a murder looked so much easier on television.

The next morning, Simon didn't paw at me until after nine. It was late for him and his urgent moves between the bed and the door made it clear he couldn't wait. I dressed as fast as I could, gathered my things and flew down the stairs. We had to hurry for Simon's sake and for mine. After the scene last night, I just wanted to go home. Simon dragged me out the door to his favorite spot and I swore I could hear him sigh.

I tossed my few belongings in the car and went back in the lobby as Lorraine stepped off the elevator. She was dressed for her role as estate owner and funeral arranger. Her rose-colored skirt of cashmere draped from her thin waist and the creamy silk blouse was so soft, the sleeves billowed.

"I'm glad I caught you," she said with a smile.

That comment worried me. She leaned down to pet Simon.

I almost shrieked. "Be careful! His claws are sharp. They can ruin your blouse."

She scratched him behind both ears and he looked like he was purring. "You wouldn't do that, would you?" She drew him near and nuzzled his neck. "Of course, you wouldn't. You're my buddy." The silence grew as she petted him. Then she said, so quietly that I almost missed it, "I'm sorry, Abby."

"Sorry? For what?" I was surprised. "You don't have to apologize for anything."

She stood up and avoided my gaze. "I, well, I wanted you to know that I'm sorry I exposed you to all this suspicion and sadness."

"Then, I'm sorry too for all that you're going through. I want you to know that I'm glad you won the silver auction on eBay and that we met."

She pulled a small card from a pocket hidden in her skirt. "This has my phone number at Fair Winds. I wrote my email address on the back. I hope you'll be in touch sometime soon." The glow was coming back to her skin and her eyes sparkled a little.

I took the card. "Yes, I will and I'll send you my contact information as soon as I get home."

We took a step toward each other and hugged with Simon between our feet. His wagging tail beat against our legs. I told her to take care of herself and to call me if she needed anything.

At that moment, Reg blew in through the front door with an armful of roses, a couple of dozen at least. He walked up to us, both of us too surprised to speak.

"There they are, my two favorite girls." He extended his floral extravaganza toward us. "These are for you." He nodded toward his aunt. "You always said a little beauty can ease just about anything life throws at you. I hope these will." He turned to me. "And roses for you, Abby, as an apology. Please forgive the way I acted last night."

Looking between the two of us, Lorraine asked, "What happened?"

"It's not important," Reg rushed to say. "I just want you to know that I'm sorry and I hope you'll stay. Now that we can go home to Fair Winds, I was hoping you would come and stay with us." He looked at Lorraine for her agreement. She nodded. "You could stay until the funeral on Wednesday."

Lorraine joined in. "Abby, if you could, I would appreciate it." Her face was flushed with hope.

"It's just a couple of days," added Reg. "It would mean a lot… to both of us."

I was such a pushover. It had been a long time since I'd been needed, not for work, but for being me. Not since Gran passed away. She'd left a big hole in my life. Maybe it would be good to fill it for a little while.

"Oh, all right you two," I said, forcing the tears out of my voice.

Simon whined, right on cue. "But only if Simon can come too."

Lorraine knelt down to tell him about her Chesapeake Bay Retriever and Labs at Fair Winds – Moses, the old guy who spent his time surveying his realm, and the two girls, Tilly and Sookie, who could romp for hours.

Reg leaned close. "I'm really glad you're staying, Abby. Thanks."

"My pleasure, but I must leave after the funeral." I insisted. "I have to get home and …" I snapped my mouth shut. This was not the time to remind Reg that I needed to find a job.

We made our plans: I would follow them to Fair Winds after I fed Simon and checked my email.

Before we got in the car, I took Simon for a quick walk along the harbor where the watermen tied up their boats. It was too early for most of them to be back from the day's crabbing. My attention was drawn by the engine roar of one boat tied up in a slip. Black smoke belched out of the tall exhaust pipe. Several guys on board leaned over the engine then one broke away from the group and shut it down. He was a young man I recognized from the Tilghman Island Festival: Jimmy Smith.

It looked like he'd gotten his boat. I maneuvered Simon in the direction of the boat and caught snatches of their conversation.

"I think you got a good deal," said the tall one. "She's not new, but she's in good shape and has a lot of years left in her."

My eyes wandered over in their direction while they talked about working on the water. Using Simon as an excuse, I walked around the area for the few minutes until Jimmy's friends left then I led Simon over to the slip. I might accomplish what Lorraine and I had set out to do the day before on Tilghman Island. It was time to start scratching some of the names off the suspects list.

"Nice boat." I tried to sound innocent.

He looked at me and nodded his head once in thanks.

Great, the man is shy. It's going to be tough getting answers out of him.

"Is she new?"

He nodded again and added, "Yes, ma'am, to me she is."

"She looks expensive." Oops, not the right thing to say since he just looked at me, his eyes smaller with a glimmer of suspicion. "I mean, it must take some money to get a boat you can trust out on the water all time." I didn't know what I was talking about and he just kept looking at me. Might as well go for it. "Your name is Jimmy Smith, isn't it?" He took a step back toward the cabin. Was it a guilty reaction? I ignored the sound of a car pulling up on the gravel behind me. Someone was coming. It was time to press. "We met yesterday. I was with Miss Lorraine, a friend of Miss Evelyn's – the woman you asked for money."

"How do you know that?" he hollered.

I took a step closer to the boat. "Did you get mad at her, Jimmy, when she turned you down? Did you hurt her when she came between you and your dream? Where did you get the money for your boat, Jimmy?"

"I gave it to him," said a voice behind me.

I whirled around and came face to face with Ryan.

He put his hands on his hips and his breathing sounded like a freight train. "Jimmy didn't hurt Miss Evelyn. He didn't have to. I gave him the money a good week before somebody killed her." He took one step toward me. "What gives you the right to come down here and make accusations? You're on the Shore for one whole weekend and you're an expert about the people here?" He leaned in and lowered his voice, the menace was clear. "Why don't you get in your car and go back where you belong."

What could I say? I wanted to say something, in self-defense, to explain, but I couldn't think of a thing. He was right. I felt like a naughty little girl who should go home and play with her dolls. I felt two inches tall as I walked away dragging Simon, who thought we were playing a new game.

CHAPTER FIFTEEN

Contact with the oils of the human hand can tarnish silver severely. It is prudent to include the wearing of white gloves in the uniform worn by a member of the staff handling any silver pieces.

—"The Butler's Guide to Fine Silver" Mr. Hollister, 1898

I held tight to Simon's leash as I hustled back to my car. I'd crossed a suspect off the list, but did I have to look like such a fool in front of Ryan?

I wanted to crawl under a rock then realized it was a glorious day – the kind that made you want to feel the wind in your hair and sing at the top of your lungs. The sky was an azure blue that you only see in Old Masters paintings. The air was warmed, not baked, by the sun. In the car, I made sure that Simon's harness was attached securely to the seat belt and put the top down. When I got to the main road and beyond all the very limiting speed signs of St. Michaels, I gave the Saab's turbo engine a little exercise. Simon barked in delight.

Before I knew it, the white fence of Fair Winds appeared and I downshifted quickly to make the turn into the entrance. And what a grand entrance it was. The white brick pillars now stripped of the yellow police tape stood like guardians on either side of the black asphalt drive. I drove toward the house through a tunnel created by tall trees that laced their branches together high over my head. A gentle breeze rustled their shimmering yellow leaves. It was wonderful with the top down. Even Simon, safe in his harness, was enthralled with this magical place.

Pools of light filtered by the trees led the way to the magnificent house at the end. Painted brilliant white, the house sparkled in the bright sunshine. Lush plantings hugged the house, not to smother it, but to embrace it. Two-story pillars held a portico over the steps. I didn't know the protocol so I parked to the side and released Simon from his seat harness. For once, he was content to stay close.

Somehow, a fond wish of mine had come true, an invitation to one of the grand old mansions along the Miles River. It's too bad the invitation was connected to a murder. With mixed emotions, we climbed the steps leading to the massive paneled front door painted glossy black and I raised the brass knocker in the shape of a sail. I was about to see what life was like inside such a house.

The door knocker landed with a heavy sound and in no more than a moment, the door swung open without a creak. A young woman barely five feet tall, wearing a black shirt and skirt and white blouse, stood dwarfed by the entry.

"Yes, may I help you?" she asked.

"I'm Abby Strickland. Miss Lorraine—"

"Oh, yes, Miss Abby, we've been expecting you," she said as she swung the door open wide. Her face was marked with sadness. Her ivory skin was pasty and dark circles ringed her tired eyes. "Please come in. My name is Ruth. I'm Miss Lorraine's…" She stumbled on the word, "housekeeper."

I wanted to say something consoling, but she went on before I could find the right words.

"Miss Lorraine has been looking forward to your arrival."

"And this is Simon." I pulled his leash as he started to wander off.

She leaned down and let him smell her hand. "Dogs are always welcome at Fair Winds, sometimes more than people," she said.

I crossed the threshold of Fair Winds into a different world with different rules and priorities. The floor of the foyer was covered with large marble tiles set on point, creating a diamond pattern in shades of dark blue and white, capturing the nautical roots of the area. In the center of the room was a large round table of golden walnut polished to such a shine that I was sure I could put on my lipstick in its reflection. A large cut-crystal vase held a huge bouquet of roses that filled the area with a sweet scent. Ruth led us through a living room that was the size of a cavern. I slowed my steps, trying to visualize the grand parties hosted there over the years, but had to scurry to keep up as Ruth opened a pair of French doors and continued outside over a large flagstone patio and on to the soft cushion of green grass.

Lorraine was sitting in one of several white wicker chairs placed in the warm sunlight. Large black sunglasses hid her eyes as she looked out at the river beyond. All was peaceful until two enormous dogs rose up to greet us – or should I say, greet Simon. It was pandemonium as her three retrievers – muscular dogs with silky coats – romped like giants around Simon.

"Take that leash off the poor boy. He'll be fine. He's part of their pack now, see?" said Lorraine.

As soon as he was free, the dogs took off across the lawn with Simon trying hard to keep up. His puppy legs were a poor match to the long, sure-footed strides of the Chessie and the Labs. In the quiet, I sat down and let the peace and calm of the place settle over me.

Without turning her gaze away from the river, Lorraine said, "I'm glad you're here, content to sit with me in this beautiful place."

Trying to lighten the mood, I said, "Simon is certainly enjoying himself."

Lorraine turned her head to see her dogs rolling around in the grass with their new friend. I caught a smile cross her face, then fade.

"I've been thinking about the arrangements for Wednesday. You might want to go see my friend at the shop in town called Charisma to get a dress for the funeral."

I agreed. For important life events like a funeral, I came down on the side of old-fashioned tradition. Out of respect, I wanted to wear something dark and conservative. It would be interesting to visit the shop that had the Angela scarecrow in the window.

With that detail addressed, we sat quietly again until another thought popped out of Lorraine. "I'm so glad the chief has a good suspect."

"Who?" *Had I missed something in the hour or so we'd been apart?*

"Jimmy Smith, of course." Lorraine sounded a little irritated that I wasn't keeping up.

I almost groaned.

She continued, "He had a good reason to get back at Evie for refusing to give him a loan."

"It wasn't Jimmy."

My statement came as such a surprise that she sat up, took off her sunglasses and squinted at me. "How do you know that?"

"He got his boat."

"Aha!" She pointed her sunglasses at me for emphasis. "That proves it. He asked her for a loan, she refused. He broke in and stole money from the safe. She caught him and…" Her voice caught, but she straightened her shoulders and went on. "And she paid for being in the wrong place at the wrong time. Case solved."

I held up a hand like a traffic cop to stop to this fictional tale she was weaving. "No, I'm afraid that's not what happened."

"Go on," she demanded.

"It seems that your friend Ryan loaned him the money. He made the boat deal days before the … the crime. He picked it up early this morning."

"I don't understand. How do you know this?"

I wished she hadn't asked. I wanted to hide what a fool I'd made of myself, but she deserved the facts. "I ran into Ryan and Jimmy at the harbor by the hotel and they told me."

Yeah, after I tried to sound like some famous detective. I was lucky Ryan didn't throw me in the water with Jimmy's assistance.

My news made Lorraine deflate like a tired, old balloon. "I was so sure," she mumbled.

I wanted to do something to help her and my mouth was working before my brain could catch up. "Look, why don't we recreate what happened Friday night?"

Lorraine stared at me with a horrified expression.

"No, no, not everything, not *that.*" I was shaking my head hard. "I mean, recreate what happened from your point of view. Maybe you forgot something, something that didn't seem important at the time or when you talked to the police." I was convinced this was a good idea and, too late, realized what the emotional toll on Lorraine might be. "Unless it's too much for you."

She sat for a moment. "No, I think it is a good idea. After all, insurance companies and the police recreate accidents all the time to make sure they didn't miss something." Her lips stopped quivering and moved into a straight line, the sign of a determined lady. "We'll do it. Lunch first to give me strength then we'll walk through what I did last Friday night."

Somehow, food on the Eastern Shore tasted better when eaten outside. A simple chicken salad sandwich was a delight. It would have been nice to sip lemonade and wait for boats to sail by, but we had work to do.

Inside, we walked into a kitchen large enough to accommodate a full staff. Bordered by an endless array of white cabinets and stainless-steel appliances, the massive center island was topped with a slab of granite in warm tones that reminded me of chocolate, cinnamon and cookie dough. The red floor tiles had been scrubbed clean.

Lorraine put her hands flat on the island to support herself. "I suppose this is where we should start." She took a deep breath. "The staff had left for the night. Ruth and Staci had gone to bed. They live out, but will stay over before and after a party. It's easier that way. Evie and I were alone here in the kitchen."

"What time was it?" I asked.

"Oh, I think the clock had just struck eleven," she said.

I'd seen the impressive old grandfather clock off the foyer. I bet everyone up and down the river could hear it chime the hour.

She went on. "I was tired and suggested that we finish up for the night. Evie told me to go on to bed. She said she still had a couple of things to do while she waited for the last batches of cookies to bake." Her voice caught as she struggled to swallow a sob. "She asked if I wanted her to bring me one when they were done. I told her no, but if I had…"

I went to her and rubbed her back gently as she leaned forward, her tears splashing on the stone. "This wasn't a good idea. I'm sorry. Let's go back outside and…"

She stood up, her muscles tense, her back straight. "No." Her voice was as hard as the granite. "No, you were right before. If I know something more than I think I do, it might lead us to whoever did this horrible thing." She poured a glass of water, took a deep drink and resumed her place by the island. This time her hands were steady as she wiped the surface dry. "Evie offered me a cookie, I declined, then I said goodnight and went upstairs to my room."

As she walked to the kitchen door, she paused by the corner of the island. "I remember when I walked by, the cake on its pedestal. I told her that she'd outdone herself. The cake was beautiful. Evie said that we'd finally achieved the perfect combination: a beautiful cake and the perfect sterling silver serving piece." Lorraine turned and gave me a little smile. "Thanks to you, Abby." Before we both started crying, she rushed out and I followed her to the foyer.

"I checked that the front door was locked. I went upstairs." She seemed to float up the graceful circular staircase carpeted in plush softness to the second floor.

I followed her down the wide hallway, past one darkened room after another until we reached the river side of the house and entered a palatial master bedroom. Palatial, because the huge four-poster bed fit comfortably under the high ceiling, the tall windows overlooking the serenity outside. Shades of lavender and amethyst created a soft, restful feeling.

Lorraine disappeared through a door and continued her report of events. "I came into my closet, got undressed and took a long hot shower. I didn't hear a thing with the water running." She reappeared.

I asked, "Are you sure you didn't hear anything like voices, an argument, anything?"

She shook her head and avoided looking me in the eye. "No, I'm sure I didn't hear anything while I was getting ready for bed."

I suspected there was something she wasn't telling me. "And you know that because…?"

She sighed, not wanting to give up her secret then admitted softly, "I didn't hear anything because I sing in the shower. Come, I'll show you."

We went through the closet into an immense bathroom tiled in warm golden stone that reminded me of my trip to Italy several years earlier. Using a stage voice, she went on. "As you can hear, the acoustics in here are fabulous. Even a rotten singer like me sounds terrific. So, that night, I was singing in the shower at the top of my lungs and heard nothing else."

Back in the bedroom, she continued. "After I put on my nightie, I got into bed with a book to help me relax. Wait!" She grabbed my arm and looked at the pillows on the bed.

"What is it?"

"I remember coming out of the closet and hearing voices."

Excited, I rattled off questions. "Did you recognize the voices? What were they saying? Was Evie arguing with someone? Who could it have been?"

She patted my arm. "Nothing as dramatic as all that. I seem to remember thinking that Evie had turned on some late-night TV show to keep her company."

I was almost overcome with disappointment. For a minute, I thought Lorraine had overheard the argument that had led to Evie's death, that she heard the voice of the murderer.

Lorraine interrupted my feelings of frustration. She moved to the windows looking over the river. "There was something else." She frowned, then squeezed her eyes shut as if she was working through a problem. "I'm not sure, but I may have heard a car or truck on the gravel driveway by the kitchen."

"That's a long way from your bedroom."

"Yes, I know, but all my windows were open. It was a cool night, great for sleeping." She bit her lip, thinking. "Yes. It was a car, not crunchy enough for a truck. At the time, I suppose I thought it was something on TV but, now that I think about it, it may have been outside."

She continued to look out the window as I wondered at the significance of this detail. She seemed to be lost in her thoughts so I asked her what happened next.

"I was in bed with the light still on when Staci started screaming. I jumped out of bed and ran down the hall to the front of the house. I found her at the bottom of the stairway with her hands covering her eyes, screaming her head off. I couldn't imagine what was wrong."

We retraced her steps down the long hallway and stood at the top of the stairway lit by the regal crystal chandelier.

Lorraine pointed. "She was down there by the front door, screaming. I yelled at her to find out what was wrong. She didn't hear me over all the noise she was making. I ran down the steps and had to shake her hard to quiet down. All she could do was point toward the kitchen." As Lorraine described what had happened, she stood glued to the spot at the top of the steps.

"That's when I..." Her voice started shaking and I put my hand on her arm.

"That's when you went down the hall and found what happened," I filled in for her.

She nodded.

"Okay, we don't have to go through that part." Her shoulders seemed to relax a little. "Was the front door open?" I asked.

"No, I remember I had to unlock it when the police came. Whoever did this didn't come in through that door," she said, clipping off each word exactly.

"Could it have been Staci, I don't know, in a fit of anger or…" The look on her face stopped me.

"If you had seen her, you'd know that she couldn't have lifted a feather let alone swing a murder weapon. Besides, there wasn't any."

Any what?" I asked.

"Blood. There wasn't any blood on her dress."

Suddenly, I saw a dress… my dress… drenched in my mother's blood. I was only five years old when the accident happened. I was riding in the back seat when the truck ran a stop sign and slammed into our car. She was killed instantly. It took every ounce of strength I had to throw off that memory and focus on Lorraine.

Lorraine was rationalizing what she'd seen. "If Staci had done it, she would have been covered in blood. It was all over the kitchen. When I walked in, I almost slipped on the wet floor. You know…" Her voice faded away.

"What? Did you remember something?"

She bent her head a little to the side. "That night, I noticed the color of the red floor tiles clashed with the color of the blood. I never realized how orange the tiles were." She shrugged to shake off the thought. "It doesn't matter. I'm going to have the whole floor replaced. It's too much of a reminder of what I saw." She hurried on and what I heard made me shudder.

"Evie was on the floor on her back. Her mouth was wide open in a silent scream. Her throat…her throat was slashed open… in shreds. Blood was soaking into her white apron. Evie always insisted on a white apron in the kitchen. It was so bloody."

She said with great sadness, "And her beautiful cake was smashed on the floor with bits of frosting on her face."

In the long silence that followed, the image etched itself in my mind. It took the wild honking of geese flying overhead to yank us out of our private thoughts. With a start, I realized there was something important I had to do.

CHAPTER SIXTEEN

Fine sterling silver speaks of elegant simplicity. It is the mark of good taste and carries a tradition from the maker who created each piece and the people who used and maintained it over the years. If one learns the history of the use and design of each piece, one's appreciation will grow as will the understanding of a Butler's responsibility to respect and preserve it.

—"The Butler's Guide to Fine Silver" Mr. Hollister, 1898

Now that I knew about the voices and sounds of a car on the gravel drive, I had to tell the police chief. He would be able to follow up on these clues. While Lorraine went to take a nap, exhausted from our little reenactment of the murder night, and Simon curled up on the floor with his new best friends, I drove into St. Michaels.

I found the police station tucked away on the street behind the Acme market. There was no high metal fence, no intimidating façade. There was only a porch stretching across the front of the building, a porch more appropriate for rocking chairs and a chat than the entrance to a police station complete with emergency equipment, guns and holding cells.

Inside, the security was tight. The precautions reminded me of a jail or prison and made me wonder how much violence and danger there was in this little town. Even the secretary was protected from casual visitors. She stood behind a thick Plexiglas window while she asked for my name and the nature of my business with the chief. Satisfied I wasn't a threat, she buzzed me in and ushered me to the chief's office. His large wooden desk was covered with file folders and papers, radios and telephones. The walls were hung with awards, commendations and a framed picture taken at the party to celebrate his retirement from the Baltimore Police Department. The large white mat surrounding the photo was covered with signatures and comments wishing him well. On one wall, a ceremonial sword and scabbard, probably from one of his more prestigious assignments, hung in a huge framed shadow box. All these things were in recognition of the man's long and honored career.

The chief burst into the office, dropped in his large black leather chair and immediately began moving paper and file folders around. He wore a starched white uniform shirt and a badge with his title of Chief prominent in the center.

"Yes, what do you want?" It wasn't a nasty question. It was more a question asked by a man who had run out of time for pleasantries.

Quickly, I filled him in on the results of our walk-through of the murder night, highlighting Lorraine's recollections about the voices and car.

"This is new information, but it's not unusual for someone to remember more details after the event. It's interesting that she thought she heard voices." He leaned back in his swivel chair. "Did she say she heard another woman?"

"No, she said it sounded like a man. Why, should it have been a woman?"

"No." But he frowned. "What size shoe do you wear?"

I was surprised by his question that came out of the blue. Without thinking, I spouted the answer. "Size 8."

He gave a little grunt.

"I assume that wasn't the answer you wanted." I said. No response. "Chief?"

He drew his eyebrows close together. He was wrestling with something.

I burst out, "You found something, didn't you?"

There was a growl deep in his throat.

"Chief, you can tell me." Silence. "Look, I didn't ask to get involved in this whole thing. I was pulled into it, because I sold Lorraine the cake breaker and the State Police questioned me. Either we can work together a little bit or I can try to figure it out on my own and if the killer hears me asking about shoes, I could get into big trouble—"

He slammed his fist down on his desk, but the impact was muted by the stack of papers. "Alright, alright. We found a small footprint in the flowerbed outside the library where Miss Lorraine's safe is. I think it was made by a woman's shoe. We haven't been able to match up the size to anyone at Fair Winds yet. Know anybody who wears size 5½?"

"No," I tried to picture Lorraine's shoes. "I don't think Lorraine does, but I'll keep a look out." When I saw his scowl, I dialed back my enthusiasm. "I can just glance down at women's feet and if I see little ones, I'll let you know." He harrumphed. "Promise. Um, how did you find the print?" I asked.

"Just plodding police work, that's all. Nothing glamorous. In a murder investigation, you have to look at everything, go over every inch of the crime scene and environs."

"What about the car? Do you think Lorraine heard the murderer drive away?"

"What kind of car do you drive?" He asked quickly.

"Oh, here we go again. First, my shoe size, now my car?" He sat as if his face was made of stone, his eyes locked on me. "Okay, I drive a Saab 9-3 Turbo. Why?" Acid churned in my stomach as I realized I was going under a microscope again. "Do you think I zipped over from Virginia, killed a woman I didn't know in a place I've never been and got home in time for a good night's sleep before the state police showed up?"

Calm down. He's fishing for information. He plays his cards close to his chest. That's his job. Breathe. And I did.

He pushed on. "Know anyone who drives a black SUV?"

I thought for a moment. "I only know you and Lorraine here on the Shore. You drive an SUV."

"Hmmmm…" He didn't look pleased with my little joke, then a little smile, more like a smirk crept over his face. He was enjoying the fact that he knew something that I didn't. I hated that game when it was played on me in grade school and I rose to the taunt now in the police station. I jumped out of the chair and cried, "So, there *was* a car! You knew there was a car. You knew before I told you."

"You're not my only source of information, young lady. Part of police work is using all the resources available, like the public." He leaned forward and folded his hands on the files in front of him.

Stop overreacting. He's a professional, trying to do his job.

Quickly, I sat down again. "Somebody saw something?" I asked in a calm voice.

"Seems so. We put out the word and worked through all the calls and tips that came in. We got a report of a car seen speeding away from Fair Winds on the night of the murder, including the license plate number."

"She really did hear a car?" He nodded. I leaned back, truly impressed at how this was coming together. "So, who was it? Was the killer driving the car?"

He folded his muscular arms and wiggled his eyebrows. "You've been down here what, 36 hours and you think you should be privy to all the information I have?"

I decided to ignore his sarcasm and raised my eyebrows. "You can't be looking for a guy who wears a size 5½ shoe?"

"How about a guy with an accomplice? There are all kinds of possibilities. That's what *I'm* going to find out."

I stood up and pretended to pout. *Maybe I should try a different tack.* "Of course, Chief. I have to go shopping anyway."

"That's a much better way for you to spend your time instead of getting under foot. Off you go. I have to get back to work."

One of his officers knocked on the door and poked his head in. "Chief, we tracked down the driver of the SUV. He is in the interrogation room."

"You caught him already? Who is it?" I couldn't wait to tell Lorraine.

He gave me an exasperated look that said I should be quiet. "Wouldn't you like to know?"

I settled back in my chair and felt a wave of cold go through me. *Lorraine must have heard the murderer driving away from the house.*

The chief turned to the officer standing in the doorway. "Good work. I want to sit with the investigating officer. I'll be along in a minute," the chief said.

"Yes, sir."

"And don't forget to take the hat off the camera lens," said the chief quietly.

"Yes, sir."

I couldn't help but ask, "A hat covers your—"

"Officers do their paperwork in that room sometimes and we don't need a recording of them working."

I turned to go then stopped. "Ah, Chief, there's one more thing," I said, feeling very meek.

He paused, instantly suspicious. "Now what have you done?"

"Noth -- Nothing."

"Spill it," he ordered.

I steeled myself for his explosive reaction. "You can take Jimmy Smith off your suspect list."

And explode he did. His fists came down on the stacks of papers on his desk. His words came at me like bullets from an automatic. "What did you do?" He shook his head slowly, deliberately, in disbelief. "Tell me you did NOT go around asking questions. These people don't know you. They don't like strangers. This is a murder investigation. And..."

I stood there and took his anger. He was right. If Jimmy had been the murderer, I could be floating around with the crabs right now. The thought sent a shiver through me.

When his anger ebbed, I said in a quiet, contrite voice, "I'm sorry. I ran into Jimmy and we talked about his new boat and where he got the money. Ask Ryan."

"Oh, Ryan was there too?" He looked down his nose inspecting me... and I felt like a bug. He sure knew how to intimidate a person.

I shrugged. "I saw an opportunity and took it. I was just trying to help."

He put his fists on his hips and looked very official. "Ms. Strickland, it's time for you to stop meddling. You could be hindering our investigation. Murder isn't a game. Asking questions could get you hurt. Let us do our job. Go shopping. Better yet, go home. Go back to Virginia where you belong." He ushered me out of his office. "But before you leave, leave your contact information with my secretary so I can find you if I need you." He pointed me back toward her desk.

With more emphasis than I thought was necessary, he said "Now, good-bye."

"Yes sir," was all I could say as I watched him walk down the short hall and disappear into a room on the right.

I stood in the hallway, looking at the door. To think that the person who murdered Miss Evelyn was on the other side. A nasty taste came up in my mouth. This was as close as I'd ever want to be to such a person. Then my mind starting churning.

Could it be someone I've met? The officer said he *so it must be a man. That leaves out the servers at the Cove and Jackie at the Crab Claw and all the women at the Tilghman Island Festival. There were a lot of men there.* A shudder ran through me. *Could it be Ryan?*

No, NO, don't let it be Ryan. I took a deep breath. *Stop that. Some of the most ruthless killers in history were very handsome men. You never know what kind of mind is behind a pretty face.*

I truly didn't want it to be Ryan and I couldn't bring myself to leave the station not knowing. I looked around to see I was alone and crept down the hall. If someone caught me, I could ask for the ladies room. As I edged closer to the interrogation room, I could hear the chief's deep vocal tones asking a question.

A man answered and he was angry. "I don't know why I was hauled in here like a common criminal! I've done nothing wrong." His voice sounded familiar, but I couldn't quite connect it to a name. "And I don't have time to waste sitting here. I have a restaurant to run."

The chef from the hotel!

It was hard to imagine that the hands of the man who'd cooked that magnificent dinner for us at the hotel had killed Evelyn ... and all for a cake recipe. It was hard for me to believe. At least it wasn't Ryan.

"Then, answer one question for me," the chief said. "Why were you at Fair Winds on Saturday night about eleven o'clock? Why were you driving like a bat out of hell when you left?" There was a gasp, then silence. "Well?"

"It wasn't me," the chef said in a small voice.

"Oh, so somebody else was driving your car?"

"Yes... no." He stopped.

"I'm waiting. The truth this time," said the chief, bearing down on the man.

"That was the night Miss Evelyn was... was killed." The man was cracking under the pressure.

"That's right." The chief paused for effect and went for the jugular. "And you were there, Mr. Blaine. You were with Miss Evelyn. Did you fight? Did she refuse your romantic advances? Were you frustrated? Did you lash out and—"

"No! Stop!" He pleaded. "It wasn't like that at all."

There were tears in his voice, not for her, but out of fear for himself, the self-centered little…

"All right, I was there, but she was alive when I left. You have to believe me." The strain in his voice made me cringe.

The chief pressed on. "Why were you there so late that night?"

"I heard she was making The Cake." He said the words with great reverence. "The Fair Winds Torte. I went to plead with her to give me the recipe. I offered her money." He gulped. "I begged her, but she refused. Again. I want, I need that recipe and she wouldn't cooperate."

"So, you lashed out with a cake breaker and killed her," said the chief calmly. "Rather a poetic weapon."

"No, NO! It was nothing like that. Sure, I was mad. She was a frustrating old biddy. But I got out of there before I said something stupid. I was so angry. But I didn't touch her. That's the truth."

Silent moments stretched out as the chief waited. I could only imagine the strain on the chef. I wanted to peek around the door, but I didn't dare. I heard a chair scrape on the floor and I started to back away. I didn't want to think what the chief would do if he caught me standing in the hallway.

As I tiptoed down the hall, I heard the chef ask the chief, "Now that Evelyn is dead, do you think Lorraine would…" I didn't dare wait to hear the rest. I scurried out of the building, disgusted by the man who had served us such a delicious dinner the night before.

Outside, I walked through the parking lot. The chief's warning rang in my ears. What did he expect me to do, take up knitting while coincidences dragged me into a murder investigation? He seemed to believe I was innocent, but something might pop up to change his mind. Things like that happened all the time, according to news stories. I didn't relish the idea of facing police officers again who treated me like a suspect, someone who could take a life. The only way I'd be safe and the world would be normal again was for the chief to find the real murderer... and maybe I could help.

I turned toward the dress shop with a sense of determination. First, I needed to buy my dress for the funeral. If I could blend in, people might feel comfortable talking to me, perhaps drop a bit of information that would reveal something important.

The small shop almost overwhelmed me with its wide array of colors and unique styles. It would be a fun place to shop but today, I was on a mission. Despite the chief's warnings, I checked out the feet of the women. They were all larger than size 5½, much larger. In no time at all, I found a dark, conservative dress and paid at the counter.

On the main street again, an old man's voice, dry as the crackling leaves on the ground, spoke my name. "Miss Abby, Miss Abby, don't be rushing off."

With all the talk about murder, I almost took off running back to my car. Instead, I turned and saw a man withered by age, propped up by scarred wooden cane. A gentle breeze could carry him away.

I relaxed and asked, "How do you know my name?"

His smile revealed brilliantly white teeth except for the one missing on the side. "You're staying at Fair Winds. The Luther Family of St. Michaels always knows what and who blows through that stately place."

A stalker. It sounded like a whole family of stalkers. My guard went up again and my nerves went on alert. Thankfully, we were on the main street, the church bells ringing two o'clock in the afternoon. I wasn't alone with this stranger. People were walking around, shopping, soaking up the atmosphere.

"No need to take fright, ma'am." He raised his fine-looking fedora. "My name is Luther, Jedidiah Luther. I used to work for Miss Lorraine and my daddy worked for her daddy at Harraway Hall. My grandson helps out when he's home from college. Like I said, we Luther's have a long history with Miss Lorraine's family."

Small town, U.S.A. – either everybody is related or knows everybody.

"Well, Mr. Luther, it's nice to meet you. I'm afraid that I—"

"Do you believe the Lord works in mysterious ways, Miss Abby?"

Before I could come up with an answer, he went right on, shaking his head, eyes lowered. "It's a terrible business, what happened at Fair Winds. Poor Miss Evelyn." The catch in his voice added emotion to his words. "And poor Miss Lorraine. I can't make sense of it. I've prayed for wisdom like I always do. The name Jedidiah was the blessing name for King Solomon. Now, I think there's a reason for you being here. I've seen you with Miss Lorraine, how you treat her with respect and kindness. You care about what she's feeling about her friend, Miss Evelyn. So, I think I need to tell you a little story. Come sit on this bench here. These bones are weary and could use a sit-down."

As I joined him, I promised myself I'd only stay a moment with this old man, out of respect for his connection to Lorraine. It did feel good to rest in the warm sunshine. We wouldn't have many more days like this before winter blew in.

"It happened right over there at the Acme." He pointed to the grocery store across the street. "It was back when my daddy was *the* Mr. Luther. I was just a teen boy. I seen Miss Evelyn in the market, 'cept she was Mrs. Truitt then and she looked bad. Her long pretty hair was dirty and all. She looked like she'd break out in tears any minute and she had a right to. Her poppa was dying, his boat was gone and her husband was dead in the ground after he done spent all their money. She was so skinny." He took a deep breath that had a wheezing sound in it. "She was skinny except for her tummy. It was round with the baby she was carrying."

Baby? When we wrote the obituary, Lorraine said Evelyn had no children. But this old man saw her pregnant. He made it sound like she was close to term. What happened to the baby?

Mr. Luther caught his breath and I wrestled my thoughts into silence. I sat quietly and waited for him to continue.

"When I saw Miss Evelyn was in the family way, I told my daddy and later heard him talking to my momma about the mess that little lady was in… and the danger at her front door."

"Danger?" I asked.

"Seems right after she buried her husband – before people could tell she was expecting a baby – a hateful woman showed up claiming to be the man's mother. She pushed her way into their house down on Tilghman, wanting money, anything of value. Said her only son promised to take care of her and now that he was gone, she'd come to get her due. It made my daddy sick when he heard that she'd gladly take a child in payment." He shook his head in disgust. "She was no Christian woman, no way. Didn't even show up for her only son's funeral. That's when my daddy took himself over to Harraway Hall and told Miss Lorraine's momma what he knew. That same day, Miss Evelyn was gathered up to Harraway Hall and her poppa was taken to the hospital so he could die comfortable. Daddy was sent to clear out the house so Miss Evelyn wouldn't lose the few things she had."

The old man's breathing sounded raspy as he told the story. I waited to give him a chance to rest. After a few minutes, I asked. "Did that awful woman ever come back?"

He paused then nodded. "Yes ma'am. Only when she came back, there was no baby for her to take."

"Then Evelyn lost the baby?" I asked.

He stared into the empty space in front of him. "Sometimes when we live close, we don't see things that are right in front of us. Sometimes we need somebody else to see things true. Keep your eyes open, Miss Abby. And you keep looking." He drew a deep breath. "Time for you to go along now. This old man needs to rest awhile." He closed his eyes and raised his head a little to take the sun.

I got up quietly, went to my car and headed in the direction away from Fair Winds and toward Tilghman Island. For some reason, that little bit of land kept coming up. It was a place at the end of the beaten track where people lived life their own way.

Maybe someone there could tell me more about Miss Evelyn's baby or the woman from Virginia. If the old lady knew to come to Tilghman, maybe Evelyn's supposed stepson knew as well. At least I might find out if he really existed.

It took me about twenty minutes to get to where I could see the island but I had to wait. The drawbridge was up to let some sailboats pass. It gave me time to figure out a plan of action.

I pulled up at Fairbanks where I'd gotten gas after the Tilghman Island Festival on Saturday. I figured I'd top off my tank and go inside to see what there was to see. When I opened the door, the bells hanging from the handle jangled and everyone looked at me. As Ryan said, it was a gathering place for the locals. They got real quiet and watched as I went to the cooler. I took my time selecting a drink and finally they picked up their conversations. There was talk about the prices paid for crabs earlier in the day. Two women were talking over the noise made by a fussy baby. It reminded me of Christine and how alert she was to little Johnny's every need. I thought of Evelyn and the fate of her baby. There was no child in her life. Had she miscarried again? Or given up the child for adoption? Or was it taken away by the Truitt family? I couldn't imagine the pain of losing a child or having it stolen. What kind of woman could storm into Evelyn's house demanding money or a child in order to have someone take the place of her own dead son? Lorraine said Evelyn's husband was no-good. With a mother like that, what would you expect? Then I remembered the rumor about a stepson who would have been that woman's grandson. If he did exist, she should have been content to latch on to him instead of threatening Evie…unless he ran away from her, too. Or maybe he'd gotten the idea from his grandmother to come up to St. Michaels and demand money. Thinking about that family made my stomach turn.

The bells on the door jangled and, when I looked over, a smile spread over my face. I recognized the bright blonde hair and long nails of the girl who slapped down some money for gas. Rita. I followed her outside where she had parked a broken-down, dark red car with Virginia plates.

"Hi," I said, pulling out the squeegee to wash my windows. "Didn't I meet you at the festival yesterday? I'm Abby."

She looked at me from top to bottom. By her bored expression, I could tell I was dismissed. *Oh no, you don't. I'm not going to play by your rules.*

"I thought you were from here, but your car is from Virginia, like mine?" I made it sound like a question, hoping she'd offer up some information. Instead, I got attitude. What a surprise.

"What of it?" she snarled and stood by the car ready for a fight.

"Oh, nothing. It's just that I heard a lot of people born on the island go away then come back. I thought maybe you were—"

Her words chopped right into me. "What I do ain't no business of yours." She opened the car door.

I rushed on to keep her from driving away. "The guy from Virginia, you know about him?" She froze. "I mean, people are saying that some guy's stepson came up here from Virginia. Maybe you know him?"

She turned slowly, her eyes drilling into me. I felt a wave of heat rush up my body warning me to run. Was this girl going to come at me? She could do some real damage with those nails.

She tossed her hair with a flip of her head. "I don't know nothing about any guy," she called out as she got into her car, slammed the door and drove away.

Yeah, right. Then why are you driving a car with a Virginia license plate?

I only got part of the plate number because of the dried mud on it, but I wrote down what I saw. I'd drop it off for the chief on my way back to Fair Winds. He had the resources to follow it up. I'd just have to suffer through his lecture about meddling the next time I saw him.

CHAPTER SEVENTEEN

The Butler has the responsibility to help protect the silver of the House and to protect the House from fakes and forgeries of silver pieces. There are simple techniques to use to detect a fraudulent piece. For example, each hallmark must be applied individually by the maker. If the marks line up perfectly, one has reason to be suspicious.

—"The Butler's Guide to Fine Silver" Mr. Hollister, 1898

I walked into the main house at Fair Winds and found Lorraine fretting over a breathtaking collection of sterling silver spread over the dining room table.

"Wow, this is beautiful. Need some help?" I asked.

"Oh, yes, thank you. We'd taken these things out of the silver closet for the dinner," she said as she put a hand on the table to steady herself. The events since that day we met in Annapolis were taking a heavy toll on my new friend.

I pulled out one of the dark walnut chairs with a needlepoint seat. "Why don't you sit down and tell me what to do."

She paused for a minute and I braced for an argument, but she came around and crumpled into the chair. To distract her, I started asking questions and commenting on the many silver pieces that shone under the light of the chandelier. There were silver serving bowls in different sizes, a silver pitcher for water, and knives, forks and spoons of every description. She showed me the Rose Stieff pattern and I agreed that it was too ornate for my taste as well.

And then I saw it, probably the most efficient eating utensil ever created: the SPORK in brilliant sterling silver. The spork combined the bowl of a spoon with the short tines of a fork. You could use it as a spoon or a fork, hence its name, SPORK.

I grabbed one of the eight lined up in a neat row in the center of the table. "I can't believe it, a spork in sterling. Now, I know you have absolutely everything, Lorraine!"

She looked confused. "What are you talking about?"

I held it out for her to see.

"Oh, you mean the ice cream fork. It really is an oddity…"

"No, it's a spork. Ever since I discovered it as a child at some fast food joint, it's been one of my favorite things. I've only seen it made of white plastic and never expected to find it in sterling, but here it is." Was I giggling? Oh, why not? A little humor would go a long way. Even Lorraine was looking a little lighter, her mouth drawn back in a smile, her cheeks tinged with a rosy hue. "I can't imagine eating ice cream with a fork."

"It comes in handy when you have cake and ice cream," she explained.

"Yes, now that makes sense."

Lorraine was determined to make me into a silver dealer. "You'll find that collectors call it an ice cream fork, so take note for your auctions if you find one in those boxes of yours."

"I don't know. If I find any sporks, I just may keep them. But it wouldn't hurt to find out the going prices. I'll be right back." I sprinted up the steps to the bedroom assigned to me, grabbed my computer tablet and ran back downstairs. I turned on the portable Wi-Fi hotspot on my phone and started my search. "What is the pattern of this ice cream fork?"

"That is my Chantilly pattern," she said.

I could understand why she preferred the simple design to the busy Rose Stieff pattern. It wasn't plain, just elegant. I plugged the information into my search and got a lot of results. "It seems that this piece is popular. Let's see, here's a listing for $65 and another for $69." I did the quick calculation in my head. "That means you have more than $500 in ice cream forks alone sitting on this table. The thief – if it was a thief who broke in that night – should have come to the dining room. He would have really cleaned up." I sighed. "I'm sorry, we were talking about something else finally and I brought it up again. I—"

"Don't be silly. We can't ignore what happened. It's like that 800 lb. gorilla sitting in the corner." There was a spark of excitement as she put her elbows on the table and rested her chin on her hands. "We've been forgetting something. If it was a burglary as the chief said, he or they would have passed on the silver for something better."

"And that would be?" I asked.

"The diamonds. Remember we found one of my diamond earrings and some loose stones on the floor of the study and in the kitchen?"

"That's right. I'd forgotten. According to the chief, it might have been a woman or a man and woman," I said, following her train of thought.

I filled her in about what the chief had said. Together, we got up and she led the way to the flowerbeds outside the study. We searched, but the only things we found were a couple of weeds which she quickly pulled out by their roots and a lot of squashed mulch and mud, stepped on by many feet. They probably found something and all the law enforcement people came to look. Any trace of a small footprint was long gone now.

We wandered into the kitchen. Just days ago, it was a very busy place. Now, it was empty and silent. She put on some coffee and, while we waited for it to brew, I mentioned the old friend of Fair Winds I'd met on the street.

"Jedidiah?! How is he? He's fighting lung cancer," she said with a sigh. "Too many people here on the Shore like to smoke and cancer is taking its toll."

"He seemed well, though a little frail. He loves his stories, doesn't he?"

"Oh yes, he's seen many things in his life, some best forgotten, I imagine," she said as she poured the coffee.

"He talked about Miss Evelyn and how she came to Fair Winds." The pouring stopped.

"Really, what did he say?"

"He talked about many of the same things you did," I shifted my position on the kitchen stool so I could see part of Lorraine's face. "And he said she was pregnant when she came to Fair Winds, something about running away from her mother-in-law?" Lorraine handed me a mug and I took a sip, hoping she would fill in the gaps.

Before she spoke, she took a long drink of her coffee. Was it thirst or was she stalling?

"Abby, it was a terrible time for Evie. I was away at school and I only remember what Momma told me. Evie never wanted to talk about that time in her life. Thanks to Mr. Luther, Jedidiah's father, Momma found Evie living in a rented house on Tilghman with barely a thing to her name. She was dirty, hungry and very pregnant. Momma brought her back to Harraway Hall and she was with us from then on."

"And what about the baby?" I asked.

Lorraine rose from the stool, a melancholy expression on her face. "Everything took a terrible toll on her. She suffered so and so did the baby. Momma sent her away afterwards to recuperate and forget." She put down her mug. "Shall we finish putting the silver away?"

And with that, the subject was closed. She must have lost the baby as well as her family and her dream of a happy home of her own. Before I followed Lorraine to the dining room, I looked around the kitchen that had been Evelyn's domain. So happy and efficient. There seemed to be everything one would ever need to create fabulous dinners and scrumptious desserts. The woman was fortunate that she landed in a house filled with such love and caring. I glanced at the floor, the spot where she died. It was so sad that her life ended violently. The person who did it had to pay.

I walked through the butler's pantry into the dining room. Instead of being attracted to the silver, I plopped into a chair as a heavy cloak of gloom wrapped itself around me. It took a moment for Lorraine to notice, but when she did, she stopped what she was doing.

"What's wrong?"

I scrunched down in the chair and let out a deep breath. "Suddenly, I'm overwhelmed by everything. Life! No matter how careful you are, no matter what you do, somebody else can mess it up or even end it."

"I'm so sorry, I've only been thinking about myself. Not about how all this must be affecting you." She sat down in the chair next to me. "I've been selfish and I'm sorry."

"It's not that. I'm glad to help in any way I can."

"And you have," she said quickly. "You've been such a great help and support to me."

I was glad to help someone in such a sad, stressful situation. To be honest, it felt good to do something that made a difference to someone. Being out of a job and undervalued or rejected so often in my job search was getting to me.

I mumbled, "At least I can help someone else if not myself."

"What did you say?" She put her hand on my arm. "Abby?"

Now it was my turn not to meet her gaze. "It's just that I feel so useless. I put all that work into the company's product and *pouf!* It's all gone. I'd like to figure out what I'm supposed to do with the rest of my life."

"The rest of your life?" There was a note of surprise in her voice. "Abby, you're not even 30 yet. You have time to figure it out."

"I'll be 29 next March. I should have a better idea of where I'm supposed to be, what I'm supposed do. All my friends from school are establishing themselves in careers they love. I've had several different kinds of jobs, none of which I'd take again. I have a college degree in computer science, a field I'm starting to hate and a useless minor in history."

"History isn't useless," she stated just above a whisper.

"You're right but how am I supposed to pay the light bill with it? There isn't exactly a section in the want ads listing jobs – Only History Minors Need Apply."

She jumped in while I took a breath. "Maybe not, but you're talented and smart. We will find something you'll love doing and you'll make money doing it."

My breath caught. She said, *We*. *We* will find. It had been years since someone had used that word when talking about my life, no one since Gran. With that simple word, Lorraine had ripped the lock off my own grief and loneliness. I started to cry. She put her arms around me and held on till I was done.

CHAPTER EIGHTEEN

Hold a silver piece in the light so you can see what you're doing. Polish one area until you see the shine come up then move on to the next area. Be vigilant. You do not want to leave tarnish on any piece.

—"The Butler's Guide to Fine Silver" Mr. Hollister, 1898

The next morning, I had to wake Simon. All that running around with the big boys – and those Labs and Chesapeake were big – had worn out the puppy. It was just the two of us for breakfast. The cook, Mrs. Clark, said Lorraine and Reg had eaten early and left to make the final arrangements for the funeral. Simon wasn't interested in staying with me. I had to laugh as he dragged himself out to the patio to curl up in the sun. In minutes, he was snoring.

I wished I could settle down like Simon. Being in the huge house of Fair Winds somehow made me restless. I sat in the breakfast room, its big windows overlooking the river. The extra cup of coffee and the slim edition of the local paper occupied my attention for a little while. I found Evelyn's obituary and was pleased to see it was printed just the way we wrote it.

The reference to her support of Naomi's House caught my eye. The police chief had mentioned that Evelyn had taken a special interest in one particular young woman there. I wondered about that while I finished my coffee. The chief had said the girl's boyfriend was rough and had an explosive temper. Had he threatened Evelyn… or worse? The chief had some questions for the man, but I didn't know if the police had caught up with him yet. I toyed with the idea of going back to the police station in St. Michaels, but suspected the chief wouldn't welcome me with open arms. He might have appreciated the license information I left in a note. I wasn't sure how would he feel about the bit of investigating I was doing.

Enough of all this speculation and sitting around. It's time to take a trip to Naomi's House.

It took some digging to find the address of the administrative offices in Easton. The ride was quick and easy now that most of the tourists had gone home. It was luck that I found the director in her cramped office.

She made a place for me to sit and said, "I'm always willing to take a few minutes to talk with someone interested in the problem of domestic violence. At least our situation isn't as bad as some of the other counties in our district, but if even one woman is hurt, our work isn't done."

We chatted about the services offered by the organization until I felt comfortable asking about Evelyn's participation.

"She was a generous contributor, both financially and personally," the director said.

"What do you mean *personally?*" I asked. "Was she involved with the abused women?"

"In a way. She participated in group discussions, offered advice and information. She was uniquely qualified and an inspiration."

"Uniquely qualified, because she was a survivor of domestic violence herself?" I asked.

The director's hand fluttered around her hair, smoothing it, pushing it behind her ear. "Oh, we don't talk about things like that. The future is what's important."

"Did she get close to someone, to provide inspiration, especially recently?" I asked, unwilling to let the subject drop.

She pursed her lips and looked off, thinking. "Now that you mention it, there is one young woman. Said she reminded her of…" The director paused and flicked her eyes toward me then away again. "Of her friend."

"Of course. She must be devastated by the news of Miss Evelyn's death." I put the most compassionate note in my voice that I could. "I'd imagine a friend to talk to might help ease the shock. I know how upsetting this has been for everyone. I'm staying at Fair Winds right now and seeing the place where it happened… well, it's very disturbing."

The director perked up. "Are you a friend of Miss Lorraine's?" She almost reminded me of Simon who liked to sit up and beg when I was close to the cookie jar.

"Yes, I am."

Now, she was excited. "Oh, well, if there's anything I can do for you," she rushed on.

I decided to go for the prize. "Do you think I might talk to this young woman, offer her some comfort over the loss of Miss Evelyn?"

The director gave me an appraising look. Had I pushed too far?

"Would you be telling Miss Lorraine about your visit?" she asked. I nodded. "Well then, I don't see any harm in a little personal visit." She stood up. "I could take you over to the shelter right now, if you'd like?"

"That would be good. Thank you."

I followed her outside where she stopped on the sidewalk and pulled out her keys. "Now that we've lost Miss Evelyn, I'm hoping to interest Miss Lorraine in getting involved. There's a big hole that we need to fill." She gave me an encouraging look.

"Yes, I'll be sure to tell Miss Lorraine about our conversation and my impressions of the work you're doing."

She gave me a huge smile.

I pulled out my own car key. "If you'll give me directions to the shelter…."

Her smile turned into a frown. "I'm afraid I can't do that. If you write down anything about the location of our shelter, it might fall into the hands of an abusive man. We guard the information very carefully. Why don't you just follow me?"

As I got to my car, I noticed a car making a quick turn at that corner. It was old and dark red like the one at the Tilghman Island gas station. All this talk about abuse and murder had me seeing ghosts and goblins. I needed to take a breath.

The director led me through the streets of Easton and parked in a quiet neighborhood. I locked my case in the trunk since I didn't know what I'd be able to take inside. We walked toward the entrance of a non-descript building. Only the fence and security cameras suggested that something needed protection – in this case, people. I wondered if those who lived and worked in the area had any idea there was a shelter close by.

The director introduced me to a coordinator who showed me into a conference room furnished with a metal table and plastic chairs. I did not want to know the stories those walls could tell. In a few minutes, a girl named Lucy came in. She didn't look old enough to buy a legal drink, but the bruises on her face and arm were proof that she had seen more of life than many twice her age. Lucy was skittish as a young colt but, considering what she'd probably been through, I wasn't surprised. We spent some time talking about my connection to Lorraine and Fair Winds. When I mentioned what a wonderful woman Miss Evelyn was, the girl broke down. I listened through her tears as she told me how Evelyn had helped her.

Once the tears trickled away, she lowered her voice and said, "You promise not to tell on me if I tell you something?"

I nodded, then shook my head, not quite sure how to respond but wanting to hear her secret.

"Nobody can find out," she insisted. "You have to promise."

I promised.

Lucy looked over at the closed door then scooted her chair closer. "Miss Evelyn gave me money. It's against the rules. You can't tell a soul," she pleaded.

"Why did she give *you* money? What was it for?" I asked, gently.

Lucy blew her nose and spilled the details. "She said I reminded her of herself. She started taking a special interest in me when I found out I'm pregnant."

Yes, that made sense if Mr. Luther's story was true and I had no reason to doubt him.

"She gave me money to get away from the Shore. She said I should go to a place near Pittsburgh where they'd help me start fresh." Then, she started to cry again. "I don't even know where that is."

I patted her back to offer some comfort and she threw her arms around me in an over-the-top hug. Not knowing what to do, I put my arms around her lightly until her trembling body calmed and the sobbing stopped. Finally, she sat back in her chair.

"Lucy, if Miss Evelyn gave you the money to leave, why are you still here?"

Her lower lip started to quiver and the tears threatened to start again.

"No, no, I don't mean..." I stumbled. Anything seemed to set her off. "I was just wondering..."

She looked at me with those deep blue eyes, one surrounded by a bruise turning a sick yellowish green. "He took it." She said it so quietly that I almost missed it.

"Somebody took the money? Who? Your boyfriend?"

"Yes," she whined. "He went through my coat pockets and found the money and wouldn't give it back. Said he needed it to take care of me and the baby."

"He knows about the baby?"

"Yeah, I found out when I was in the emergency room with this." She pointed to her eye. "I told him and ever since, he's been so sweet." She reached inside her shirt and pulled out a cheap necklace with a little heart dangling from the chain. "He bought this for me. Isn't it pretty? He was trying to show he loves me."

I wasn't sure if she was trying to make me believe that he had changed or if she was trying to persuade herself.

"Then what are you doing back here in the shelter?" I asked softly.

Lucy hunched over, her fingers playing with her lower lip. "He got mad again." She gripped my arm. "But it was all my fault." She rambled on with the details. I wasn't sure I wanted to listen until I heard her say Evelyn's name.

"She saw me on the street a couple of days after she gave me the money and wanted to know why I hadn't left. I couldn't lie to her. I told her what happened, how he took the money from me. She was so mad, called me a silly girl. Then she calmed down and asked me if I still wanted to leave, start a new life and all. I told her I did, I swore to her I did." Lucy took her time blowing her nose.

"Then what happened?" I asked to urge her on with the story.

"She said she'd give me more money, but she didn't have it on her and she didn't have time to go to the bank right then. She said if I came to the kitchen door at Fair Winds later that night, she'd give me the money. She told me to pack up my things and be ready to leave."

"Which night was that?"

Her eyes filled with tears again. "The night she got killed."

The room filled with the sound of her sobs and the tension of my frustration. I wanted to shake the sniveling girl to get the details of what happened that night. Instead, I took a deep breath and lowered my voice. The last thing I wanted to do was spook her.

"Did you go to Fair Winds?" She nodded. "Did you tell the

police?" She whipped her head back and forth in an emphatic NO. "Okay, that's okay. When did you see Miss Evelyn that night?"

"That's just it, I didn't see her. I borrowed Linda's car … she's my friend…and I drove down to Fair Winds. I used the gravel road on the side just like she told me. I got out of the car and was walking up to the kitchen door and…" She started to cry again.

I pushed my chair back a little to avoid her leaping into my arms and asked quietly, "You were walking up to the kitchen door and…?"

"I—I chickened out. I couldn't go into that grand house. I didn't want to stay in Easton, but I wasn't sure I could leave my friends on the Shore and go to a strange place what with the baby coming and all."

"So, what happened then?"

"Nothing." Her tears stopped all of a sudden. "I got in the car and went back to Linda's house."

"And you didn't see anything… or anybody?" She shook her head, but wouldn't look me in the eye.

I suspected that there was more to the story so I gave Lucy my cell phone number to call if she remembered anything else. After all, I knew where I could find her.

I didn't have much time to mull over what I'd learned as I walked to my car alone.

"Hey!" A young, thin man with stringy hair jumped out from behind a tree. "You the bitch from Virginia been botherin' my girl?" He planted his feet, put his fists on his hips and stood between me and my car.

Is he talking about Lucy? Did I lead her abusive boyfriend to the safe haven?

My stomach churned. Was there somebody – anybody – around to help me? My eyes darted around looking everywhere. The street was empty. The houses were quiet. The shelter was too far away. I had nothing, not even my case, to defend myself. I could run right at him, but I didn't like the looks of his well-developed biceps. If I could only distract him so I make a dash for my car…

"Yes, I'm from Virginia. But I'm afraid I don't know you or your girlfriend." I glanced at the old beat-up car parked behind mine. I realized with a start that it was the same one Rita had at Fairbanks down on Tilghman. And the same one outside the director's office.

Could Rita's boyfriend be Evelyn's stepson?

On Tilghman Day, Rita's mom said she'd gone down to Virginia. Had he come back with her to the Maryland Eastern Shore to find Evelyn and collect?

His thick Southern accent cut into my thoughts. "You seem a little nervous. Do I scare you?"

"You surprised me, jumping out like that. That wasn't very nice." *Not nice? NOT NICE? What was I saying?*

He jerked his head in surprise.

Got to keep talking.

"I thought you were someone else." I started moving toward the curb to go to the passenger door of my car. "You're not, so that's okay."

He moved quickly to the curb to block my way. I turned back toward the shelter house. He jumped in my path.

I stepped to the left. He mirrored my move.

"What are you doing?"

He gave me a slow smile, filled with menace. "You're gonna listen to what I got to say."

I started to turn away. He moved again, closer.

"Okay, say it and we're done." I hoped the anger in my voice hid my growing fear.

"You ain't to talk to my girl no more, understand?" He growled. His finger pointed right at me.

I shook my head. "I don't know who your girl is. Now…" I turned and pulled my car remote out of my pocket.

He sprinted around me again. "Don't play dumb with me. Rita don't like you. Stay away from her!"

Slowly, I raised my eyes to his face. Yes, I'd remember him if I ever saw him again. "Are you threatening me?"

He put his arms out wide, the picture of innocence and took a step back. "Me? I wouldn't hurt a fly, ma'am."

I took a step forward. He backed up. I touched the remote to unlock the door. The beeps surprised him. He tripped over a tree root and staggered off-balance. He fell against my car for support.

I lunged for the door, got it open, slid inside and hit the lock. My hand shook so badly, I almost couldn't get the key to go in the slot.

He stood there watching me

Safe inside with the engine running, I lowered the window a little. "Is your name Truitt?" I shouted.

He straightened up quick and started to snarl again. "My name ain't no interest of yours. Just remember what I said. Leave Rita alone." He turned around, got in his poor excuse for a car and tried to squeal his tires as he sped away.

With the threat gone, I held on to the steering wheel, trying to calm down. It took a lot of deep breaths before I could drive back to Fair Winds.

CHAPTER NINETEEN

When polishing a silver vessel, such as a bowl or goblet, begin with the inside area first so bits of polish do not mar the polished area. After, put the piece on a table and tilt it away from you as you work your way around the outside.

—"The Butler's Guide to Fine Silver" Mr. Hollister, 1898

As I made the turn on the Fair Winds driveway, I tried to leave my fears from the confrontation with the Virginia man behind me. It was clear that he had enough anger pent up inside to threaten someone. How big a leap was it to go from intimidation to murder? Thankfully, the chief had ignored Lorraine's wishes and worked with the farm manager to assign a couple of men close to the house. Once inside, my tensed-up muscles started to relax. Lorraine said that Fair Winds was always an island of safety and comfort for her. Evelyn's murder had threatened that belief, but, even with the memory of blood and violence so fresh in her mind, all Lorraine wanted to do was go to Fair Winds. As I walked through the house, I felt its warmth and protection wrap around me. Over the more than a century of its existence, the house had weathered many storms, both outside and inside its brick walls. It felt anchored in its history marked by old portrait paintings, sailboat models graced the wall under the main staircase and a stately grandfather clock that chimed in a deep resonant voice. Delicious aromas lured me down the hall to the kitchen where I left the historic heritage behind and slipped into the 21st century. Here, all the appliance readouts – timer count-downs, oven temperatures, stovetop settings – were digital. Four women were working in beautiful choreographed movements so there were no collisions or mishaps. Little bowls of ingredients stood ready for blending into more scrumptious desserts like those sitting on the counters near the butler's pantry. Lorraine's big dogs and Simon had stationed themselves strategically around the large kitchen ready to pounce on anything that fell on the floor.

Ruth rushed up to greet me and offered a small plate of cookies. "Have one! They're still warm, Oatmeal-Raisin-Nut-Chocolate Chip cookies." One whiff of the textured goodies had me reaching for one. I'm not a big fan of chocolate – yes, I know I'm weird – but this combination of flavors was heaven to my taste buds. "We call them Reggie's Nuggets because they're so bumpy. When Mr. Reggie was a little boy, he spent hours with Miss Evelyn here in the kitchen concocting the recipe. It's his favorite."

As I finished the last bite, I mumbled, "I can understand why. You ladies are magicians."

Ruth lowered her voice. "We're making things for the reception after the service tomorrow. It gives us something to do. It's better to think about baking than on what happened."

I agreed and wished I had something to occupy my hands. I didn't want to intrude on the kitchen activities, because I was all fumble-fingers when it came to baking. The thought of working on my job applications or silver auctions was more than I could handle.

Ruth reported that Lorraine and Reg were still out making arrangements for the service. I wandered into the sunlit breakfast room overlooking the river. I'd already worried holes in what happened in Easton and knew I needed Lorraine's insight to make sense of it all. I was too edgy to work on the computer. I wanted to move around.

Between the breakfast room and the kitchen, a hallway led away from the main house. I followed it in hopes of locating Miss Evelyn's room. Who knows what I might find there? Oh, I wouldn't go through her drawers or anything like that. I just wanted to see where she spent her private time off the job and away from her good friend Lorraine.

The sounds of a busy kitchen faded as I moved down the hall. By the windows on the left, a little seating area overlooked a small garden that seemed tired after a long summer. On my right was a closed door. I tried the knob. Locked. There were three more doors, one open to a bathroom and the others closed tight. I found myself creeping up to the next door on the river side. My hand closed around the knob and it turned.

Inside, there was a cozy sitting room with a large window overlooking the lawn that ran down to the water. Along one wall, there was a TV and music center with shelving. Country music CDs jockeyed for space on the crowded bookshelves filled with cookbooks and framed photographs. A collection of pictures featured the governor and Evelyn's famous cake. One black-and-white shot showed a man creased and toughened by exposure to the weather. He had his arms around a little girl. Based on Lorraine's stories, it must have been a very young Evelyn and her father when he worked the water. Another black-and-white photo of a woman holding a baby might have been Evelyn's mother. There were a few pictures of Evie and Lorraine together, close-up shots of two friends smiling together over the years. On the end of one shelf was a formal portrait of a young woman alongside some baby pictures. I suspected it was a sad reminder of Lorraine's sister. I stepped back to take in the whole array of lifetime moments important to someone I'd never meet.

That's when I noticed the pictures of Reg, from the time he was a toddler through the years to the day he graduated from college. So many pictures. I reasoned that she probably felt a connection with him because of his tragic beginning – losing his mother and father shortly after his birth – then brought first to Harraway Hall then Fair Winds to be raised by his grandparents, aunt and loyal housekeeper. It was easy to imagine the young boy standing at Evie's elbow ready to sample another recipe for Reggie's Cookies. They both had something to give to fill the voids that life had made.

Footsteps down the hall and a door closing brought me out of my daydream. Somebody was using the bathroom, somebody who would not expect or appreciate finding me in this part of the house reserved for the staff. I stood at the door and listened. When all was quiet again, I poked my head out slowly to find the hallway empty. Ever so carefully, I closed the door to Evie's suite and sprinted back to the breakfast room on tiptoes.

I stood at the window enjoying the view until my breathing calmed. I wasn't cut out for illegal activity. My physical reactions would let a blind man know I'd done something I shouldn't. Once I calmed down, I was bored again. I got my tablet and sat in the afternoon sun pouring in through the breakfast room windows. It was funny how I seemed to gravitate back to this room. One couldn't deny that the view was fabulous: water reflecting the white fluffy clouds sailing through the blue sky, lush green grass invaded by some Canada geese along the shore and tall trees with leaves of vibrant colors in a farewell salute to the season. What was happening outside went along with the baking frenzy going on across the hall where Evelyn's recipes were in use to make cookies, cakes and tarts for the final gathering of her friends. Both happenings signaled an ending. Those thoughts reminded me of the silver Aunt Agnes had sent and Lorraine's invitation to explore her silver closet any time.

Imagine needing a whole closet for one's silver.

I went down the main hall and stepped into the butler's pantry just beyond the kitchen. The silver closet door was unlocked so I flipped on the lights and was dazzled. I had underestimated the amount of silver Lorraine owned. The closet was more like a small room with all the walls lined with glass-enclosed shelves that went from floor to ceiling. There were chests that held silver flatware—the basic knife-fork-spoon table settings—stacked in a special partitioned area. The rest of the shelves, lined with anti-tarnish cloth, held every type of silver tableware imaginable. Silver serving trays were stacked carefully with felt between to prevent scratching. As I wandered deeper into the closet, I lost count of the number and types of different candlesticks with their candelabra configurations. There were bowls of all sizes and shapes along with several gravy boats. I made a mental note to research why gravy was served in a *boat.*

"It wasn't poisoned." The words whispered in little puffs of air against my ear.

CHAPTER TWENTY

The tea kettle is vital since tea is infused at the table, not in the kitchen. This practice came about when tea was so dear in price that even in the finer Houses, all effort was made to prevent waste.

—"The Butler's Guide to Fine Silver" Mr. Hollister, 1898

"Stop sneaking up on me," I insisted as I whirled around. "You scared me half to death."

Reg stepped back and held his hands up in surrender. "Hey, take it easy."

I started breathing again. Maybe I had overreacted, but after what happened in Easton and the scary stepson, I had every reason to be on edge.

Trying to calm down, I said, "Okay, okay, I'm sorry." No, I was letting him off too easy. I pointed my finger at him. "You have to STOP coming up on me without warning. Let me know you're around, okay?"

"Okay, okay." He put his hands down slowly. He seemed uncomfortable and started to back out of the closet.

"Wait!" I said.

He froze.

"Sorry," I took a deep breath and began again. "You said something wasn't poisoned. What?"

He gave me an exasperated look. "What do you think? The cake, of course."

Of course. The Fair Winds Torte Evelyn made the night of the murder had gone to a lab in Baltimore for testing. The State Police were hoping to find poison to support their theory that the governor's stalker was responsible for the murder.

Reg filled in the details. "We dropped by the police station in St. Michaels after we finished making the arrangements for tomorrow. The chief got the report and said the state boys were disappointed. Seems they have to start back at square one and they descended on the chief to catch up on the angles he was exploring." Reg walked slowly past the silver shelves toward me. "Too bad, it would have tied a nice ribbon on this whole thing. I don't know how much more Lorraine can take."

"I suspect she's tougher than you think."

He folded his arms. "I don't know how much more I can take… of your contribution to the investigation."

"What?" His comment took me completely by surprise.

"Yes, the chief had an interesting question for me. He wanted to know where I was between eleven and one the night she was killed."

I shrugged. "I guess…"

"You guess? *I* guess you had to tell the chief that I drive a new black SUV." His anger was boiling to the surface.

In defense, I sputtered, "He asked me if I knew anybody—"

He nodded impatiently. "Yeah, I know. You were just trying to be helpful. Or was it payback for what happened with the company? How convenient that I drive a black SUV like the one seen leaving Fair Winds that night. It made it easy for you to dump me smack in the middle of the suspect pool?"

Horrified, I raced to explain. "I'd never do that. Not out of spite, never. I told the chief there were a lot of SUV's on the Shore.

He even drives one." I turned to look at a tea set. "What are you worried about anyway? You were at home that night, miles away across the bridge."

"Yes, I was home that night, but it was awkward being questioned like I was a common criminal," he complained.

"Yeah, tell me about it." I didn't know what else to say so I apologized again.

He looked around at all the silver and shook his head. "I guess I don't understand women." He gestured at the shelves full of silver. "Take your fascination with this stuff. I grew up with it, but I don't get it. People were always fussing over it: polishing it, setting the table so carefully, afraid to get a spoon in the wrong place and, after dinner, washing every piece by hand as if it was a precious baby. Evelyn was a fanatic about it. Never could I understand why. It wasn't hers. She was a servant paid to take care of it."

"Reg, she was more than a servant… to Lorraine, to you."

He looked at me in complete confusion. "No, she wasn't."

Now, I was annoyed. "Come off it. You grew up with her. She made your Reggie Cookies. They're making dozens of them right now in the kitchen. I had one. They're delicious. I heard how you and Evelyn made up the recipe together when you were a little boy." Reg started to back out of the closet. "Face it, Reg, she cared about you or why did she have pictures of you growing up all over her suite?"

"How do you know that?" he asked.

This was not the time to confess to a little snooping. My friend needed to face his grief. "She cared about you and you cared for her. You don't have to admit it to me, but you should admit it to yourself. It'll make all this easier, believe me."

He'd backed out to the butler's pantry. "I don't know what you're talking about. I have to go now. Sorry, Abby. Have to make some calls."

As he walked away, a blanket of sadness engulfed me. If Reg couldn't cry now about what had happened, he'd cry later and it would be harder on him. I knew this from experience. I was sad about Evie's death and its effects on my friends, but I had to throw off their sadness and get on with things before I suffocated from the grief around me. I turned around to consider the rows and rows of silver.

Not everybody has to like it, but I do.

Something at the far end of a shelf, sitting in its own spotlight, took my breath away – a formal tea service that belonged in an old English drawing room. I counted eight pieces in all: two pots with beautiful lines – one gracefully tall and the other short and squat, a covered sugar bowl, a milk pitcher and an open bowl used for waste or excess hot water once the teapot was heated. A huge oval tray rimmed in the same pattern stood ready to carry all the pieces to the hostess. It seemed that the pattern was Rose Stieff, the favorite pattern of Lorraine's family. Each piece covered in a mad design of roses, leaves and vines reminded me of the busyness of a Laura Ashley print. Actually, that was probably unfair when I stopped to think that each one of the delicate flowers and leaves was created by hand, hammered slowly and carefully. The most amazing piece of all was standing next to the collection on the tray. It was a tall large pot like an oversized teapot on its own stand above a burner. I'd only seen something like it in a silver reference book.

I grabbed my tablet and synced it for internet access. I soon found that the regal piece was known as a kettle used to warm the water for making tea in one of the pots. The reference said that to find a kettle, stand and burner in the same pattern as an original set was rare. I believed it when I saw an auction bid for the same pieces I was looking at: $4,750 and there were still two days to go before the auction closed. Curious, I looked up the value of the rest of the set and gasped when I saw the asking price from one reputable, well-known retailer: $25,999! This tea service was worth more than $30,000! That would buy a nice car in today's world. I shook my head to think that in the Victorian drawing room, a hostess was expected to serve tea each afternoon from a set such as this. It was amazing how priorities changed, not only from one historical era to another, but from one day to the next for a single individual affected by extraordinary events. Later, I told Lorraine about the value of the set. For a little while, the information distracted her from all the sadness and uncertainty surrounding the murder.

After dinner, we all decided to go to bed early. The next morning promised to be charged with emotions. After I checked my auctions, Simon and I were tucking in for the night when Lorraine knocked softly on my bedroom door.

"I'm sorry to disturb you. I know that Reggie will use one of our cars to get home later, but I know you're leaving right after the service tomorrow," she said. "It'll be so hectic with the service and reception that I wanted to come and say good-bye now. If I start telling you how much I appreciate everything you've done, I'll start crying."

"No! Don't do that." I came across the room and gave her a soft hug. "You don't have to say a word."

"I knew you'd understand." We parted, then she waggled her index finger at me. "But don't you be a stranger. I'd love to see you here at Fair Winds as often as you can get away."

I smiled. "I'd like that…" I motioned to a ball of black fur snoring in the corner. "And so would Simon. He has to go home to get some rest." We both laughed and Simon snuffled in his sleep.

"He's probably chasing rabbits in his dreams." She put her hand in the pocket of her robe and turned to leave. "Oh, I almost forgot." She pulled out and held it out to me. "Would you do a huge favor for me and see that this little package gets to Mr. Shaw, my jeweler in Georgetown? I put the information inside."

I looked and my eyes grew large. It was the evidence bag with the diamond earring and loose stones inside. "Oh no, I can't be responsible for this."

"Don't be silly," she said. "I trust you implicitly. And a good friend of Reggie's is as good and trustworthy as he is." She added with a chuckle, "If the diamonds don't make to Mr. Shaw, Chief

Lucky will just send the police to your home again. Remember, we know where you live." She curled my fingers around the bag and gave me a little kiss on the cheek.

It should have been a peaceful night's sleep, but I lay awake thinking about the little bag sitting in my purse.

CHAPTER TWENTY-ONE

Handle flatware pieces carefully. If knife blades, for example, come in contact with other utensils, small scratches or nicks may result.
—"The Butler's Guide to Fine Silver" Mr. Hollister, 1898

The day of the funeral dawned bright and cool. I followed the cars to the center of
St. Michaels to the large brick church. It was hard to find a parking place even though I got there early. The minister led a service that focused on the joys of Evelyn's life, not the mystery of her death. After the hymns were sung and the blessings were said, we followed the casket outside to the large cemetery behind the church. Evelyn was laid to rest next to the simple stones marking the graves of her father, mother and baby brother.

People retraced their steps to the Fellowship Hall and the crowd quickly spilled out to the large courtyard outside. I spotted Jimmy Smith, the new boat captain. When he saw me, his icy look made me wince. As he walked outside, I saw Ryan across the room. His eyes held mine. I was drawn to him, ready to move through the crush of people to explain, to make things right. I started to take a step toward him. His eyes fell and he walked away from me, too. I wanted to call out, but I wasn't sure he'd hear me above the noise in the room or even if he wanted to.

Reg popped up in my line of vision.

"See?" he said with a smile. "I didn't come up behind you this time, but it took me long enough to work my way around this crowd. Who would have thought so many people would come to honor a woman who worked on our staff?"

I gently shook my head, feeling sad for my friend who didn't seem to get it. "Reg, a lot of people loved her." I held up my small dish piled with all kinds of goodies made from Evelyn's recipes. "If not for the person she was, they loved her for her incredible desserts." I picked up a cookie and held it out to him. "Want one of your cookies?" He looked at it with a pained expression, shook his head and walked away from me as well.

The chattering mass of people in the room had a history with Evelyn of one kind or another. The director of Naomi's House was talking seriously with three people. Word was she wanted to start a memorial fund in Evelyn's name. Though I might not agree that this was the time or place, I had to admire the woman for her dedication. The busybody Harriet was standing in the middle of the room, rolling up on her toes, trying to see who was who and what they were doing. She looked right at me, or should I say right through me. My face didn't register with her, but someone else's did. Harriet was off like a shot elbowing her way to a white-haired man standing near the coffee. Miss Constance from the hotel was talking with her chef. She was holding up one of the pastries, evidently the subject of their animated conversation, except it seemed that she was talking happily about the confection while her chef's face was growing pale. The chef must live a life of desperation, always looking for the next best recipe to maintain his reputation. Did the stress make him crack? Did the police chief still think of him as a person-of-interest, I wondered?

A thin voice interrupted my thoughts. "Miss Abby, we meet again."

I turned to see the friendly face of Mr. Luther as he swayed from the bumping of the crowd flowing around him. His face looked strained so I ran interference for him to some chairs along the wall. He sat down with a great sigh of relief.

"May I get you some water or…" I asked.

"No, no," he barely shook his head slick with perspiration. He rested a moment then continued. "I'm so glad to see that you're still here."

I smiled. At least someone was willing to talk to me. I quickly banished the thought. I knew Lorraine was glad though people surrounded her from the moment she stepped from the car.

"Miss Abby, are you still looking?" Mr. Luther asked. His eyes flashed with interest. "And, more importantly, have you seen anything?"

His question brought me back from my musings about desserts, busybodies and Ryan to the chilling subject of murder. I glanced at the throng of well-wishers. One of them might know exactly what happened that night. One of them might be the killer, attending out of curiosity. Didn't the experts say that people guilty of a crime liked to see the effects of their deeds? A new thought surfaced. Maybe the guilty person was here, because his or her absence would be noticed.

My face must have shown the effect of this new thought, because Mr. Luther challenged me. "I see that you have seen something that others have missed." He held up his lined hand. "No, don't tell me. When the time is right, you'll know what to do. Take care." He pulled himself up off the chair with the use of his cane and, with a courteous nod, worked his way back into the crowd.

His words made the roomful of bodies seem to press against me, making it hard to breathe. It wasn't my responsibility. It was the chief's job to find the killer, not mine. I'd passed on everything I'd discovered to the chief. Well, almost everything. He didn't know about Evelyn giving money to Lucy, but I couldn't see how that was important. The girl knew more than she was letting on and I figured the chief would wring it out of her and that boyfriend of hers when he questioned them. I hoped he closed this case fast. If someone had killed once, it could happen again. Suddenly, every person around me was a threat or a target. A friend, a stranger could be a murdered. The thought was too much. Struggling for air, I moved to the door and escaped to my car. It was time to grab Simon from Fair Winds and go home, time to leave the specter of murder behind.

CHAPTER TWENTY-TWO

When one opens a silver storage cupboard, one may make an unhappy discovery: tarnish buildup on the pieces, though they were ever so carefully put away. This is especially true in cold weather when there is less ventilation and wood or coal is burned for heat.

—"The Butler's Guide to Fine Silver" Mr. Hollister, 1898

Once I'd strapped Simon in the backseat, drove away from St. Michaels and got on Route 50, that desperate urge to flee dissipated. In fact, I felt a little stupid, but so glad I was on my way home. Questions about murder, motive and abuse whirling around in my head were draining all my energy. The crazed drivers forced me to concentrate on the road. They used Route 50 like a racetrack, whipping across lanes of traffic to get a little farther ahead, jumping on and off exit ramps. After navigating my way through the traffic snarl around Annapolis, I started to calm down. Then, my phone rang.

"Hey, girlfriend!" Gwen's voice exploded with energy. Simon's owner had reappeared and it sounded like California was rubbing off on her. "What's shakin'?"

"Hey, yourself." I tried to match her excitement, but I was just worn out. Thank goodness she didn't notice.

"I have some good news!" She cried.

"Okay, I'm ready."

"I got called back for two interviews. I'm on my way to one right now."

She babbled on about job possibilities. It was good to hear her so happy. The company closing had been tough on her, and for some reason, she hadn't considered staying in Washington.

"I should have everything squared away very soon! You know, Abby, you should come out here for a job. We could get a place together and everything."

I was glad she couldn't see me shaking my head. The thought of living with Gwen who ran at full speed all the time had the makings of a nightmare. "You forget that I've done the West Coast thing. Think I'll stay here for a while. I'll be fine." *I hope,* I added silently. "Hey, I've got a question for you. I came across something about Reg and..."

She cut me off like a guillotine. "I don't want to talk about him." Her happiness and energy drained away.

"I just wanted to ask you..."

"I don't have anything to say." There was something in Gwen's voice, was it fear? Then I remembered that the day Reg announced he was closing the doors of the business, she wasn't at the meeting. She'd left the week before, without warning. Didn't even come to the office to say good-bye. She just disappeared. That wasn't like her at all. Reg said she'd decided to move back to California right away. Now that I thought about it, Gwen was pretty upset the night she'd brought Simon over to my house. She didn't explain why she was leaving on such short notice. Said she didn't want to talk about it. Evidently, the subject still upset her.

She was on her way to an important job interview so I wanted to sound reassuring. "Okay, I hope –"

Gwen cut in. "I've got an important call coming in. Gotta take it. Later."

In that instant, she hung up.

There was no telltale beep of Call Waiting. I tried to shrug it off, but I guessed that she hung up on purpose. And Gwen hadn't asked about Simon. Talking to my friend raised questions and reminded me that she had options. And so did I. It was about time for me to take advantage of them.

I managed to touch the right buttons on the phone to bring up my voicemail. First, there was a message reminding me to meet Mr. Warren. He'd suggested we talk about possible job opportunities with his company over lunch which sounded very promising. The voice on the next message made me cringe. It was Angela, who was neither an angel nor a trusted friend. She handled potential clients in a way that frankly made me sick: With her long red hair, probably not natural, falling in soft waves around a perfect makeup job, she used her deep, smoky voice to assure the male clients that she'd take care of everything. Her huge emerald green eyes, accented with smoky shadows and rimmed with black-black mascara, held the men in her spell until they agreed to do just about anything she wanted. Her approach got some initial results that made Reg very happy. The only problem was that within a few months of her appearance, Reg shut our doors for good. The real reason was still a mystery.

Her message was warm and caring. "Hi, Abby. Sorry I couldn't reach you." *Yeah, I bet you are.* "I ran into David Garrison. They're making some changes in his shop and there may be something there for you. Call me. We'll chat and catch up. I want to hear about everything you're doing. Bye."

Angela wanted to chat? Fat chance. She wanted something, that's *why she dangled that carrot of a job lead.*

The voicemail system demanded action: "Press 7 to erase. Press 8 to return this call." I was happy to erase her message. I'd decide later if I wanted to return Angela's call. With my mind focused on real possibilities, I speeded up as I entered the Washington Beltway, intent on getting home and locking my door.

Once Simon and I settled in, I took a long hot shower then checked the status of my eBay auctions. I was both elated and horrified. While I was busy running around the Eastern Shore asking people if they'd murdered a woman I didn't know, being threatened by Rita's bully boyfriend and sneaking into a dead woman's apartment, almost all of my silver auctions had closed. That was a good thing as reflected by my growing PayPal account balance, but if the auction activity stopped, two things happened: My income would stop and my house would remain a warehouse. The chaotic state of my home really hit me after being in the clean, neat and beautifully-decorated rooms of Fair Winds. With Simon safely curled up in the kitchen still recovering from his romps with his huge friends, I went to work on another box of silver.

After removing the shipping tape and packing materials from yet another carton, I pulled out a stack of boxes that were different from the wood boxes used to store flatware. These were smaller and thinner, covered in leather with simple brass closures that looked like they should cradle an expensive diamond or pearl necklace. I carried them to the kitchen table to see what treasures they held. Inside were collections of forks and knives made in very funny shapes. What made these pieces worthy of luxury leather boxes? The answer was underneath each box, written on Aunt Agnes's labels. Each box held a fish serving set. The Victorians had come up with the odd designs for the knives and forks used to serve and eat fish. When I checked some internet sites, I had a big surprise. The prices for a two-piece serving set ranged from $650 to $950, depending on the pattern.

As I poked around, I found out why using a regular knife and fork to eat fish was a no-no. It was so much easier using the curved fish knife to work the tip under the bones and remove them. If the fish was served already filleted, the knife could flake it into natural bites. I had to agree that it was nicer to eat a delicate fish in flakes rather than smashed into chunks. It was the same principle solved by the cake breaker, except applied to fish.

Remembering the cake breaker, my thoughts about silver auctions were pushed aside by my concern for Lorraine and events on the Shore. I looked at my watch. Yes, all the activities connected with the funeral should be over by now. I hoped she was home with her shoes off, maybe throwing the ball for her dogs. I wondered if the chief had followed up on any of my leads.

Maybe I could call him and ask? Fat chance! I was right where the chief wanted me, off the Shore and back in Virginia.

I resolved that the best thing I could do for myself was organize the fish sets and put them up for auction. As I reached over to pull the rest of the leather-bound boxes out of the shipping carton, I saw a large manila envelope, brown with age, with a bulge at the bottom. I cleared space on the kitchen table, laid it down and undid the metal clasp. Inside were some notes about a few sales Aunt Agnes made during the summer before I left for college. The carefully-recorded notes written in her round, flowing hand showed some sizeable transactions. One listed her purchase of a set of Tiffany sterling flatware in the Colonial pattern, four-piece place settings for 24. Twenty-four? Who entertains twenty-four people at a formal dinner party anymore? No one had a dining room large enough to accommodate a party like that.

Obviously not many because the next entry showed that Auntie had broken up the lot and sold it as two twelve-place-setting sets that yielded a tidy profit. Also, she'd sold an impressive and perplexing list of serving pieces. What made a baked potato fork different from a regular serving fork? I had so much to learn.

Next, I read *Caviar Scoop.* At least that one made sense to me. The next entry raised another question. Were people supposed to eat every morsel of the expensive delicacy with the *caviar forks* also listed?

Another curious item caught my attention: a serving spoon for peas. Two weeks ago, reading about a pea spoon would have bored me to tears, but now, I expected that people living in a slower, more elegant time would have a pea server in their silver collection. Why had it disappeared from the list of modern serving pieces? I gasped when I found the answer: $795! The priorities for the family dollar had definitely shifted. Of course, sterling may be more expensive today, because it's not used as often. I resolved to research the point at another time. I reached inside the envelope again, grasped the lump at the bottom and pulled it out, not knowing what new questions I'd face.

CHAPTER TWENTY-THREE

The Butler of the House is more than a protector of the family's sterling silver collection. Though the collection is probably quite valuable, the sterling silver pieces possess more than the monetary worth of the silver metal. Therefore, the Butler must be the guardian of the work of craftsmen as well as the memories and traditions of the family he serves.

—"The Butler's Guide to Fine Silver" Mr. Hollister, 1898

It was a small checkbook with a soft suede cover. It held the checks for Auntie's hobby-turned-incorporated business. I paged through the check register. There were the random checks written to dealers, private individuals and auction houses. Some of the deposits were sizeable. What stood out were the entries that appeared regularly every month, checks made out to Gran. I took the checkbook upstairs and stretched out on my bed to look at it carefully. Simon followed me and plopped his head on my foot. One of the entries included the notation, real estate taxes included.

While I was growing up, I never thought about where the money came from to keep our big, drafty house toasty warm and allowed Gran to do volunteer work in the community instead of working at a paying job. I attended private school, then four years of college. My dad must have sent something for my expenses but the Navy was not a high-paying employer and he had a new family to support. When I was in high school, I suggested to Gran that I work at the mall at a higher hourly summer wage than the historical center that had offered me an internship. The money would help pay some of my upcoming college expenses. It was a warm spring day when we sat in the sunroom overlooking the garden and talked about it. She told me to take the internship and not worry about the money. She reminded me that she and Auntie had always taken care of the expenses and would continue to do so.

I got up and started to pace. I always assumed Auntie lived with Gran because she was the older sister, never married, who couldn't afford to live on her own. They never talked about it. In our family, money was a necessity of course, but not an obvious part of our lives. Other things occupied our minds and hearts.

I'd had two strong women in my life who quietly did what they thought was right. That weekend so long ago, my parents and I had driven to Gran's house where I was going to stay while my parents took a long romantic weekend. At the last minute, I went with them. After the accident, Gran came to the hospital to find her daughter in the morgue, my dad in surgery and a frightened little me in the children's wing. I don't know how they found the strength to meet the challenges in the coming weeks. What was their source of strength to handle the logistics of a funeral and recovery plan for my father? Where did they find the patience to deal with the non-stop antics of a little girl missing her mother? Together, they gave me something worth more than money. They set an example of what strength and determination could do. If they could find a way through that difficult time, so could I.

"Simon, things are not always how they appear." I went downstairs with him on my heels and looked at the brimming cartons.

"I guess if silver took good care of us then, Simon, it should take very good care of us now." I paused and scratched behind his ears in his favorite place. "I should say, me. You're going back to live with Gwen." He nuzzled my leg. "Now, don't get too attached to me. I bet when Gwen comes back, you'll forget me in a flash."

I wasn't sure it would be that easy for me. But now was not the time to think about saying good-bye. I was time to think about making changes happen.

I went to the fridge for a bottle of cold water and stood looking at the magnets on the door. I hadn't played with them since the police showed up and I took a daytrip to the Eastern Shore. Make that a many-days-trip. I cleared the center space and pondered. What was swirling around in my mind right now?

I moved the big green dollar-sign magnet to the center. Money was the chief motivator in my life right now. I wondered if it was at the center of the situation on the Eastern Shore. Money seemed to make people do strange things. If there was a lot, a person spent a lot of time and energy protecting it. If someone needed money desperately, there was no way to tell what a person would do. Money was at the center. It bought shelter, food – a lifestyle. I almost never talked about money in my family, but Reg was different. He was always flashing large bills, flaunting his expensive shoes and clothes, driving pricey cars. I had to admit that he was willing to work hard to get it. From what he told me over the years, his career was successful in banking and finance. Having money seemed to define him. I put a top-hat-magnet next to the dollar sign to represent his attitude towards money.

At the other extreme was the so-called Truitt stepson. He wanted money handed to him for no other reason than he existed. Somehow, he'd gotten the idea that the world *owed* him. Maybe he learned that at his grandmother's knee. I moved the Teddy bear magnet on the opposite side from Reg's top hat. Two different people, two different mind-sets.

I moved the little birthday-cake-magnet under the dollar sign. It stood for the hotel chef whose career rose and fell on his ability to offer intriguing, mouth-watering, gourmet dishes. Having Evelyn's cake recipe could bring him national prestige.

There was one more—no, two more people—to add to this picture. I looked over my magnet collection and found a cartoon character holding barbells to stand in for that bully-boyfriend of Lucy's. It was important to add Lucy to this mix of personalities. She didn't seem to have a clue about handling money. Fortunately, there was no magnet of a woman with a black eye so I moved a heart next to the muscle-builder. It reminded me of her heart necklace and her blindness about love.

I crossed my arms and looked over the arrangement. Someone was missing. Lorraine! Her attitude about money was very different, and admirable. It had bought her freedom to run her farms, provide jobs, contribute to the community and, yes, surround herself with interesting people and nice things. I picked up the little magnet with a plastic silver spoon I made after Aunt Agnes's silver arrived. Yes, that was an appropriate magnet for Lorraine. I put it above the dollar sign.

The picture was complete. There were seven people with different viewpoints about money. Reg had access to buckets of it. The stepson thought he deserved it. The bully figured he was entitled to it. The chef saw it as a reward for his work. The only one who really needed it was Lucy, for herself and her baby, yet she was tangled up in her boyfriend's abuse. And of course, Lorraine.

Seven very different people—all connected with Fair Winds. What was their connection, if any, to an open safe and a very bloody scene in the kitchen? It felt like the answer was sitting right there in front of me but I couldn't... WAIT! Open safe. Diamonds. I'd forgotten about Lorraine's diamond earring that I'd promised to take to Shaw's Jeweler. I rubbed my face. Forgetting about a valuable earring was a sign of how tired I was. I pushed all the magnets together, made something to eat and went to bed early that night.

The next morning, after breakfast and a quick walk with Simon, I was back at it – researching, selecting, polishing, photographing and finally, opening another auction. I lost count of how many auctions were open or how many cups of coffee I drained. When the phone rang and I reached for it, my body was almost too stiff to move.

"Hey, how's it going?" Reg sounded calm and carefree, and I was jealous.

I filled him in on my activities on the computer since I'd gotten home.

"It's time for a little fun. Let me take you out for dinner. Nothing fancy," he said quickly sensing my attitude.

"No, I don't feel like getting dressed up, going out and all. Thanks, but no—"

"I have a better idea. What if I bring over a pizza, from your favorite restaurant? Maybe sausage, mushroom, extra sauce and… fresh basil, all on thick crust?"

I laughed. "You know my weakness. It's gotta be thick crust. Okay, you win. Can we make it early, say six?"

"Six it is and you don't have to do a thing. I know you've been working with all that silver, turning it into gold." He laughed at his little joke and so did I. "I'll bring the plates, salad, wine and the utensils."

"No," I said.

"No, what?"

"Leave the utensils to me. See you at six." I ended the call and walked into the dining room with a spring in my step. I found one of the silver chests of flatware, pulled out a two knives and forks along with a silver spatula. Aunt Agnes called it a lasagna server but I thought it would work well to dish up the pizza. After carefully washing and drying the silver and clearing away my papers and computer, I set the kitchen table for dinner.

With mouth-watering smells filling the kitchen, Reg said he felt a little strange serving a pizza out of a cardboard box with sterling silver. He was a good sport about it and the time I spent with my old friend was just what I needed. The tension and stress seemed to roll off both of us so we could enjoy each other's company again.

After demolishing the pizza and feeding Simon tiny bits of

cheese under the table, we tried to relax in the wooden kitchen chairs to finish the wine. I offered to clear off some space in the living room but he shrugged it off. His eyes strayed over to the refrigerator door.

"Is it my imagination or is your magnet collection growing?" he asked.

I shrugged. "I haven't added any since… lately. Haven't been getting out much except to walk Simon or go to interviews."

"Or visit the Eastern Shore." He looked at me with his eyebrows raised in a high arch. "How did you get started doing this crazy magnet thing?"

"It became very important to me a long time ago. You know I lost my mom when I was little."

"Tough for someone so young. It was hard enough on me when my grandfather died and I was almost a teenager," he said. "I can't imagine what it was like for you."

"I don't think losing someone you love is ever easy no matter when it happens. In my case, it was traumatic. After the accident, the police found me in the backseat covered in my mom's blood. I had a few bumps and bruises but nothing serious, except I stopped talking. There wasn't anything physically wrong, the doctors said. They thought I'd grow out of it. Gran waited months and decided to take things in her own hands. She'd always kept magnets of different kinds on the refrigerator. She bought more and moved them all down to my level. Instead of trying to guess what I wanted all the time, she told me to use the magnets to communicate with her. For example, she'd say, if you want some ice cream, put the ice-cream-cone magnet in the middle."

Reg got up to inspect the magnets. He pointed at one. "Is this the magnet?"

"As a matter of fact, it is. It's all beat up because ice cream is one of my favorite things but I don't have the heart to throw it away."

"You must have used it a lot over the years."

I laughed. "It's the magnet that led to the breakthrough. The day I moved a magnet for the first time, she had trouble hiding her tears. Once we got into a rhythm of using the magnets, she changed the game rules. If I wanted something, I was to move the magnet but I had to say please."

"What a smart lady," Reg said.

"Yes, she was. She figured if she could get me to speak one word, others wouldn't be far behind. It took a while before I finally spoke up, but once I started talking again, I haven't stopped." I pointed at him and chuckled. "That wasn't a straight line for you to tease me."

We both laughed as he held up his hands in submission. "Me? Tease you? Never."

"Over the years, we kept collecting and using the magnets. It was our little thing." I took another magnet and put it in the center. "This one got a lot of use, too." It was a heart.

He looked at me with a sad smile. "You miss her, don't you?"

The wave of sadness took me by surprise. I didn't want to cry so I only nodded.

"I bet if she were here," he went on. "She'd give you a little bit of advice."

"Oh, she was always good at that." The tears that threatened turned into a nervous laugh.

"Let me see if I can *channel* your grandmother." He went over and started moving magnets around. Finally, he stepped away and waited for me to get the message.

There was a hand, a sailboat, a plus sign in bright red, a bicycle, the letter A, a wine glass and a pair of lips in the shape of a smile.

Reg poured the last of the wine. I stared at the magnets and played with different meanings while he finished his wine and cleaned up our mess. Thankfully, he remembered not to put the silver in the dishwasher.

With everything washed or tossed in the trash, he plopped down in his chair. "Either my message is too deep or I'm really lousy at this game. Give up?"

I gave him a weak smile. "Yes, I'm afraid so. Sorry."

"No problem. See if you can follow my screwball logic." He pointed to the hand. "This was the closest I could come to a wave good-bye, *Good-by to the Shore*." He pointed to the sailboat, then the plus sign.

"Does the plus sign mean *and*?"

"Yes, at least you got that one. Now, the bicycle means *move on*."

"And the letter A stands for my name?" I asked.

"Right and it's blue-green, just like your car. That color always reminds me of you."

"But I haven't a clue what the wine glass means," I said, shaking my head.

Reg sighed. "That one is a stretch. You know when the Jews make a toast, they say, *To Life!* Just like in the "Fiddler on the Roof" movie."

"I see. You're using the wine glass to make a toast?"

"Right! The smile is obvious, *Be happy*."

"So, the message is, *Forget the Shore, Abby, and get on with your life. Be happy.* Is that right?"

He applauded and then, with his hands on his hips, he looked at the message he'd concocted. "I'm not so bad at your little game, am I?"

"Don't get cocky," I said with a big smile.

He looked from the magnets to me. His smile faded. "You've been through a lot lately, Abby." He leaned down and gave Simon a full-body rub, much to his delight. "This guy here is all the excitement you need right now." He pulled me up and into his arms. "I seem to be at the middle of all this upset in your life and I'm sorry. I care about you. I want you to be happy. Forget about the mess in St. Michaels. Let the chief sort it out. Take care of my friend, Abby, okay?" He kissed my nose.

We'd come to another crossroads. I wasn't sure which way I wanted it to go. Reg made the decision for us.

He said, "And on that note, I'm off."

I walked him to the door and just as he headed down the sidewalk, he turned. "Oh, I almost forgot. Do you still have Lorraine's earring? Now that I'm back in town, I can take care of that errand. You don't need to worry about it."

"The earring? Oh, I'm sorry I already dropped it off."

He paused then waved good night.

As I closed the door and locked it, I wondered why I'd lied to him.

CHAPTER TWENTY-FOUR

A large table centerpiece of silver, like an epergne filled with flowers, fruit or desserts, makes a strong statement in the dining room of any House. Inspect it thoroughly as the tiniest spot of tarnish can ruin its appearance. When the silver gleams, there is nothing to match the effect.

—"The Butler's Guide to Fine Silver" Mr. Hollister, 1898

The next day, I was scheduled to meet Mr. Warren, the man Angela said may have a senior position open on his software development team. I wasn't sure how keen I was for a tech job anymore. Maybe hearing the details about the work would spark my interest. Anyway, we were having lunch at Clyde's and that alone would make the trip worth it. According to its advertising, Clyde's is where prominent government, business and academic figures meet. The Clyde's in the heart of Georgetown was part of a chic mall with tiled floors, an Italian fountain and indoor garden. I rode the escalator up clutching my parking receipt. When I saw the parking rates, I hoped the restaurant would validate or I'd need a small mortgage to retrieve my car.

Focus! You're here to nail down a new job so you don't have to worry about every little dollar. You may not like the work but it's the safest way to support yourself.

I felt awkward about the place, the parking and the navy-blue suit with a skirt I was wearing to look professional. Even as a department head at the startup, I often wore just a jacket and pants or nice jeans. Anything else would have been overdressed. I looked at the watch Gran had given me and felt a little boost of confidence as I rushed upstairs. If I got this job, I pledged to be nice and thank Angela for the referral.

Inside, the hostess led me through the bar area where a gold record hung on the wall. It was for the Starland Vocal Band's hit song *Afternoon Delight.* Everybody thought the song was about getting it on with your sweetie in the afternoon. The real inspiration was Clyde's afternoon menu titled *Afternoon Delights.* We walked into the Atrium Dining Room where vintage model airplanes hung from the ceiling. Mr. Warren sat at a table close to the warmth of a crackling fire in a towering stone fireplace. We shook hands. He didn't get up. That should have been a clue to how things would go. I sat down on the Bentwood chair and almost fell over. My chair wobbled on the uneven so I had to concentrate on keeping my balance as well as making a good impression.

We sat in silence, looking at the menu. I bypassed the expensive entrees and ordered a grilled cheese sandwich and tomato soup, a little comfort food to calm my nerves. Mr. Warren announced his selection of the pan-roasted rockfish to the waiter. While he discussed the nuances of his order, I peeked at the menu price for his little lunch with sautéed spinach, Yukon gold potato puree, romesco sauce and tapenade… $16.95! Maybe I could have picked something a little more gourmet. After all, I could make tomato soup and a grilled cheese sandwich at home. Too late now.

We talked about general things to get a feel for each other. When I was ready to discuss the job opportunities, he'd implied might be available during our phone conversation, our lunch appeared. Between bites of his expensive lunch, he talked about delayed projects and tightening budgets. He referenced pending RFPs and RFBs – alphabet-soup shorthand for government Requests for Proposals and Requests for Bids. As he savored the last bite, he declared that his company would not be hiring for months. My delicious three-cheese sandwich turned to sawdust in my mouth. Why had we bothered to meet? His stream of bad news stopped only when he answered his phone. He spoke quietly, dabbed his lips with his napkin, mumbled something about an emergency meeting, got up and left.

I was dumbstruck, especially when the waiter put the bill down in front of me.

The oh-so-important executive who had suggested lunch had stuck me with the bill. One look at the total almost made me gag. Seething inside, I pulled out my strained credit card and when I signed my name with a flourish, it was from anger, not flair. I had to escape the stuffy atmosphere filled with people on expense accounts, so busy name-dropping. When I jostled someone's chair by accident, I didn't bother to apologize.

On my way out, I passed some cozy tables-for-two along a paneled wall. My steps slowed as I neared one particular table. Tired of being a victim and without thinking twice, I slid into the vacant seat across from the stunning woman wearing a stylish and expensive-looking turquoise dress that set off her long red hair.

"Hello Angela. What is a bitch like you doing in a nice place like this?" I asked.

"And yet, here you are," she said with an ironic chuckle. She smiled in amusement as if faced with an inferior adversary.

Was there nothing that unnerved her?

Since the first day she walked into one of our staff meetings at the startup, her superior attitude had been infuriating. She always made us feel inadequate, that if we put in a little more effort, the company would be a success. But no one ever challenged what she was doing to contribute. If we had held her accountable for her marketing efforts, we might still be in business today. Well, her time had come.

"Yes, here I am, after having lunch with Mr. Warren, the guy you recommended." My hands were shaking from anger so I put them in my lap.

She opened her sapphire blue eyes wide as she asked, "How did that go?" Her syrupy attempt at concern oozed across the table and made me gag.

"You were right, it was a good fit." *Was there a flash of surprise under her flawless make-up?* "A good fit for a sucker. He doesn't have a job opening and he stiffed me with the check at this expensive restaurant – not exactly an affordable choice for an out-of-work girl but, here I am... thanks to you."

If I'd seen you before I paid the bill, I would have dropped it on your table and said, I believe this is yours.

With a little pout, she said, "That's unfortunate."

"Unfortunate circumstances seem to pop up wherever you go." My eyes narrowed, digging for the truth about her work with the company and her hold over Reg. "It was unfortunate our startup closed after you showed up," I said.

"Yes, it was," she chirped. Her eyes strayed to the tabletop as she straightened the silverware.

"Unfortunate that good people are out of work," I continued.

"Yes, it is," she cooed as she pouted those really thick lips men seemed to like.

"Unfortunate that we were doing fine until you appeared," I charged.

"Reg wanted help market his product and—"

I didn't let her finish and raised my voice to drown out her words. "Oh yes, the minute you started whispering in Reg's ear, everything came crashing down."

The woman at the next table glanced over, filled with curiosity. I stared at her and she turned away. I wasn't finished.

"Why did the bottom fall out? Did you make Reg do something dirty, something illegal?"

She bristled. *Had I hit a nerve?*

"I have better things to do than listen to your groundless accusations." She glanced up over my shoulder. "Much better things to do, as you can see." She smiled a slow "cat that ate the canary" smile.

I turned and saw a gorgeous man with a little silver at the temples. In his custom-made suit and silk tie, he oozed money and power.

"Should I have made a reservation for three, darling?" he asked.

As I stood up, my eyes surveyed him from head to toe, then I turned back at Angela and said, "A little old for you, isn't he?" She might be dismissing me but I hadn't scored, yet. I cocked my head and gave her a silent appraising look. "Maybe not."

Calmly, I turned and glanced at the man. "She's all yours." As I brushed past him, I murmured for his ears only, "You poor bastard."

Behind me, I heard her ask in an almost desperate voice, "What did she say?"

I didn't wait to hear his reply. A smile of victory spread over my face. I had to control the urge to do a victory dance. It was the one moment everyone dreams of, when you come up with the perfect scathing comment at the right time, and walk away. This was my moment and oh, it felt so good!

CHAPTER TWENTY-FIVE

Be sure to make purchases and repairs with a reliable and reputable dealer to avoid fakes, shoddy work or switching out of the original piece.

—"The Butler's Guide to Fine Silver" Mr. Hollister, 1898

I took my time strutting between restaurant tables and out the door, only to discover I'd made a wrong turn. Instead of standing by an escalator, I was outside the boutique mall on a crowded sidewalk. It was as if an invisible hand had guided me outside toward Lorraine's jeweler, the man I'd forgotten. I'd feel so much better when the diamonds were passed along to Mr. Shaw.

I checked the address and found the shop wasn't too far down M Street. Once, the old port town of Georgetown on the Potomac was filled with grand sailing ships, tough sailors and rats. Now, the streets were lined with graceful tall trees and very expensive real estate. The area attracted money— from the Four Seasons Hotel to the limos, the direct-from-London baby buggies and the price tags in the chic shops. People on the crowded sidewalk jostled for space, people like evening news anchors, government people and the ever-present gaggle of noisy tourists, so it was hard to walk without bumping into someone.

"HEY!" snapped a large man. "Be careful of Rascal!"

"Rascal?"

He pointed down at my feet. Rascal, a long-haired dachshund, was busy winding his leash around my ankles.

"Please remove yourself," demanded his owner.

I almost lost my balance as I untangled my feet. The man walked off in a huff with Rascal dutifully prancing beside him. I went in the other direction to find Lorraine's jeweler, clutching my purse with the diamond earring inside.

The shop was in a narrow two-story building paneled painted Federal blue. The heavy Colonial-style molding around the two windows and main door was the color of rich cream. A historical landmark plaque hung above the discreet sign that simply read, SHAW'S – Jewelers. Inside, the cozy shop was decorated in shades of blue, from carpeting the color of a sapphire to the walls papered in a lighter shade. Diamonds, gold and platinum in antique-styled cases sparkled in the light of a dignified crystal chandelier.

A courtly, older gentleman, wearing a starched dress shirt, dark tie and a vest with a watch chain draped across his round middle, was seated at a small desk. The inner workings of a watch were spread out in front of him. "Good morning, may I help you?"

"Hello," I said. "I'm looking for Mr. Shaw."

"Mr. Shaw, at your service," he said with a little bow of his head. "What can I do for the lovely young lady today?"

"Lorraine Andrews asked me to deliver an earring to you for repair."

"She called." He shook his head. "A tragic thing about Miss Evelyn. Such a nice lady."

"You knew her?" I hadn't expected that.

"Yes, I've known them both for years. Miss Evelyn would bring things to the shop – for appraisals, cleaning and repairs."

So, she knew about the diamonds. That might be important to know.

He looked surprised when I asked, "Why do you think someone would want to hurt her?"

He took off his glasses and cleaned them. "I can't believe anyone would want to hurt her. She was a good friend to Lorraine, to everyone." He put his glasses back on and peered at me. "You're a friend of Miss Lorraine?"

"Yes, I am," I said.

He gave me an appraising look then made his decision. "You two have something in common." He glanced down at my wrist. "You both have excellent taste in timepieces. A lady's Piaget Tanagra 18K round face gold watch with twenty-eight diamonds, I believe?"

"Mr. Shaw, you are very good. It was a gift from my grandmother."

"A woman of discriminating taste. It is good to see a young person wearing quality workmanship every day. Many of your generation prefer those plastic things in fuchsia and daisy prints." He screwed up his face in distaste. "They feel so slimy."

"I agree. Tell me, Mr. Shaw, what kind of woman was Miss Evelyn? Was she happy living at Fair Winds with Miss Lorraine?"

"Those two were closer than close." Mr. Shaw smiled, distracted by a personal memory. "It wasn't a rich-girl, poor-employee sort of thing. They were more like sisters, watching out for each other, helping and supporting each other..." He drifted away to his own thoughts.

I waited politely, but valuable parking lot time was passing. "Mr. Shaw?"

"I'm sorry. I can't imagine how Miss Lorraine feels. For the first time in her life, she is truly alone."

"She has her nephew Reg," I reminded him.

Mr. Shaw huffed. "He puts on a show but he's not really close to his aunt. He's more interested in..." Mr. Shaw took a deep breath and shook his head. "It's not for me to say." Straightening up, he put his glasses on. "Now, show me this package Miss Lorraine entrusted to you."

I handed him the little evidence bag and when he took out the earring and loose stones, a kaleidoscope of colors exploded in the intense light of the shop. He picked up the earring, held it close to his right eye and frowned. In one fluid motion, he pushed his glasses up on top of his head and settled a loupe, the jeweler's magnifying glass, in front of his eye. He made a close examination of the earring and each loose stone. Then, he put everything on a velvet-covered pad and made a sound deep in his throat. "One moment, Miss."

He called to the back of the shop and a petite, young woman with lustrous caramel-colored hair came and stood next to the jeweler. "Michelle, one of my gemologists," he said by way of introduction.

She glanced down at the earring, looked closer and mumbled one word. "Oh."

She pulled out her loupe. "May I?" Cradling the earring in her hand, she moved the loupe over each stone and a frown developed on her face, too. Michelle lowered her loupe, turned to Mr. Shaw and gave him a tiny shake of her head.

I watched in confusion and had to ask, "Is something wrong?"

Finally, Mr. Shaw said, "I'm afraid there is a problem. I've appraised this earring and its mate on several occasions. They are quite valuable based on the design of the settings and quality of the stones. At least they were. As it sits right now, only some of these stones are real diamonds."

"Only some? They all look like real diamonds." My voice rose an octave.

"Yes, they do, to the untrained eye. Since I last appraised this piece, many of the stones have been replaced."

My jaw dropped as I stared at the man. "Mr. Shaw, are you sure?" He began to scowl, so I quickly added, "I'm no expert, but . . ."

He said in a deep tone. "I am an expert. So is Michelle. They are good quality replicas, but they are not diamonds."

Michelle took out a small mirror. "Let's do a little test." She unlocked the display case and selected a large diamond solitaire ring. My breath caught as she touched the sparkling stone to the mirror and pulled it across the surface leaving a deep, clear scratch on the mirror glass. She returned the ring to its place in the case.

"Now, let's try a stone in the earring." She angled the large stone that dangled at the bottom of the setting and dragged it across the glass. Only the faintest of a line appeared.

"How can that be?" I asked.

"On the Mohs Scale of one to ten used to compare the hardness of different substances, the diamond is the hardest natural material on earth. The plate glass of a mirror is much softer so a diamond leaves a deep scratch. A cubic zirconia, a substance often used to replace a diamond, is much softer." She pointed to the mirror. "So, you get a faint line."

"Mr. Shaw, when Miss Lorraine gave me the earring, she said it was a *diamond* earring. You said that when you appraised it, all the stones were diamonds. Now, they're not. Why?"

The jeweler shrugged. "It's quite simple. Someone changed out the stones."

He raised his eyes to my face. His expression tinged with suspicion made me squirm a little though there was no reason for me to feel guilty.

Michelle broke the spell. "Whoever did this was an amateur." She handed me a large magnifying glass. "Look at the metal around the fake stones."

"There are scratches," I observed.

Mr. Shaw nodded with emphasis. "That's right, young lady. You have found the telltale sign of an amateur. A true craftsman would never leave a mark."

"It's not the first time an owner has made a swap," said Michelle.

"Do you think Lorraine…?" I couldn't finish the question. The idea was too shocking to say aloud.

"Maybe she needs cash. These days, fakes can look good in a piece of jewelry for a fraction of the cost. Swap out a few diamonds and when no one notices, replace more."

"And no one is the wiser," Mr. Shaw added. "Almost no one."

It didn't make sense. The earring was stored in Lorraine's safe. Why would she lock up fake diamonds?

"Can you just buy fake stones to fit a setting?" I asked, still not convinced.

Michelle continued my education. "Yes. It's not the kind of work we do here at Shaw's, of course. You might learn more at the store down the street with a burgundy awning. Their windows are filled with sparkly stones that are as phony as most of the stones in this earring."

Mr. Shaw put the stones and earring back in the evidence bag and held it out to me. "Miss, I will not accept this piece."

"But why?" I exclaimed.

"I have no protection against a charge of theft. Someone could say I was the one who made the switch." He laid the bag on the counter. "I am sorry."

I recoiled. "What am I supposed to do with it?"

Mr. Shaw sighed. "I suggest you return it to Miss Lorraine," He arched one eyebrow. "And hope she does not make that allegation against you. I'm afraid you are in a very difficult position. Perhaps you are the one who made the switch."

"Me?! No, I…" My words faded when I saw the look on his face and reality sunk in.

He pushed the bag across the counter. "I'm afraid you'll have to leave now. There's nothing more I can do."

I slid the package into my purse and went out on the street again. Possibilities rattled around in my head. If the stones weren't real, why didn't Lorraine tell the police when the chief suspected an attempt to steal the jewelry was connected to the murder? Another thought brought me up short. What if Lorraine knew the stones were counterfeit? She could double-dip by making an insurance claim. If the chief found out, it would undermine her reputation and worse. No, it didn't jive with my impression of the woman. I wanted to believe that Lorraine didn't know the stones were imitations. But if she did, there was another suspect in Evie's murder.

CHAPTER TWENTY-SIX

The official content measurement of sterling is quite strict. The silver fineness must be 92.5% in combination with other metals. Any other level of purity constitutes a fake.

—"The Butler's Guide to Fine Silver" Mr. Hollister, 1898

I staggered a little and put my hand against a tree trunk to steady myself. The suspicions about Evelyn's murder were starting to get to me. First, it was the Virginia State cops and their pointed questions: Where were you last night when the woman was murdered? The St. Michaels police chief hitting me with questions out of the blue: What kind of a car do you drive? Why were you talking to Jimmy Smith? Now, the Georgetown jeweler. One minute he was warm and welcoming; the next, he all but accused me of switching out the diamonds.

This situation could get ugly very quickly and I was right in the middle of it. I could call a lawyer, there were so many in Washington I could have my pick, but who could I trust? I didn't know any criminal lawyers. More importantly, there was no one who knew me. If I was charged, I'd need someone to fight for me, not just go through the motions of defense. My representative had to *believe* I was telling the truth. Newspapers were filled with stories about innocent people convicted of major crimes being released after spending years in prison. I never dreamed it might happen to me, but the police had never questioned me about a murder. No one ever thought I may have stolen diamonds.

No, this is real. If it comes down to it, can I make people believe I didn't steal anything … or murder anybody?

That thought took the breath right out of me and I propped my body against the tree.

Come on, Abby. What are you going to do? Think!

I couldn't prove that I was home alone with Simon on the night of the murder. I couldn't prove that the stones were imitations when Lorraine gave me the earring in the evidence bag. Gran used to say that if you couldn't depend on someone else to figure things out, it was time to take care of yourself. It was time for me to do just that.

I pushed myself away from the tree and looked down the street at the burgundy awning emblazoned with the words *Windsor Jewels* in white on the next block. It was time for me to get to the bottom of this mess… for myself and Lorraine.

Windsor Jewels stuck out like a carnival on this historic, elegant street. The display windows were filled with stones sparkling on burgundy velvet: searchlight-size diamond studs, mammoth solitaires rings and intricate necklaces as big as horse collars. Among the other differences between this store and Mr. Shaw's was that every stone was a fake.

Inside, the carpeting was so thick I looked down to see if my shoes had disappeared. The walls were burgundy, obviously their signature color. Display cases scattered throughout the store sat in floods of high-intensity lighting to coax out the maximum sparkle of the pieces inside. And sparkle they did. Flashes of red, blue and yellow were everywhere.

"Good afternoon." The man with the English accent looked

more like an earl than a salesperson. "My name is Mr. Cutler. How may I make your day beautiful?"

Did that kind of line really work with customers?

"Why don't I show you some pieces that might interest you? Let's start over here."

He walked to a case in the middle of the shop and unlocked it. Dutifully, I followed along, determined to learn all I needed to know before I fell for his sales pitch. I'd always had a soft spot for shiny, beautiful things so I had to work fast.

I pulled out my spacey California-blonde routine I'd learned growing up on the West Coast. With all due respect to blondes, it was a ploy that worked time and again. I thought a Southern accent would add a nice touch.

"What a lovely store y'all have," I gushed. "This is the first time I've been here."

"Allow me to welcome you. Though it might be your first time to visit Windsor Jewels, I trust it won't be your last."

I needed a good story so I used the first thing that popped in my head.

"Mr. Cutler, I was doing a little shopping and the strangest thing happened. I saw my best girlfriend's beau near y'all's fine shop. If he was shopping here, well…" I glanced down then back up at him through my eyelashes. "I just had to come in and ask you, was he shopping for a ring?" I rushed on. "It's okay. You can tell me. I won't breathe a word to anyone, I promise!"

Mr. Cutler stared at me, blinked twice then stammered a response. "Well, I… It seems that…" Then he shook his head and clasped his hands together as if he was going to say a prayer. "No, I think your gentleman would not shop for an engagement ring in our shop."

"Oh, are you sure?" I pleaded.

"Yes, I feel fairly confident that is the case."

I gave him my best Southern-belle pout. "Oh, she'll be so disappointed. You have so many beautiful things."

"Yes, we do, but young men usually light up the heart of their lady love with the real thing."

"The real thing?" I looked at the cases again. "But…"

"Yes, they are lovely, but they are lovely *Lady Windsor* Diamonds." He tried again when he thought I didn't understand. "Lady Windsors, the Counterfeit Diamonds."

Gotcha!

I tried to look shocked. "You mean everything is fake?"

"We prefer to call them Lady Windsors." He gave a little chuckle. "Don't feel bad. We've even fooled diamond thieves. It happened several years ago. It's our practice to leave our jewelry in the shop windows overnight to attract people out for an evening stroll. If they see something they like, they'll come back to shop the next day. Late one Saturday night, some jewel thieves smashed the windows and absconded with the jewels."

"Oh my! What happened?"

"We felt a responsibility to warn the people so we ran a large newspaper ad, 'BEWARE of DIAMOND CROOKS.' You see, the Lady Windsor Diamond is virtually indistinguishable from a real thing." He chuckled. "It was better than an avalanche of advertising. Our sales went through the roof."

"With all due respect, who would buy counterfeit stones?"

He raised his eyebrows and smiled. "You'd be surprised. The prices for natural diamonds are breathtaking and insurance rates are blowing through the roof. Why should people deny themselves a pretty bauble or two?" He winked at me.

"Mr. Cutler," I almost forgot the Southern accent but recovered quickly. "Is that the only reason?"

"Oh, no. Say you own a family heirloom of exquisite stones and you want to wear it to an event. What if you were held up at gun point and the thieves demand the necklace… or your life?" He leaned toward me and lowered his voice. "What would you do?"

"I'd give it to them," I said quickly.

"Oh? Your grandmother's treasure?"

"It would be covered by insurance," I insisted, "so I could replace it."

"If you could afford the astronomical rates and if you were willing to give up the necklace that had graced your own grandmother's neck. Why put yourself in harm's way when I can protect what's precious to you?" He paused for dramatic effect. "I can duplicate any stone to create a copy for you to wear in complete safety while the real thing sits safely in the vault."

"So, I could hand it over without losing a thing?" I made my eyes as big as saucers.

He nodded.

Now, to get the information I needed. "Could someone replace a real stone with a Lady Windsor then sell the diamond?"

He looked around again to make sure our conversation was still private. "Of course. It happens all the time."

Pay dirt!

"A woman might not want her husband or paramour to know that she's milking his gifts for cash. She has the flash of diamonds and the value in her pocket for whatever she might want." He leaned closer, about to reveal a big secret. "I'm been told from a reliable source, if it's a good stone, she could expect to get only 25% to 33% of the appraised value and that would have to be a true appraisal, not one inflated for insurance purposes."

"That's all?" I was surprised. "People talk about investing in diamonds. Getting so little of the value doesn't sound like a good deal to me."

"If you think about it, it makes sense. Unless a dealer has an order for a stone of that size and shape, it would end up in his inventory and no one wants to tie up his money like that."

I didn't want to push my luck with Mr. Cutler, so I looked at my watch and squealed, "Why, look at the time! I'm so late. Thank you so much, Mr. Cutler."

"When you want to dazzle, come back and see me," he called out as I slipped out the door.

CHAPTER TWENTY-SEVEN

An intricate design requires additional time and concentration. Never assign the job of cleaning silver to an individual who is impatient, may shirk the work or perform the work in a careless manner. Attention to detail and careful work shall pay great rewards.

—"The Butler's Guide to Fine Silver" Mr. Hollister, 1898

I hustled down the street and redeemed my car for a small fortune. Rush hour traffic was starting to build as I scooted over the Key Bridge crossing the Potomac from Georgetown to Northern Virginia and home. Simon was delighted to see me and ready for us to play with his ball and his bone and his squeaky toy. He didn't know which to pick up first. I cleared off a living room chair and sank into its comfort, so welcome after the stress of the day and weeks of sitting on the hard kitchen chairs.

My phone beeped to remind me I had a voicemail from the call I'd ignored while driving in traffic. I listened to the message and tensed up all over again. It was from Reg and he was furious. Angela had called him and complained about our little conversation at Clyde's. He went on and on about how wrong I was to blame Angela for the failure of the company. He was appalled that I'd act so childish in public. He was shocked by my behavior. So was I! His behavior didn't make sense. Why was he still taking her side in everything?

Anger was tying my stomach into knots. I was beginning to wonder if I was getting an ulcer out of this whole mess. Fear added a layer of anxiety. What would Lorraine do when she found out about the altered diamond earring? I tasted bile from my overactive stomach as I considered for a moment that Lorraine already knew about the fake diamonds. I really wanted her to be innocent of everything. I figured we'd have to tell the police. I hoped I wouldn't have to face that rigid Virginia detective Collins. Facing the St. Michaels police chief would be bad enough. My skin crawled when I thought about the way Mr. Shaw looked at me. It was sheer luck that *he* didn't call the police while I was in his shop. I went in the kitchen and dug around the cabinets and drawers until I found a little bottle of almost-expired antacids.

Waiting for some relief, I looked at my magnets set up on the refrigerator door. Maybe they'd give me a better perspective. At the center was the dollar sign, because money seemed to be at the center of everything. All around it were magnets for the chef, the man hanging around with Rita who may or may not be Evelyn's stepson, Lucy, her abusive boyfriend along with one for Lorraine. I added a magnet of the Capitol representing the man allegedly stalking the governor. I left Reg's top-hat magnet in place even though he wasn't on the Shore the night of the murder. He might know something about the others and just hadn't realized it yet. I added the wine glass Reg had picked the night before to represent my life. I wasn't guilty of anything – except selling the murder weapon – but maybe I'd seen or heard something that could be important.

Should I add something to represent a gang or random thief? I wondered. No, the police had used their resources and dismissed those possibilities. There were still plenty of suspects.

I stepped back and looked at the crowded field of people the police would say had motive and opportunity for murder or had some connection. But, wait. I was forgetting something. I was forgetting the diamonds. I took a clunky plastic engagement-ring magnet I'd bought when a college roommate got engaged and put it in the middle with the dollar sign. What a mess of possibilities. It was time to narrow things down.

First, I removed my wine glass magnet. I knew I hadn't killed anybody. Everything I knew about the situation I'd passed to the police chief who was getting impatient with me stumbling around in his case. I frowned. Well, almost everything. There was the bit about my visit with Lucy, but I reasoned to myself that didn't yield any new information. Oh, and there was that confrontation with the guy from Virginia. I promised myself to tell the chief about that.

I shifted by gaze to the silver spoon magnet that represented Lorraine then I looked away toward the kitchen window that faced the street. No, I didn't want to face the possibility that she might be a… I shook my head. No, I couldn't, wouldn't believe she'd killed her best friend. All my instincts told me she was innocent. My rational side couldn't see a reason for her to steal her own diamonds. Wait, not true. Maybe she did it to claim the insurance money. But, I argued silently, if she needed money, why do something that could send her to jail? She could sell off some land… or even sell the diamonds outright.

No, I refused to believe Lorraine did anything wrong.

To be honest, I didn't want my new friend to be guilty of anything bad. No, she didn't belong among the suspects. I pulled off her silver spoon magnet and put it back in my collection.

Simon started running around the house, his little feet scrabbling on the bare wood floors. I was making progress and I didn't want to be distracted. I looked up just in time to see him hit a throw rug and ride it all the way into a wall. I lured him into the kitchen with a chew toy and he settled down in the corner.

Next, I thought about Lucy. Could she have put this scheme

together let alone have the strength to attack Evie? The girl was so little and seemed like a weakling. I moved her magnet out of the center ... paused... then put it back but next to her boyfriend's magnet. She might not have committed the actual murder but she could have been involved with him in some way. I remembered noticing that she had tiny feet. Maybe she wore a size 5½ shoe. If he was strong and mean enough to knock Lucy around, he would have no trouble hurting Evelyn. No, both of their magnets stayed in place. I moved the stalker's magnet out to the edge. There wasn't anything to support the idea that he was involved. My hand hovered over Chef's magnet. I remembered his interview in the police station. He was upset. He was melodramatic. Did he have the grit to kill for a recipe? I moved him to the edge as well.

One good suspect stood out, the mysterious stepson who threatened me on a public street. I moved his magnet along with Rita's toward the center. Yes, that felt right. I could follow up with the chief to see what he'd found out from Birdnest, Virginia. I grimaced thinking that I had to tell him about my confrontation on the street with that man.

Simon pawed my leg. He had his leash in his mouth. Where had he learned such a cute trick? Or was it a signal?

"Can you wait a few minutes so I can finish? Then I'll take you for a walk."

He barked and pawed. Stupid me. I'd said the magic word *walk* and he heard *walk right now.*

As I clipped the leash to his collar, I noticed that Reg's magnet was still next to the diamond magnet. That didn't work. I couldn't imagine that the man I knew would kill a woman who helped raise him and made his favorite cookies. I reached out to move it, but Simon jerked me toward the door. It wasn't worth a tugging match. I'd move it when we got back.

CHAPTER TWENTY-EIGHT

To polish silver, one may use a finely powdered form of rouge used by silversmiths and jewelers to polish metal. Choose carefully. Different types of rouge will create different looks. For example, red rouge produces a high color and luster. Black rouge will create a darker appearance.

—"The Butler's Guide to Fine Silver" Mr. Hollister, 1898

We charged into the chilly fall air. It wasn't a bad thing to have someone drag me away from murder and missing diamonds.

"Come on, you little hellion! Let's walk before you break your neck running around the house or drive me crazy."

Simon sniffed every leaf, bush and invisible trail across the grass and marked his favorite spots, as usual. He tugged hard on the leash. A clump of ornamental grasses in someone's garden was irresistible.

"No, Mister, you may not trespass." He insisted and pulled harder. "Tell you what, we'll go down to the park where you can snuffle all you want."

When Gwen had first brought Simon to me, his little legs worked hard to keep up with me on a fast walk. Now, he was stretching out those legs at an easy pace as I started jogging. And they say children grow up fast.

The park held all kinds of mysteries for him to explore. We went around the perimeter to avoid other walkers, dogs and children. It was easier to handle him that way. Not only were his legs longer, his muscles were getting stronger. I suspected that Gwen would have to buy a new leash before he snapped this thin one in two. There was a twinge of sadness. I was going to miss the little guy when he went to live in California. Tired, I plopped down on a wooden bench and Simon planted himself on my right foot. I guess he wanted to make sure I didn't sneak away.

My grip tightened on his leash as his head came up and turned toward the singing and laughing at a picnic table close by. A group of mothers and children were gathered for a party and the birthday girl had just blown out the candles on her cake. It made me think how a cake is at the center of important celebrations: birthdays, weddings, anniversaries, retirement, graduation, christenings, bar mitzvahs. Each cake had to be special, like the Fair Winds Torte the governor loved so much. How could the cake be connected to the diamonds? Could there have been TWO people in the house that night for different reasons? I closed my eyes and rubbed my forehead. All these disconnected thoughts were giving me a headache.

"DOGGIE!" A child's squeal flipped my eyes open.

It was Baby John from next door on a trip to the park, one of Christine's favorite afternoon outings. She leaned over her child who was safely strapped in his stroller and said, "You're right, sweetie. Let's go pet the doggie."

I groaned. In moments, Simon was surrounded by strollers, giggling children and Christine's entourage of play-date mommies. The kids pulled Simon's ears and poked their fingers in his eyes to my growing terror. Instead of moving their children safely away, the mothers used it as a teaching moment. Calmly, they took control by teaching the older ones how to pet a dog while keeping the littlest hands out of harm's way. Christine gave me a big smile that reminded me of our early days as neighbors. When I first moved in, she'd made lists of recommended stores, pointed out shortcuts to avoid traffic congestion and occasionally brought over a bottle of wine at the end of a long day. Of course, that was when she worked as an attorney downtown, before she became a wife and mother. We were still friends, only we now had so little in common.

"Abby," Christine said over the commotion. "I made banana bread today. I'll bring over a loaf when I get home."

I thanked her as I pulled Simon out of the group before the puppy could take a nibble out of a chubby arm. We took our time going home. Simon had earned the right to sniff and smell and mark as much as he wanted. By the time we got home, he was worn out and dragged himself up to my front walk. Without warning, he started barking and straining to get to the front door. He wanted to get inside and fast. Trying to hold on, I fumbled with my house key ring and dropped it, as usual.

"Simon! Settle down. I have to unlock the door first." Barking, he lunged and almost knocked me down. "Simon!" He jumped up and started scratching at the paint. "Stop that!"

There was no way he was going to listen to me so I braced myself, jammed the key in the lock and opened the door. Simon lurched forward pulling his leash right out of my hand. He skittered down the hall messing up the rug again and ran around the corner to the living room, barking the whole way.

"Stop making that racket. We're home now. Quiet!" My scolding had no effect. I pulled off my jacket and hung it on a hook in the closet. A chilly breeze felt good on my overheated skin. I felt better. The walk had cleared my mind and relaxed the strain out of my muscles. But the barking had to stop. I followed the trail of the crazy dog.

"Simon, I really don't understand you. You were so calm with the kids, now …" As I came around the corner, I gasped.

"It's about time you got home." Sitting in my living room was Reg.

He looked comfortable in the chair I cleared off earlier. "I was beginning to think I'd have to wait all evening." He acted as if I was late for a date.

"W-what are you doing here? How did you get in?" My eyes followed the breeze of cold air to the source: a broken windowpane in the French door right by the lock. "You broke into my house? You broke into MY HOUSE?!"

He shrugged. "I had to. I didn't think you'd let me in if I rang the doorbell. Abby, I'm sorry I yelled at you. I know it was wrong. Please forgive me."

Again, I thought. This man was starting to scare me. His erratic behavior was bad enough, but he looked *wrong.* Always immaculate, now he was a mess. He hadn't shaved, his shirt was wrinkled and he needed a haircut. I took a step backward and Simon came to stand next to me, a growl rumbling deep in his chest.

Reg sprang from the chair. "Abby, don't back away from me. I need you."

My hands shot up in self-defense. Too combative. I tried to calm down. "It's okay," I said, hoping to mask my feeling that it was definitely not okay. "Why don't you tell me what's going on?"

He started to pace, "They cancelled my tour."

"Your tour?"

He stopped and stared at me, impatience written all over his face. "The speaking tour… to meet with entrepreneurs all over the country? I told you about it at dinner Sunday night."

Ah yes, the tour that made me see red, I remembered. *You're being honored as a great success while I'm turning interviewing for a job into a career.*

I tried to put concern into my voice. "Why would they cancel the tour?"

"They found out my startup went bust." He dragged his fingers across the top of his head leaving wedges in his dirty hair.

"I don't know what I'm going to do." He paced nervously around the room.

I turned toward the hall.

"Where are you going? You can't leave me. I need you."

He jumped, blocking my way to the front door.

"Really, Reg. I want to go to my kitchen."

We moved around the cluttered living room like pieces on a chessboard. I suspected I had to avoid checkmate. I put my hands on my hips. "Look, I just took a long walk and want a glass of water, if you don't mind."

I took a step forward and he took a step back. All the way to the kitchen, he maintained a position between me and the front door. When we got to the kitchen, I slid over to the sink to run the water and look out the window to the street. Where were those play-date mothers when I needed them?

"Abby, don't you need a glass?" Reg asked quietly.

"Of course." I took out a glass from the cabinet. Willing my hands not to shake, I filled it and took a sip. I almost choked when I saw he'd stepped into the kitchen and was standing next to the refrigerator where the magnets were set up around the money and diamond symbols. If he looked around, he'd see them. He was good at my little game. If he figured out the meaning, I didn't know how he'd react and I didn't want to find out. I had to get him out of the kitchen and out of my house. I took a quick step toward him.

"Ab-by," Reg said my name slowly. "We have to talk."

My stomach twisted. "Okay." I grabbed one of Simon's cookies. "Let's go back in the living room." I stepped forward. He stood, blocking my way. I willed my face to stay calm though tension crackled around us. His eyes held mine. I didn't dare look away even though every muscle in my body wanted to run. After what seemed like forever, he slowly stepped back into the hall. I almost cried with relief then realized that he was still blocking my way to the front door. The only option was to lead the way back to the living room.

"Why don't you sit there?" He pointed to the chair he'd occupied when I'd walked in. I gave Simon his cookie, but he left it on the floor, unwilling to take his eyes off the man. Reg swept some silver packets off another chair and sat down. I almost snapped at him but reined in my anger.

"I'm sorry, Abby."

"Don't worry about the door, Reg." I tried to sound unconcerned. "I'll get it fixed." I took another sip of water.

"You know, it was your fault they cancelled the tour," he said.

I gagged in surprise. "How do you figure?"

"You shouldn't have gotten mixed up in the mess on the Shore."

"It wasn't my choice," I said with a little nervous laugh. "It was the police who dragged me into the investigation."

"You didn't have to hang around with Lorraine. Because you were there, I had to stay instead of coming back to Washington to head off the negative news about the company."

"Reg, how did you expect them to react? We failed." If I ever wanted to cram words back in my mouth, it was at that very moment.

"That's not fair, Abby. People didn't do what they were supposed to. Things happened. It wasn't me who failed." He choked on the last word.

"People like Angela?"

"Never mind," he shot back.

I leaned forward, putting my elbows on my knees. "Maybe if you'd been in the office more toward the end instead of out with Angela…"

"I had to see potential clients and make trips to the Shore," he barked.

The Shore? My confusion must have shown on my face.

He crossed his arms across his chest and tilted his head like a pose. "Lorraine was sick and I had to be there, okay?"

"Sick? She didn't—"

"Not now, back then." He got up and started pacing again. "You have no idea what I did for that business... and you."

"Now you're blaming me for the company going under?" Anger was burning away my fear. I couldn't seem to keep my mouth shut.

He plopped down in the chair again and clasped his hands in his lap. With a heavy sigh, he said, "Can't you just accept that I'm under a lot of stress right now? I'm not myself."

I sat without moving a muscle.

Suddenly, he flung his arm out toward the broken glass in the French door, the wind whistling through the gaping hole. "Look what I did here today. I broke into your home!" His face filled with pleading. "Come on, Abby, you've known me for a long time. You know that's not something I'd ever do." He ran his hand through his hair again.

A little part of me wanted to comfort him, but my fear and anger overwhelmed that inclination. I stayed in my chair and stoked the top of Simon's head.

In a muffled voice, he said, "Help me. There are people putting pressure on me, making me do things that I don't want to do." He reached out to me.

Was this the missing piece of the puzzle?

"Who is trying to hurt you?"

"They're bad people, Abby."

"Did they... did you have anything to do with the murder?" I asked very carefully.

"Me? ME! I wasn't even there. Oh Abby, why would you ever think..."

"Reg, I don't what to think. Maybe we should go to the police."

"NO!" He cried. He took an exaggerated breath and lowered his eyes. "No, they didn't have anything to do with that." He glanced at me. "At least, I don't think so."

The doorbell rang

"Don't answer it," he hissed.

"Why?" I was whispering. I cleared my throat and repeated in a normal voice, "Why?"

The doorbell rang again twice.

I got up. "I'm sure it has nothing to do with you. It's probably my next-door neighbor." I prayed I was right.

When I opened the door, Christine beamed a brilliant smile at me and marched right into my home, never a more welcome visitor.

"Abby, the banana bread is just the right temperature now. I think..." She walked into the living room and saw Reg. "Oh, hello." She flashed her high-wattage smile only it didn't quite reach her eyes.

Reg scowled in response and turned away.

"Hmm," she said and turned toward me. "I brought you this loaf of bread because everybody says my recipe is the best." Her eyes strayed back to Reg. "Maybe we could all have a piece?"

Her eyes darted around the room and landed on the French door.

"Oh, Abby!" squealed Christine. "Your door is broken!" She looked between the door and me making her little flip hairstyle bounce around. "Are you okay?" She gave Reg a good hard look. "Is everything all right?"

"Oh yes," I said quickly. "My friend and I were talking."

"But how was your door broken?" Her eyes squinted a little in suspicion as she glanced at Reg.

"Oh that," I tried to shrug but it felt more like a spastic move. "I, ah, broke the glass earlier when I was mopping the floor. Guess I got a little too enthusiastic."

"I see." Her eyes traveled down around her feet, noticing traces of dust. "Hmm, well, I thought you'd like some bread and..."

Reg snapped. "Okay, I'm outta here. I can't take another meddling female." He stomped out the front door and slammed it behind him.

Surprised, Christine turned to me with raised eyebrows. I didn't say a word. I couldn't get her involved. Instead of answering her unspoken questions, I reached over and took the bread. The heat coming through the foil wrapping felt good, soothing.

"Thank you so much for bringing me the bread." I stammered. "I-I'm sorry."

She leaned close and said in a whisper, "I don't like the looks of him. I know you said he was your friend, but I don't trust him. He reminds me of Bobby, a guy back home. If I were you, I wouldn't believe a thing he says. Bobby was always lying."

She scooted out the door and as I closed it, her words ricocheted around in my head.

CHAPTER TWENTY-NINE

If the silver piece has an intricate design, take the time to gather the proper tools and materials to clean it properly to reveal its hidden beauty.

—"The Butler's Guide to Fine Silver" Mr. Hollister, 1898

Early the next morning, the phone rang at an ungodly hour though it didn't really matter. I was already awake and had been most of the night. All my tossing and turning must have kept Simon awake. About 3 o'clock, he jumped off the bed and lay down on the bathroom floor, leaving me all alone in the dark. The call went to voicemail and I snuggled down into the pillow. I wasn't ready to face the day. Then the phone started ringing again.

I fumbled with it and looked at the Caller ID. I didn't recognize the number and almost let it go to voicemail again when my finger hit the answer button by accident.

"Abby? Abby, are you there?" The voice was strained, pleading. "Abby, please answer."

"Yes, I'm here, who is this?" I said, pulling myself up to sit on the edge of the bed.

"Thank goodness. It's me, Lucy."

"Lucy?" I hoped her bully boyfriend hadn't beaten her up again. "What's wrong? Do you know what time—?"

"Abby, I've got to talk to you. I can't lie anymore. You're the only one I could think of to tell. You won't yell at me, will you? I…"

I was on my feet and waking up fast. "Whoa, slow down. What do you mean, lied? Lied about what?" Silence made it sound like the call dropped. "Lucy? Are you still there?"

"I lied," she muttered. "I lied about that night."

"The night Miss Evelyn was killed?" I tried to sound calm and non-threatening. I worried that she'd scamper away any minute.

"Yes, yes! That night. I'm sorry," she wailed. "I don't know what to do. I'm so scared."

"Okay, take a deep breath and tell me what happened." I grabbed a pencil ready to make notes, not sure I could keep everything straight without my coffee.

Her words tumbled out. "Oh no, I can't do that. No way. I can't." She was about to bolt.

"It's all right. Trust me, we'll work this out." I heard her suck in a gulp of air. "That's better, Lucy. What do you want to tell me?"

"I want to tell you something important, but I'm afraid."

"I'm right here for you," I said, willing myself not to be shocked by whatever I heard.

"But I can't tell you over the phone," she whispered. "You never know who is listening. I might be next!"

"Don't worry. You'll be fine," I hope, I added silently. "What do you want me to do?"

"I need to see you. I have to tell you in person, face to face."

"But Lucy, I'm in…" I paused. "Lucy, listen to me. It might be better for you to talk to Chief Lucan who—"

"NO!" she screamed. "He'll lock me up for lying. It's gotta be you. You'll protect me."

I started moving to the bathroom. "Okay, okay. I'm up in

Washington so it will take me a couple of hours to get to you, but I'll come. Will you promise to talk to me when I get there?"

"Yes, yes, I promise." I could feel her relief through the phone. "You've saved my life."

After agreeing to call her when I was close to Easton, I hustled a sleepy Simon outside for his morning ritual, threw myself in the shower to get my eyes open and brewed a gallon of coffee-to-go for the same reason. Simon found his breakfast bowl in the backseat and we were off. Yes, *we.* I couldn't leave Simon in the house alone. The last time we went for a drive to the Eastern Shore, we stayed five days and that was supposed to be a leisurely daytrip. I had no idea what would happen this time.

CHAPTER THIRTY

Carefully apply polish to all the cracks and interstices in the silver work. A cloth may not reach all portions of metalwork. Consider the use of a soft brush to attend those parts that are not easily accessible.
—"The Butler's Guide to Fine Silver" Mr. Hollister, 1898

As I maneuvered through the ever-present traffic around Washington, I talked to Simon. My conversations with him seemed to soothe my mind and I needed to relax right now and to think clearly.

"Remember how you went crazy when we got to the door yesterday and…" I added sheepishly, "I yelled at you? I'm sorry. You were only trying to protect me."

I caught a glimpse of him in the rear-view mirror, sitting tall and proud in the back seat.

"I promise I'll never ignore your warning again."

I jumped when a car honked and sped around me. Evidently, while I was talking to Simon, my car drifted into the next lane. Time to pay attention to my driving and what lay ahead.

At the Chesapeake Bay Bridge toll plaza, a small gust of salty air sent a chill through the car. Mother Nature declared it was time to bring the season to an end and I was to follow her example. It was time to meet with Lucy and discover the rest of the story.

Once we crossed the broad expanse of water, traffic settled into a rhythm and I could look around. The gray skies made the water look like molten silver working its way in to fill the empty spaces along the natural shoreline. It brought to mind the Miles River that flowed gently by Fair Winds in sharp contrast to the chaos, emotions and fear inside the big house. Fog lay over Kent Narrows, the waterway between Kent Island and the peninsula of the Eastern Shore. As I drove over the high arch of the bridge, the details of the land lay hidden under the hazy blanket below… just like the truth of what happened that awful night.

The exit ramp for Route 50 took me by the discount shopping mall still sleeping before the onslaught of shoppers. Perhaps a time would come when Lorraine and I would join them in search of great deals on clothes, shoes and purses, not dealing with abused women, fake diamonds and murder.

I sighed. I should call Lorraine to return her earring and deliver the news about the counterfeit stones. It was still too early to call, as if any time was right to talk of such things. That's why I jumped when my phone rang. Tired, I answered without checking the Caller ID.

"Abby, are you okay?" It was Gwen.

"Yes, yes, I'm fine. Are you all right? It's so early in California."

I hoped this wasn't a report of bad news. I had about all I could handle.

"Oh, I'm fine, better than fine! I left you a couple of messages, but you didn't call back. I've been worried. That's not like you."

She was right, I was usually very good about returning calls from friends. With all the craziness in my life, voicemails had dropped in priority. Here was another good reason for getting things figured out in St. Michaels today.

"I'm sorry, kiddo. I've just been busy," I apologized.

"I have news, big news. I got a job!"

She chattered on as I got lost in the all the details.

"What? Wait, Gwen, I didn't catch that last part."

She sighed. "I said I'm not coming back for Simon. You have to understand, Abby. They want me to start the new job right away and, in a few months, I might be transferred to the main office in Palo Alto. Isn't that awesome? I don't know where I'm going live yet, so it doesn't make sense to get an apartment… for a dog."

A dog. Ouch! I looked over at the furry ball with lanky legs hanging over the seat. He had become much more to me than just a dog. Though I knew I should sound disappointed, I couldn't help but smile that Simon would be staying.

I cut into her rambling explanation. "Don't worry, Gwen, I'll take care of Simon. He'll be fine. Good luck with your new job." We promised to stay in touch.

As I clicked off the call, Simon raised his head and looked at me with those sleepy baby brown eyes.

"Oh, you caught what I said, eh? Your selective hearing is working again? You can hear a snippet of a phone conversation, but you can't hear me say 'Come'?"

I ruffled his neck behind his ears and my hand came away with short strands of his black hair. Where did I ever get the idea that a Lab didn't shed?

"You're a handful all right, in more ways than one." He barked. "And loveable. I guess I'm stuck with you." He barked again. "Okay, okay, I admit it! I like having you around." My voice took on a mock stern tone. "Now, go back to sleep. It's time to call Lucy." He put his head down on his paws right on cue.

Lucy answered on the first ring and gave me directions to her friend's house in Easton. In the past week, I was starting to learn my way around the Shore with a little help from my GPS. It led me to a small walkup apartment that wasn't in the best part of town. When I knocked on the door, a woman on the other side demanded that I identify myself. When I did, she flipped several locks, removed a chain and opened the door just wide enough for me to slip through.

As I stepped inside the sparsely furnished living room, Lucy threw herself into my arms, sobbing. Tears carved their way down pale cheeks that should have been rosy with youth and the new life she was carrying. She wore a large, ratty T-shirt that couldn't camouflage her swelling body. After many minutes of reassurance and tissues, we settle on a threadbare sofa and she started her story, the true and complete one this time.

"Remember, I told you that when Miss Evelyn found out I was pregnant, she gave me money to leave the Shore?"

I nodded, careful not to interrupt.

"Before I could escape, Paulie found the money and took it. He said I'd never get away from him." She looked at the tissue in her lap that she had torn to shreds. "I went back to Miss Evelyn and she said that she would give me one more chance. That I had to promise to leave the Shore as soon as she gave me the money."

She stated to cry again so I eased her back into the story. "She gave you some more cash and…"

She shook her head. "No, she didn't have any cash on her right then and said she didn't have time to go to the ATM. There was some big party she was getting ready for and all. She told me to pack up and go to Fair Winds late that night. Paulie would be at the bars until real late so I could take off without him knowin'. She was real careful, told me to go down the gravel drive to the kitchen door on the side of the big house."

Her friend Linda jumped in. "Lucy told me what was going on and I loaned her my car that night." She banged her fist on the table. "I knew I should have gone with her."

"No, no, Linda. You couldn't have known." Lucy went on trying to reassure her friend until I wanted scream.

"But," I interrupted as gently as I could. I didn't want to spook her. "You went to Fair Winds by yourself, right?"

She nodded. "That's right. I went just like she told me. I

parked in the little lot they have there." Her voice shook a little. "I was walking up to the door and I – I..." She clammed up.

"You what?" Oh, how I wanted to yank the rest of the story out of her. Instead, I patted her knee and said, "It's all right, Lucy. You can tell me. What did you do?"

"I chickened out. I couldn't take her money again. I didn't know if I could leave the Shore and all my friends, with the baby coming and all. I turned around and that's when Paulie jumped out of the bushes!"

"Your boyfriend?" She nodded. "What happened then?"

Tears started to leak out of her eyes again. "He grabbed my arm. He wanted to know what I was doing. He guessed I was gonna get more money and he wanted it. I told him I didn't have nothing." Her voice trembled and her words came out in little breaths. "He told me... get inside... get the money... bring it to him pronto. I pulled away from him... said I was done taking money from nice people like Miss Evelyn. He raised his hand to smack me," she wailed, "I ran to the car, but he got here first. He... he grabbed my wrist. He squeezed it so hard I thought he'd break it right off. He threw me against the car and I went down. He said, 'If you don't get the money, I will.' And he went on up to the door."

She caught her breath. Her voice was just above a whisper. "That was my chance. The car keys had gone flying when I fell so I ran. I figured I'd hide in the bushes on the other side of the house till after Paulie left. Then, I'd track back to the car, find the keys and get out of there. But he came after me."

Lucy pulled out another tissue and blew her nose. She was calmer as she went on.

"I tripped in the dark and he caught my arm. We were outside a room with big windows. The lights were on and we saw Miss Evelyn come in. She went to a picture of a lady on the wall. Paulie pulled me down and we watched her."

"What was she doing, Lucy? Tell me everything," I insisted.

"There was a safe behind the picture. She opened it and took out some money and counted it. Paulie got all excited. Said it was his big payday. He pushed me into the bushes, opened one of those fancy glass doors and walked right in. Just like he owned the place. It was awful."

She put her face in her hands. Her words were garbled. Gently, I pulled her hands down and steeled myself to hear about Miss Evelyn's last moments.

Lucy took a ragged breath. "Paulie says to her that he'll have whatever's in that safe. And then… it was so amazin'. She turned on him and gave him what-for! Told him he had a lot of nerve coming into the house, told him to take himself right back out before he got hurt. He came right back at her saying he'd come to pick up the money she was gonna give me. She called him awful names, yelling at him when she realized he was the one beating up on me." She shook her head at the memory. "Then Paulie gets all mean, tells her I deserved everything I got and if she didn't give him the money, he'd teach *her* a lesson."

"I bet Miss Evelyn didn't appreciate being threatened. What did she do?" I asked.

"Nothing." Lucy looked like she couldn't believe what she'd seen.

"Nothing?"

She was shaking her head.

"Did she give him the money or pull out a gun or –"

"Somebody else came in, told Paulie to get out." Lucy said.

"Was it Miss Lorraine?" I almost didn't want to hear the answer, because it would mean she had lied and –

"Nope, it was a man," said Lucy.

"A man?" Now, I was very confused. Had the chef still been in the house? Had he killed her? I put my hand on Lucy's knee and quietly asked, "Who was the man?" I held my breath.

"I don't know." She looked at me, pleading in her eyes. "I couldn't see him but heard his voice. It was a man all right. He was yelling at Paulie."

"Did you recognize his voice?"

"No, 'fraid not."

I leaned back against the sofa pillows. "Then what happened?"

"He must have scared Paulie real bad 'cause he backs up and comes toward the door and me. I wasn't gonna stay in the middle of that. I ran to the car, found the keys and drove back here."

Linda chimed in. "She was shaking like a leaf when she got here. Wouldn't tell me why. I'm glad she didn't. I don't know what I would have done."

Her comment pulled me back to reality. "Lucy, you have to tell your story to Chief Lucan." She wiggled away from me. I gently grabbed her hand to get her attention and hold her on the sofa. "Listen, he needs to know about the man. He might have been the killer."

Great move, Abby. The girl is shaking like a scared rabbit, ready to bolt. She's got Paulie trying to hurt her and you just added a killer on her trail.

Desperate, I turned to her friend Linda for help. She bit her lower lip as she considered what I said. Lucy was fortunate in one way, she had a friend who really cared.

"Do you really think that's the right thing to do? I could hide her here and—"

"Yes, it's best for Lucy and the baby to catch this killer," I said quickly.

She paused for a moment then nodded. "Okay, what do we do?"

We came up with a plan to drive Lucy to the shelter so she could be with her counselor while she talked to the police. Assured that she would be safe, I watched them drive away.

CHAPTER THIRTY-ONE

The heritage of fine sterling silver carries a heavy responsibility. Understanding the history, purpose and proper maintenance techniques of each piece in your charge help preserve it in excellent condition for coming generations.

—"The Butler's Guide to Fine Silver" Mr. Hollister, 1898

With Simon securely strapped in the car, I took a chance and put the top down. It would be a short ride down the St. Michaels Road to Fair Winds. I angled the mirror so I could keep an eye on him. I should have known he'd curl up and start snoring before we'd gone a few blocks. With a smile, I called Lorraine to let her know I was on my way with stories she wouldn't believe. She said she'd put on a pot of coffee.

On the way to the big house, as Lucy had called it, my mind was full of everything she'd told me. If she'd only talked to the police sooner, the killer might be in custody. Thankfully, the counselor at the shelter would make sure Lucy did the right thing now. Still, there was one detail that didn't fit: the diamonds. Mr. Cutler at Lady Windsor had said the person switching out and selling the real stones would only get a fraction of their value. It made sense that someone would need access to a lot of stones to make the effort worthwhile. It was hard to imagine anyone having a lot of diamond jewelry in this day and age and those kind of big-money people seemed to live in New York, Los Angeles, London and places like that. Could a ring of jewel thieves be hitting some of the big houses in the area? But if that were the case, the chief would have said something, wouldn't he?

Before long, I made the turn at the grand entrance to Fair Winds and sped down the driveway. I parked the car in the front, released Simon from his harness and he followed me to the door. Ruth answered my knock and just as she was about to close the door, another car came down the drive and pulled in next to mine. I grabbed Simon's collar and as I pulled him into the hallway so he wouldn't accost the visitor, I looked to see who it was.

Harriet, the busybody from the Crab Claw, was carrying a cake, of all things.

As she rushed up the steps, she said to Ruth, "Oh, thank you. I'm here to see Miss Lorraine." She was about to take a step over the threshold, but Ruth barred the way.

"I'm afraid Miss Lorraine isn't at home," she said in a dignified tone.

"Then, I'll wait for her." She moved again to enter the house, but to no avail. Ruth didn't budge.

"I'm sorry, ma'am, I don't believe Miss Lorraine is expecting you."

The permed white head cocked to one side. "How do you know that?" There was a sneer in Harriet's voice.

"Because someone is already here waiting to see Miss Lorraine. She has an appointment."

"Good, then I'll wait with her." I could see the top of Harriet's permed white hair bobbing around, trying to see who had an appointment with Lorraine.

I knelt down and willed Simon to be quiet. I hoped Ruth was successful in barring Harriet, because I didn't want to deal with a woman Lorraine had described as harmless as some kind of hungry fish.

Ruth stood her ground. "I'm sorry, ma'am, that won't be possible."

"But I brought her a cake," Harriet pleaded as if that was the ticket of admission.

"I'll be happy to take the cake and tell Miss Lorraine you brought it. I believe you're new to Fair Winds. May I have your name please?"

New to Fair Winds? Oh, that comment must have smarted.

Moments later, Ruth closed the door, holding the cake.

"Persistent, wasn't she?" I said.

Ruth nodded, but kept her opinion to herself. She seemed to be growing into her new job. Then, something Ruth said penetrated my tired brain.

"Did you say that Miss Lorraine isn't here?"

"That's right. She received a phone call, got her things and said she wouldn't be gone long. She thought you might like to wait in the library. Please follow me."

We went down the long hallway, Simon on my heels, toward the river side of the house and turned into a room with expansive windows and French doors overlooking the water. Was this the room where Lucy and Paulie had watched Evelyn go to a safe?

Ruth asked, "Is there anything you need?"

"No, thank you," I said in a whisper as I looked around. With a nod, she closed the door.

During my short stay earlier in the week, I'd just poked my head into this room. Now, I savored what I missed. The walls that were not made of glass held bookshelves filled from floor to ceiling except for the space taken by an exquisite marble fireplace framed by two overstuffed chairs that beckoned readers to come and get comfortable. A heavy mahogany library table with carved legs looked large enough to handle the most complicated research project. On the wall behind it was the portrait of a young woman with platinum blonde curls. I cocked my head to side considering her face. It reminded me of Lorraine, but the resemblance was vague. Her lost sister? Whoever she was, she was guarding the safe tucked behind the canvas, of that I was sure.

The musings about the girl in the portrait reminded me why I'd come. I started pacing, too nervous to sit down. Where was Lorraine? I was anxious to tell her Lucy's story. It filled in so many blanks.

I went over to the large windows with mullions dividing the glass into many small panes. Ignoring the view of the Miles River, I searched the flowerbeds just outside where Lucy must have left her tiny footprint. The mulch looked trampled now by the feet of the many investigators. The police chief would want to know how I'd found Lucy. When the time came to talk to him, I wanted Lorraine with me.

Where was she?

CHAPTER THIRTY-TWO

When polishing a candlestick or candelabra, begin at the top and work your way down to protect the work you've already completed from drips and dirt. Inspect each surface as you go.

—"The Butler's Guide to Fine Silver" Mr. Hollister, 1898

As I paced the library, my eyes crawled around the room taking in the leather-bound books with titles printed in gold gilt, a stack of wood logs in the fireplace and silver picture frames on a table behind the door. A smile crept over my face as I thought how funny it was that Aunt Agnes's bequest had me gravitating to anything silver. I went over to look at the frames. My smile faded slowly as I took a closer look at the pictures in the frames.

One heavy ornate frame held a photograph of a young Lorraine posed in an exquisite wedding gown, but what drew my eye was a necklace of breathtaking diamonds around her neck. Hanging from the center of the circle of diamonds was a teardrop-shaped diamond the size of a baby's fist.

In a photo with President Reagan, a young Lorraine was

wearing a dramatic pin on the lapel of her dark suit. An abstract swirl of diamonds supported with three diamonds dangling from the bottom. They must have been huge for them to stand out like that.

There were more photos of Lorraine wearing diamonds. There was a choker with five emerald-cut diamonds, the earrings one of which I delivered to Mr. Shaw, a bracelet that looked like a cuff of diamonds and more. I looked past the baby pictures and graduation shots of Reg on the table until my eyes fell on a shot of Reg and Lorraine beaming at the camera. I couldn't tell the occasion but Lorraine was wearing some impressive diamond pieces to celebrate.

So, the vast collection of diamonds did exist. If just the diamonds in the photographs were swapped out and sold, there would be enough cash to fund ten startup companies, buy acres of land or do just about anything else. Lorraine had access to the safe, of course. She had the connections. Was she the one converting the stones to cash?

Then, I remembered what Lorraine said at the Crab Claw when she took off her diamond engagement ring.

"Wearing them brings me such joy. I'd be devastated if I didn't have my diamonds."

Lorraine wasn't switching out the diamonds.

Then, who?

Where is Lorraine? What made her leave suddenly? Or who?

My head was starting to hurt. The day had been a roller coaster from the early-morning phone call from Lucy to her harrowing story that filled in the gaps of what happened the night Evelyn was killed.

There had been another man at Fair Winds. Not the slime bag who was Lucy's boyfriend.

Another man. In the library.

Someone Evelyn knew. One person who might have access to Lorraine's diamonds. One person who was welcome at Fair Winds anytime, day or night.

A chill burned through me. I knew. I knew who Lucy heard. He was my friend for many years running. He'd grown up with advantages and love.

And on one fateful night, he'd swung a silver cake breaker ending a life.

A noise made me jump.

CHAPTER THIRTY-THREE

Some silver pieces are altered to increase their value. Know that the true value of an altered piece is its worth without the alternation. Any change to a finished piece, once discovered, reduces the value of the piece substantially.

—"The Butler's Guide to Fine Silver" Mr. Hollister, 1898

Mrs. Clark, the cook, walked into the room carrying a tray laden with dishes, jam and a white linen napkin,

"Hello, Miss Abby." There was tension in each syllable. I was suddenly alert because she was always so laid back.

"I heard you were coming and remembered how much you like my biscuits. These are hot out of the oven." She waddled over and put the tray down on the table in front of the fireplace.

"Thank you, Mrs. Clark, but have you heard from Miss Lorraine? Do you know where she went?"

The woman paused, looking very uncomfortable.

"It's okay, you can tell me," I said, trying to keep the panic out of my voice.

"Well," the cook smoothed her white apron. "She said something very strange just before she left. She said that if she wasn't back by noon, I should call the chief. She said it was a *delicate* matter and he would know what to do."

"The chief? Police Chief Lucan?"

"Yes, I was to tell him that she'd gone to MEBA and there might be trouble."

My skin tingled. "Do you have any idea why she'd go there?

Reluctantly, she said, "I think she was going to meet someone."

"Who, Mrs. Clark? Who? It's really important."

She concentrated for a moment. "I do believe it was Mr. Reggie. That boy, I don't know…" She shook her head.

Reg. The one person Lorraine would drop everything for and go. Reg might break again under the stress. Look what happened yesterday when he broke into my house. Was a gang forcing him to do these awful things? I wouldn't let myself think about that night with Miss Evelyn.

I took out my cell phone and dialed Lorraine's cell number. It rang over and over again. No answer. When her voicemail kicked in, I pressed the button to take me directly to the beep.

"Lorraine, this is Abby. Call me right away! It's important."

I saw Mrs. Clark go pale. Worry was contagious. The Grandfather clock in the foyer chimed.

"What time is it?" I asked in a voice strangled with worry.

"11:30," said the cook.

I forced down my panic. "Close enough to noon, don't you think?"

Cook heaved a great sigh and smiled with relief. "Yes, it is."

I pulled out my keys. "You call the chief. I'm going to find Lorraine." I took three steps and circled back. "I don't know where I'm going. What's MEBA?"

"MEBA is the maritime engineering school up the road. Take the road towards Easton, past the Oak Creek Bridge at Newcomb. MEBA will be up the road on your left. You can't miss it," she called after me as I headed out toward my car. "Look for the bow of the big black ship in the field. The entrance is just beyond it by the two white brick walls."

A black ship in the field? Yes, I heard her right, I thought, but I didn't stop for clarification. I'd probably know it when I saw it. I just hoped I'd know what to do when I got there.

Simon was hot on my heels as I ran to the car and jumped in as soon as I opened the door. There was no time to argue so I strapped him in. We roared down the drive leaving a whirling cloud of golden leaves in our wake. The tires squealed as the car leaned into a sharp left and raced toward the bridge and MEBA. Getting stopped for speeding would be a good thing.

I watched the road, but I could still see the photo of Lorraine and Reg on that special occasion. Then, they were two people beaming happiness. Now, their faces had become masks: one hiding sadness, the other hiding guilt. The awful proof was dangling from her ears, the earrings that Mr. Shaw had declared vandalized for its fine stones.

After we flew over the Oak Creek Bridge, I kept glancing to the left. I didn't want to miss the entrance to MEBA and have to backtrack. My palms were sweating on the leather steering wheel. I tried to rub them dry on my jeans, first one and then the other.

"Come on, come on, where is it?" I mumbled. Simon raised his head, sniffed the air, but stayed quiet. Did he sense that this was no time to play? We passed field after field once filled with green crops, now brittle with the coming cold.

There was no black ship anywhere. Could it be hidden by dried cornstalks? I let up on the accelerator and sat up straighter trying to see. Nothing.

A line of pine trees bordered yet another field and there! Just on the other side was the black bow of a real ship as if it had run aground.

I stabbed the brakes. Just beyond, a narrow roadway marked the entrance.

I made the turn.

CHAPTER THIRTY-FOUR

Use special care when polishing a large tray with feet. The pressure one applies during the polishing process may bend the flat tray area or worse, twist the feet. Stress can damage the tray out of proportion, ruining its original lines. It is nigh on impossible to return a tray so stressed to its original form. To prevent such an occurrence, build a pedestal out of cloths raising the tray's feet off the table during the polishing process to create a soft support to protect it.

—"The Butler's Guide to Fine Silver" Mr. Hollister, 1898

Dark red leaves covered the black asphalt and fluttered around the car as I drove along. I almost felt like I was cruising through a stream of blood. It made my skin crawl. I gave myself a shake.

No time for creepy feelings. I've got to find them.

A sign to the Memorial Garden pointed to left. It was a place to start. A black anchor stood like a sentry by the side of the road and tall ornamental grasses ringed the empty parking lot, empty except for two cars: a big black BMW with tinted windows, Reg's new car, and a white SUV. I pulled into a marked space, shifted into park and turned off the engine. After I pulled the key, I gripped the steering wheel to keep my hands from shaking.

Reg. How could you?

I just knew he hadn't planned to hurt Evelyn. The police chief had it right: She was in the wrong place at the wrong time. She must have caught him with his hand in the cookie jar, the safe where the diamonds were kept. It was a moment of passion, of anger. That would explain his deterioration in the past week. Unkempt, moody.

But now, was he a threat to Lorraine? They were here, someplace close. I hoped the chief was on his way, but the tingling along my skin warned that I couldn't wait, couldn't sit in my car hoping he wouldn't hurt Lorraine. If I moved, I might keep something horrible from happening.

But first, I had to get out of the car.

A breeze kicked up and sent my curls swirling into my face. I opened the barrette and, using the palms of my hands, pulled my hair back and tight in the clamp again. This was no time to be blinded by my curls.

In a soft but intense voice, I said, "Simon, I want you to stay here."

His ears wilted and he whined a little. "No, you must be very quiet. Be a good boy. Stay."

I said it just the way Lorraine did when he behaved for her. I hoped he would be good. His barking always irritated Reg. Right now, he had to stay calm.

Go, GO! The voice in my head screamed. I took a deep breath, opened the car door and closed it gently until it clicked. As my heart thumped in my chest, I jogged toward a path leading up to a thin line of trees. Towering high above the path was a huge brass daisy standing on its petal tips, modern art in the extreme. A goose cried out to his flock. I too wanted to call for help, hoping to hear a police siren.

Nervous, random thoughts shot through my brain. Glancing at a memorial plaque by the path, I read, *"Give us the goods, and we'll deliver."* I'd given Reg friendship. Lorraine had given him love and support. What had he delivered? Nothing. He took from everyone and when he was done, he cast them aside: his staff, his friends, me.

Would he throw away his family?

As I climbed a small hill, I heard voices from the other side of the trees. A little leap got me over a ditch filled with weeds and water. I avoided the black gravel path and stepped on the grass to muffle my footsteps. A gust of wind and a shower of crackling, crumbling leaves swirled around me. Their fragments floated to the ground.

Up ahead, voices were loud and filled with anger. I crept up to a tree trunk and peeked around it. Up ahead, as the walk topped the hill, I saw them sitting on a park bench.

"Stop avoiding my question." Lorraine's voice was hard. "I want the truth, Reggie. Did you kill Evelyn?"

He sighed, defeated. "It was self-defense, okay?"

"Self-defense? You're a big, tall man. She was only 5-4. How was she going to hurt you?" Her voice was strident in her fury.

"I just wanted what was mine. But no, she was going to tell you what I was doing and ruin my life in the process. I couldn't let her do that," Reggie whined, appealing for understanding. "She wouldn't listen to reason. I had to stop her. I grabbed the first thing I saw, that silver thing on the counter. I only meant to scare her. I didn't mean to hit her with it. She made me so mad. It was an accident."

"Oh, Reggie," Lorraine moaned. She covered her face with her hands. "What a waste."

Reg sighed with relief. "Thank goodness you understand. I couldn't let her hurt me. I'm young, I'm smart. There's so much I can do. I..." His words trailed off when she slowly raised her head. Her face was etched with grief and anger.

"No, Reggie, you ruined your life all by yourself and wasted the life of a good woman in the process. To do that to your own mother."

"What?" Reg stared at Lorraine with his mouth hanging open, then shook his head violently in disbelief. "No, you're lying. You're trying to disinherit me because of what I did. It was self-defense." His voice took on a sharp edge like steel. "Nice try, but you can't change the fact that my mother was your own sister. You can't deny I'm your nephew."

A black crow cawed in the silence.

Lorraine turned and faced him. "You are Evelyn's son."

He erupted. "It's a lie. You want to keep all that money for yourself. You never loved me. You… you…" His mouth worked but words failed him.

Ignoring his accusations, she said, "If anyone would know, it would be me."

"It can't be. A servant!" he screamed. "MY mother, a SERVANT!" He jumped up and marched around in jerky steps yelling, "No, NO!"

Lorraine looked at him and scoffed. "It seems that you are everything she feared you'd be… just like her husband, your father."

"W-w-who?" he stammered.

"Your father—a liar, a drug-runner and a thief who beat up a good woman and raped her. You are the product of that act."

"No, no." He ran his fingers through his stringy hair. Tightening down on his emotions, he spoke each work carefully. "I know what you're doing, but you can't. You can't take away what is mine." His index finger stabbed toward Lorraine with each word. "I'm your nephew. I know it. You know it. That's all there is to it."

Slowly, I hung my head as two people, once part of a loving family, tore each other apart.

"Everything I've said is true." She paused, allowing her words to penetrate his tortured mind.

Slowly, he sank down to the bench and put his elbows on his knees, his hands cradling his head and let the words wash over him.

"Evelyn was married to your father. He raped her in a drunken rage. She was pregnant with you when he was murdered by some drug runners. Your grandmother came up from Virginia demanding everything her son had. She hoped there was a child to take his place, to take care of her, wait on her every need like a slave. Evelyn needed to protect you. Momma brought her to Harraway Hall."

"Servants all have messy lives. It doesn't change a thing. I'm your sister's child," he insisted.

Lorraine sighed and closed her eyes. "My sister. Another woman who fell for the wrong man." She crossed her arms. "Here's the truth about my sister. She trusted a suave and sleazy man who was sniffing her money instead of her perfume. Against Daddy's wishes, they eloped and ran off to England. On a lark, they took a ferry to Ireland that was caught in a storm and sank. They drowned along with everyone else on board. When word came, Daddy was devastated. The last time he'd seen his youngest daughter, his baby, they'd had a terrible fight, said some awful things. He blamed himself for everything. Momma and I went over to England, hoping they'd find her body so we could bring her home."

"You did. I know. I've gone to my mother's grave in the family plot many times," he mumbled.

"You went to my sister's grave, yes. But not your mother's. We dug the grave for your mother a few days ago in the church cemetery."

"No, no..." He moaned.

"When we went to England, we took Evelyn with us to keep her safe from her mother-in-law. We were afraid she might show up any minute. We waited weeks and weeks for word from the authorities. Your mother went into early labor and you were born in London. We had a baby to fill our days and nights while we waited for news. It was a bittersweet time."

"See? Now, I know you're lying. You went to London and found that they'd left me with a nanny. You've told me the story for years."

"And I've been lying to you for years. Oh, the part about you being born in London was true, but the part about the identity of your real mother was a lie. It was Evelyn, not my sister." She took a tissue out of her pocket and wiped her eyes.

"We knew we had to keep your real identity a secret to protect you. Somehow, Momma got you a passport in the name of Lambert, my sister's married name. You lost your real identity when we boarded the ship to come home.

"I can still see Momma walking into Daddy's study with you all wrapped up in a blue blanket. He'd always wanted a son—now she was giving him one."

Reg's cheeks glistened with tears.

"You brought Daddy back to life that day." Tears clogged Lorraine's voice. "He only wanted the best for you. All he asked was for you to grow up to be a man he could be proud of, to know right from wrong and to help others, especially those less fortunate. But you couldn't even do that, Reg. You broke my heart when you refused to attend the funeral service for Evelyn. Then you showed up for coffee and cake."

"She was the housekeeper." Reg's voice was shrill. He got up and started pacing.

"She was part of our family. She helped raise you." Her voice shimmered with pain. "At the very least, you could have stood with me and been a comfort."

Reg looked up at the blue sky, took a deep breath then let it out in a slow sigh. "It's always about you, the wealthy, do-goodie Miss Lorraine. I'm Little Reggie, Errand Boy, the Obedient Nephew." He planted his fists on his hips and stood over Lorraine. "Well, dear auntie, things have changed. Now, I'm in charge. I'm taking what's mine. Don't look so shocked. If you're so smart, you should have known this would happen. It's all your fault. Everything I've done is because you wouldn't help me."

"What? I've helped —"

He cut Lorraine off. "Helped me?" He laughed. "Yeah, I guess you and Mom-Mom… whoa, wait a minute. Your momma really wasn't my grandmother. I've gotta get used to that little fact you've kept secret all these years." His words dripped with sarcasm. "Yeah, you and your mother helped me? Like when Granddaddy died suddenly? He was the one person who ever loved me. How do you think I felt when he dropped dead? Damn it, I was only eleven! But you helped me deal with his death, oh yes…"

He whipped around and got down in her face. "You helped by shipping me off to a boarding school in the hills of Pennsylvania. Did you really think it would help me to be among strangers? To live in a place where there wasn't a sailboat, not even a puddle of water for miles?"

"We couldn't handle you. You were wild after he died."

"Of course, I was. What did you expect? I'd lost the most important person in my life. Granddaddy taught me things I needed to know, said someday I would fill his shoes as head of the family."

She sat up with a jolt. "Is that why you kept walking around the house with his shoes on?"

"What do you think? He was gone so I put my feet in his shoes." He looked stricken. "But they were so big." He choked down the tears and grief and looked to the heavens.

When he dropped his face to look at Lorraine again, it was twisted into a sneer. "Do you remember what your momma did when she caught me with his shoes?"

Lorraine said quietly, "She yelled at you."

"That's right, she yelled at me. Said I was going to ruin them. What did it matter? They were mine, just like Granddaddy told me they would be." He started pacing again. "But noooooo, suddenly *she* was in charge and I couldn't have his shoes. They were mine, MINE!"

His voice dropped almost to a whisper. "Remember the day the shoes disappeared?"

Lorraine nodded slowly.

"That's right," he snarled. "I went wild. She'd given away MY shoes."

"That was the day we decided that we couldn't do anything with you. I had no idea. We thought you were a brat. We moved up the timetable and sent you to the boarding school Daddy had picked out for you."

"No," he snapped. "He never said anything about sending me away. That was your idea."

The hurt rolled over the grass in waves to my hiding place behind the tree trunk, tears welling up in my eyes. The truth didn't excuse what he'd done, but the hurt, the hurt was so raw.

Lorraine's shoulders sagged. "Reggie, I'm telling you the truth, I've always told you the truth."

"Except for that little bitty lie about the true identity of my mother. I guess I'm supposed to overlook that."

The sigh came from the bottom of her toes. "Reggie, I've loved you like a son and only wanted the best for you."

"Really?" He sat down on the bench next to Lorraine and put his arm around the back of the seat.

The gesture was threatening, not warm.

"Is that why you didn't give me a substantial block of your money to manage when I was working as an investment broker in New York? The people at the firm expected me to set up an account for you, more than the measly fifty thousand dollars you gave me."

"Reggie, for heaven's sake. You'd just started in business. You had a lot to learn. I expected some losses, of course, but I wanted to limit them."

"It was my money, too," he snapped.

"Yes, and your share is still safe and intact."

He bounced up from the bench. "Don't act so smart like you know everything."

She looked at him and shook her head. "To think that on the day of the funeral I was going to transfer control of half of everything to you. That amount, plus everything your real mother put aside for you would give you the independence you crave. Thank goodness I didn't. You'll have your mother's inheritance, of course, but I can still do something about what's mine." Lorraine moved to get up from the bench.

Reg stood in front of her with his feet spread apart, crowding her. "Oh no, you don't. You're not going to change a thing."

"Oh yes, I am. Now, get out of my way." She tried to get up again but Reg didn't move.

"I'm afraid I can't let you do that. If you take away what is mine, who would be the thief? It's nothing personal." He chuckled and shook his head. "I just have to have to do what I have to do."

CHAPTER THIRTY-FIVE

How one handles silver is vitally important. Always pick up the piece at the edges and support it from underneath.

—"The Butler's Guide to Fine Silver" Mr. Hollister, 1898

"Reg, stop!" I couldn't stand it anymore, all the lying, the pain and now, the threat. I lurched out from my hiding place and sprinted up to the top of the hill. He whipped around and looked at me in disbelief.

"Step away from her, you lying thief." My demand slapped the surprise off his face.

"What the hell are you doing here?" Spittle flew from his lips.

"Trying to keep you from doing something really stupid," I fired back.

"I have no idea what you're talking about." he said airily, looking around the gardens at the fountain, the plants and the geese flying toward the river.

But he didn't move from in front of Lorraine to let her stand up. I dug my fingernails into my hand to control of my temper.

"I know about the diamonds, Reg." He ignored me.

"Diamonds?" asked Lorraine. She looked at me, then the man she'd raised as her nephew, then back at me for answers.

"Your diamonds. The diamonds from your diamond jewelry that you wore in the pictures framed in your library." I walked closer. "He's been taking them out of the safe, removing the stones a few at a time, having copies made and putting the fakes back in the settings."

"Is that why there were loose stones on the floor everywhere?" Lorraine asked. "Were they fakes?"

"Yes, they were." I turned to Reg. "And you knew it, didn't you?"

He waved his hand in the air, dismissing my question.

Retaliating, I shaped each word with acid. "Shall I tell her how you've used her… used me and everyone else in your life?"

I didn't wait for his permission. "I believed in you until I saw the pictures of Lorraine wearing all those fabulous diamonds. You couldn't stand letting all those thousands of dollars sit in a safe doing nothing. You couldn't stop with a pendant or a few stones from an earring. No, not when you could get your hands on a treasure trove of diamonds and you meant to have every one of them. But you couldn't take the chance of getting caught so you swapped the fakes for the real stones."

Reg looked me over from head to toe and back again. "Well, give the bitch a prize. I told you to mind your own business. I told you, you don't belong here."

"You stole those diamonds." I shot back.

The look on Lorraine's face was stone cold. She turned toward me and said, "Maybe I loaned them to him."

I stopped breathing as if hit by gallons of ice water. What? Did I get it wrong? Had she really given him the diamonds? Was she in on the switch? Was she closing ranks to protect him? How far would she go?

I summoned up the courage and demanded, "What about Miss Evie?"

Lorraine straightened the sweater she was wearing. "Evelyn."

She spoke the word as if I didn't deserve to use her nickname. "It seems she might have been in the wrong place at the wrong time."

Reg smiled at Lorraine and turned back on me with a sick, know-it-all grin.

"You see, you nosey bitch, you can't go against family. Blood is thicker than anything. We stick together."

What Lorraine said didn't ring true to me.

I pressed again. "But she just told you. You're not related. You're Miss Evelyn's son."

"Abby, I think it's time for you to go," Lorraine said in a tone that clearly said she expected to be obeyed.

"That's not a good idea." Reg said. Anger rolled off his body like ripples in a calm lake smacked by a boulder.

"No!" Lorraine blurted out as she jumped up in his face. "Let her go."

I'm such an idiot! She's trying to save me.

I started to walk backwards, back down the path.

Reg would have none of it. "On second thought, there's no reason to send her away. She's a friend and she should come and sit on this bench. Look what it says there." He pointed to a brass nameplate screwed onto the back and read it aloud. "It says, 'Doug E. Birt's Bench, Instructor & Loyal Friend.'"

He patted the weathered wooden slats of the bench. "Tell me, Abby, are you a loyal friend?"

He looked at the surrounding garden and smiled a little. "This is a memorial garden, about death and remembering. Or remembering and death." The way he flipped the phrase around made me very afraid.

He opened his arms and held them out to his sides. "Abby, Abby, we were so close once. We were friends, Abby, real friends." He took a step toward me as if he wanted to fold his arms around me in a caring hug.

I wanted to step away, but I couldn't seem to move. He cast a spell over me as he switched from a brute to my old, dear friend.

He took another step toward me. "Remember how I always

said that you were the company and the company was you? You've always been at the heart of everything I've done." He let his arms drop and shrugged his shoulders. "That's why when I came to your place, I…"

He snapped me out of the trance. "You broke into my house," I snarled. I was rising to his bait. *Stop playing his game,* I told myself.

"I didn't want to, but you made me." His meek voice transferred the fault to my shoulders.

Reg looked around again, enjoying the garden, the expansive blue sky, the gently swaying pine trees. Then, his voice and his words tore the park's serenity to shreds.

"*My dear aunt* made me into an animal from the very beginning. It had to be the best restaurants in Georgetown or Great Falls, center orchestra seats at the Kennedy Center." He twisted around and thrust his finger in my face. "And you were just like her, always wanting special birthday presents and to be fed all the time. If I wasn't taking you to a swanky restaurant, I was paying for pizza and Thai food late at night at the office."

"I never—" I sputtered, but he wouldn't let me interrupt.

"I was the good guy from the very beginning, listening to your endless complaints about an old boss or some client." He slapped the palm of his hand against his forehead. "You went on and on, until I finally got it. You wanted your own shot, a startup of your own. It was an amusing idea so I went along. The only thing is I needed money to keep you happy. And I needed more and more each month. You thought you could pull it off as an entrepreneur."

Reg took a step toward me and jabbed his index finger in my face.

"Well, you couldn't. You were failing miserably and pulling me down with you. I know why you resent Angela so much." He tilted his head to the side and took a few steps away from me. "Poor girl, she doesn't deserve the Wrath of Abby."

He spun around in a flash. "You resented her from the first

moment she walked into the office, because you knew why she was there."

"Reg, please tell us why." I was getting lost in his fairy tale and needed a moment to clear my mind.

"I brought her in to help me save the sinking ship so maybe – just maybe – I could recoup some of my money and get rid of you. The only thing is I waited too long. Then you left me no choice. I was desperate and took things that belonged to my family."

I was shocked into silence by his skewed impression of our friendship and the business. My hesitation was all he needed. He stood and took a threatening step toward me making the gravel walk growl.

"It was you. YOU!" His accusing finger stabbed the air between us like a scorpion's tail. "Everything I've done was to make you happy and when it wasn't enough, I had to stop you before you stirred up any more trouble, before you ruined me." He started to pace, as if his emotions wouldn't let him be still. "I was taking care of things, trying to make things right. Then you started poking around."

He came up and put his face close to mine. It was twisted as if he had gotten a whiff of three-day-old fish. "You're pathetic. I fired you to get away from you, but no, you had to keep sticking your nose where it doesn't belong."

Maybe if I talked to him logically, he'd at least stop this tirade of make-believe.

Quietly, I began, "Reg, I—"

"Reg, I—." He repeated my words reeking with sarcasm. "Reg, I—." He walked, jamming each step into the loose gravel, the crunch adding venom to each word. "It's always about you, isn't it? You've never stopped to think how your actions might affect, might hurt others. Case in point, I bet you thought I'd put every dime I had into the business." His eyes narrowed then he burst out laughing. "Do you think I'd bet my future on the likes of you and your pathetic work? Did you expect me to stop living my high quality of life?"

"Like the new car over there? The condo?"

"How insightful you are."

I shot back. "When you weren't making money by working for it so you started stealing from your own family?" The emotion in my voice made the question come out like a croak.

"Ha! I didn't steal from anybody. I just took what was mine. I'm Lorraine's heir."

He faced her while he said with a snarl, "And that's not ever going to change. It's all going to be mine—the land, the diamonds, the investments, everything. Why should I wait until you keel over? I needed the money now so I took it. You wouldn't have missed those things anyway. You're old and decrepit. You don't even dress up anymore. Those diamonds were wasting away in that old safe, not doing anyone any good. So, I put them to work. After all, I just took what was mine."

Beyond the trees came the distant sounds of Simon's yips from the car. My head snapped around at the sound.

"What is that noise?" demanded Reg.

"That's Simon, the black lab puppy that used to belong to Gwen. You remember Gwen, don't you?" I asked.

"Of course, another meddling female," he said.

I had to ask. "Is that why she left, Reg, because she meddled?"

"Of course, all the females in my life get in my way. That little airhead sashayed into my office one day. The door was closed! No thought, no respect. She saw me taking stones out of a setting." He shrugged his shoulders in a dramatic way. "Well, I couldn't exactly explain what jewelry repair had to do with software, could I? So, I took her out for coffee and fired her before she could order a latté."

"You must have threatened her, too. She was so upset when she brought Simon to me." I was playing up the fact that I knew more than he did. Maybe he'd get frustrated and walk away the way he had at other times.

"Well," he shrugged again. "A guy has to do what a guy has to do. Just like now. I have to take care of myself."

He swung around on Lorraine. His stare drilled into her face. "Because nobody else will."

Simon's barking became more insistent.

"What wrong with that pest?" demanded Reg.

"He's probably tired of waiting in the car," I said.

Was he trying to warn me again? Could a puppy, belted into a car yards away, sense danger?

Lorraine started to walk around. "Where do you think you're going?" Reg roared.

"Nowhere. I have to move around. Sitting on that bench is hard on this old body," she said drily.

"Sit! You're not going anywhere. I'll get to you when I'm done with Abby."

"Reg, I think—" Lorraine started to say.

"Oh, shut up! You always talk too much." Reg sat down and draped his arm over the back of the bench, a king surveying his realm. "I just have to make Abby understand that she's not as smart as she thinks she is." His arm flew out toward me. "*You* are on unemployment, begging for a job. *I* have the software. When I sell it to the highest bidder, *I* will keep the money. And *I* have the diamonds." A broad smile filled his face and a chuckle gurgled in his throat.

Lorraine made her small hands into fists. "You think this is funny?"

"Amusing, yes," said Reg.

She frowned. "So, explain something to me, Reg. If you wanted diamonds, why didn't you take the loose stones kept in little envelopes in the back of the safe instead of going to all that trouble to substitute them? It would have been much easier and cheaper for you."

His smile faded. "Loose stones? Where?"

Now, Lorraine was the one who smiled. "I keep them in a special place where they've always been. Don't you remember?"

"Remember what?" he demanded.

"The secret latch to open the hidden compartment at the back of the safe."

His face took on a faraway look. "You showed it to me when I was little."

"That's right. I showed a secret compartment to a little boy, a boy I loved and trusted. That where I keep my most precious things like the Harrison Necklace given to me on the day of my wedding. That's where I put the silver cross your mother always wore."

"Don't call her that!" he snarled.

She was getting to him and I suspected she would try to use that to get us out of danger.

"Evelyn always wore a silver cross around her neck. She called it her second most precious possession. My mother gave it to her when you were born."

Reg didn't respond.

She went on with the story. "The police took it as evidence, but the chief returned it to me in one of the little packages the night we had dinner at the hotel. I was going to bury it with her but changed my mind at the last minute. I thought you'd like to have something special of your mother's to keep."

Reg curled his lip in disgust and turned away.

In the distance, Simon was barking furiously.

"Shut that mutt up. He's getting on my nerves just like you," Reg added.

I turned to go to the car.

"Where do you think you're going?" he demanded.

"To the car to take care of the dog… like you said." I tried to sound submissive.

"No. Just tell him to be quiet."

"But I…"

"NO!" He screamed. "You're not going anywhere."

That statement scared me. Reg was a thief and a murderer and he wasn't letting us out of his sight. I had to do something, but what? For now, I played along.

I turned toward the car and yelled, "Simon, it's okay. That's a good boy. Be quiet!"

I was surprised when the barking stopped. "There, I guess he's learning..." My words froze in my throat when I turned and saw the hatred on Reg's face.

"You two have been conspiring against me and now I'm going to do something about that. I'm going to teach you a lesson."

Reg reached into his pocket, pulled out a gun and pointed at my chest.

CHAPTER THIRTY-SIX

Silver is sensitive to light. Its shine and surface will disintegrate under intense, prolonged exposure.

—"The Butler's Guide to Fine Silver" Mr. Hollister, 1898

"Reggie, NO!" Lorraine screamed.

He whirled toward her.

"Put that thing down," she insisted. "Someone could get…" The words died in her throat.

"Ah," he said. "Now, that might be the idea, don't you think?"

Quickly, I spoke up and he turned toward me again. "Reg, it doesn't have to be like this."

Lorraine overcame her shock. "Where did you get that thing?" She pointed toward the shiny silver barrel of what looked like a six-shooter.

"From you… where I get everything else. In the beginning, when I was desperate for money, I went through your desk looking for cash. You know how you always keep a wad for an emergency? That's when I found the keys to the safe. The whole scheme fell into place. You really should have been more careful. I saw Granddaddy's gun so I took it, too. After all, I couldn't walk around with thousands of dollars in diamonds in my pocket without a little protection." He waved the gun between the two of us. "You never know when you might need a little muscle."

"Put it down," Lorraine pleaded. "You know nothing about guns. Put it down before you hurt yourself."

"No, dear auntie." His words dripped with spite. "This gun is going to protect me."

I saw the end of the barrel sag a little as if the weapon was too heavy to hold. I took a slow step backwards while he focused on Lorraine.

If I can get to the car and my phone…

"All you needed were keys to get your hands on the diamonds?" I asked.

Reggie laughed aloud. "Oh, sometimes things come together." He looked at Lorraine. "Remember when you challenged the tax assessment on the farms and asked me to help you?" I was in and out of the safe all the time, checking the records… and helping myself. You thought I was such a thoughtful nephew."

He kept focusing on Lorraine. If I could keep him talking while I backed off the gravel, I could move without making that awful crunching noise. Thank goodness, there was a lot of soft grass around. I took another step.

"How did you arrange to get the fake stones to replace the real ones?"

"Oh, that part worked out very well. Lady Windsor Jewels has a reputation for pretentious jewelry that can fool any Washington snob. I told them that I was making a copy of some heirloom jewelry for a client."

"Clever." I continued to move backwards, away from Reg.

"Oh yes, it was. They were falling all over themselves to help. I guess they figured that where there was one rich client, there might be more."

I took another step. I didn't dare look to see where I was going. It was enough to know it was away from him and toward the trees.

"I wove quite a story for them." Reg pitched his voice to sound like a melodramatic actor on a soap opera. "My dear client is scared to wear the family jewels, afraid someone will steal them. I want to make copies so she can wear them with confidence that she'll be safe. If she's held up, she can let the robbers have the fakes.' They sold me synthetic stones and I replaced the real ones in the settings."

Did he just giggle?

Another step.

"I even have my own jeweler's loupe, tweezers and prong tool to do the work myself."

I agreed. "Of course. You are always..."

"Shut up! Everything was going fine until people started butting in. Now, everything's a mess," he moaned.

While he was complaining, I tried to steal a look behind me.

Reg perked up. "What are you looking at?"

I whipped my head back around. "Nothing, I just wanted to see if Simon was alright. He's awfully quiet."

"Good, maybe he's not such a dumb mutt after all, not like you pesky women, always getting in my way."

Lorraine asked in a small voice. "Is that what happened that night? Did Evelyn butt into what you were doing?"

Reg leaned his head back to look at the wispy clouds in the sky and sighed. "I guess there's no harm in telling you the whole story. It's not like you're going to tell anyone." He chortled. "I came down to the Shore that night to swap out some more stones like I'd done many times before. When I got there, some man was in the library, threatening the woman. Would she back down? Oh no, she had to get all up in his face. I should have backed out to return another night, but, when I looked in to see what was going on and saw the safe was open..." He shook his head. "I knew I had to get in the middle of it. I threw the idiot out of the house and went to get a sandwich. She came in the kitchen wanting to talk.

"I didn't have time for that so I told her I needed some papers, said good-night and went in the library. Did she mind her own business? Oh, no. She came in the library asking if I wanted some brownies and caught me with some diamonds on the desk. I told her to go back to the kitchen where she belonged. She said she was going to take a batch of brownies out of the oven – to give me time to put things back the way they should be. She said if things weren't right by the time she came back, she would march upstairs and tell you what she'd caught me doing. I couldn't let her do that, spoil my clever little game. I followed her to the kitchen to reason with her. She wouldn't listen. I had to stop her."

I cleared my throat and tried to sound contrite. "I guess you're right, Reg. We didn't realize how difficult things were for you. I'm sorry." The words almost strangled me. "Maybe Lorraine is right. Why don't you put that gun away and we can work something out together?"

Reg looked almost surprised to see a gun in his hand. He lowered it a little. "I'm so confused. Everything's happening so fast."

"Take a deep breath. You'll be okay. We can work this out," Lorraine said. She kept talking as she saw me moving away.

I was a few feet away from the big brass daisy I'd seen on my way in. A little sign identified it as a propeller of a ship. The irony almost made me laugh. Nothing was as it seemed.

"Reggie, you certainly picked a beautiful spot to talk and on such a nice day," Lorraine said to distract him.

He lowered the gun. He seemed to forget about me. If I could get those big brass propeller blades between me and that gun, maybe we'd have a chance.

"Abby, where are you going?" He asked, more curious than threatening.

I hoped I could stay upright my knees were shaking so badly. "I've never seen a ship's propeller up close."

I continued to stroll over to the blades. "I thought it was a sculpture of a daisy when I drove in." I tried to laugh lightly. "See? I'm not perfect. Everybody makes mistakes."

Each word took me closer to the propeller and safety. "Admitting you're wrong can be the first step to making things right. I bet Lorraine..." I knew I'd made a terrible mistake as soon as her name slipped out.

"Lorraine!" He spat out her name like it was a bad oyster and whirled around waving the gun at her. "You'd never let it be alright. You always have to control everything, keep everything in your tight little grip. Even me. Imagine me, the son of an old servant! If that nosy biddy had gone to bed that night..."

I froze.

"She had no right to question me, challenge me. I had to stop her. What happened was her own fault. She gave me no choice. Your cake server did the job, Abby, but it really made a mess." His face scrunched up as if he smelled something awful.

Simon started barking wildly, waking me from the trance Reggie's confession created. He'd killed her... in cold blood. It was one thing to think about it, another to hear him admit it. Now, he was pointing a gun at us!

I ran.

Time slowed down, every moment distinct. My legs moved as if through water. I ducked behind one blade of the propeller, then another, closer to the path and the car.

"Hey. HEY!" Reg yelled. "Where are you going?' He raised the gun and waved it around in crazy circles. "Come back here. Why is that dog barking?"

Reg was yelling. Simon was making a racket. Had the chief come at last?

I hugged the brass blade and shivered... from its coolness and from fear. I had to move. If I could get across the little space of open grass to the trees and high weeds, I'd have a clear run.

"Hey, where did you go?" Reg yelled. I heard the sound of gravel. "Abby?"

Lorraine chimed in. "Reggie! Come back here, Reggie. Please."

His voice was getting louder. He was getting closer. The pounding of my heart filled my ears.

"Where did she go?" It sounded like he'd turned toward Lorraine.

I sprinted, trying to keep the blade between Reg and me.

"Hey! Stop!" He yelled.

SCH-WINGGG! A bullet hit the brass behind me and flew off somewhere. I flinched, losing the sense of which way to go.

SCH-WINGGG! The propeller rang like fine crystal.

By instinct, I turned away from the sound of the bullet and saw the line of trees ahead. The line was safety, the finish line in the race for my life.

I took off.

Gulping for air, I got to the trees and kept running toward the car. That's when my foot hit wet ground and stuck like glue in the muck. I toppled over into a ditch. My face sank into the mud up to my nostrils. I didn't dare move.

But I listened, hard. The only sound was the wind causing the fall leaves to flutter down on my body. Where was Reg? Was Lorraine safe? Why was Simon so quiet?

Then, the world erupted.

Simon barked wildly, but the noise wasn't coming from my car. It was coming from the propeller.

Simon! NO!

"Get away from me, you mutt!" Reg screamed.

BAM!

"Get away!"

BAM!

Then silence.

I held my breath.

No! NO! The words roared in my mind. *SIMON! He didn't hurt Simon, he didn't hurt Simon,* I kept repeating to myself. I squeezed my eyes shut against the sting of tears.

Simon.

I shouldn't have yelled when he ran around with my sock. Why was I so mad when piddled on the carpet? It was only that one time. *Oh, Simon.*

Suddenly, hot air blasted against my face. I opened my eyes and looked into two deep brown eyes. A pink tongue licked my face from chin to forehead, mud and all. I grabbed Simon and pulled him into a strong hug.

I ran my hands ran over his wiggly body. *Was he hurt?* No, he just wanted to tussle in the mud. I held him close. Reg hadn't hurt him.

Reg!

Lorraine?

I grabbed Simon and struggled to hold him quiet against me.

There was a crunching sound. Footsteps on the gravel path. Coming closer.

Snap! A stick broke. Someone was coming closer. Then he was standing over me.

Slowly, I turned my head. A man's black shoes with a mirror shine were a few feet away from my nose. My eyes climbed up the tan pant leg to the wide leather belt loaded with attachments.

Then, the giant squatted down to my level.

"Well, young lady. Seems like you found yourself a bunch of trouble."

I almost swooned. It was Chief Lucan.

"Chief," I panted. "Reg—"

"I know. It's over. He won't hurt you."

"Lorraine?" I asked, frightened of his answer.

"She's shaken up, but not hurt."

"Is he…"

"He's gone." The Chief shook his head. "Probably died instantly. Such a waste. She asked for a few minutes alone with…" His words trailed off as he held out his hand. "If you're ready to get out of the muck, maybe you can tell me what happened here."

As he pulled me up, Simon wandered over to a tree. Slowly, we walked toward the hill together while I tried to catch my breath. I watched as Lorraine walked to the body of her nephew lying on the grass.

No, not her nephew. Son of her closest friend.

I didn't know what to feel. A few moments ago, he'd been a human being, a friend turned monster, who threatened me, a puppy, even the woman who loved and helped raise him.

The chief stood next to me. "That's one brave dog you have there." I looked at Simon jumping and chasing a butterfly that stayed just out of his reach.

I shook my head trying to clear the confusion. "What happened?"

"When I got Cook's call, I tore over here as fast as I could and came in by the back road. I heard shots and then saw a black streak run up the path and jump up on Reg. The gun discharged and they both went down. I didn't know if he'd gotten the dog or what."

I staggered. He caught my arm and held me steady.

"Easy there, girl."

"I'm okay. Then what happened?

"Your dog wiggled clear of the body and ran off toward the ditch. That's how I found you."

I started to shake and weave again. Chief grabbed my shoulders.

"Steady, just sit down here on the grass. Gently." He guided me down. "Better?"

I nodded.

"What happened here wasn't your fault. It was a tragic accident." Chief held up Reg's gun in an evidence bag. "A classic Colt .38 revolver – too much gun for Mr. Reg to handle."

I recoiled from the weapon that threatened my life, my friend and my dog.

"It's okay, it's empty now." He lowered his hand and held the gun behind his leg, out of sight. "Reg picked the wrong gun. It's heavy for a beginner. When he saw the dog coming at him, he fired. The shots went wild or this situation would have had a very different ending. Simon had time to jump on him going full speed and knock him down." He shook his head sadly. "That's when the gun discharged one last time, killing Reg instantly."

Words started tumbling out of my mouth. "It was him. He killed her. He was going to—"

He patted my shoulder. "Don't you worry about that. It's over now." He leaned down and looked into my eyes. "It's over. That's all you have to think about."

He straightened up and looked off in the distance. "Besides, you have a bigger problem to deal with."

I sat up and followed him arm pointing toward the black ship prow. Simon, bored with the butterfly, was following a scent that headed away from us.

"Oh, no!" I staggered to my feet.

"That's a fine dog you have there. Guess that little guy wasn't going to let anyone hurt his momma." He chuckled.

"Oh, he's not little anymore. He's almost full grown."

The Chief's belly laugh echoed around the garden. "Not even close! He's got a whole lot more growing to do."

"He does? How much bigger?" I wasn't sure I wanted to hear the answer.

"Oh, if I had to guess, I'd say he'll top out between 90 and 100 pounds." The Chief raised eyebrows and tried not to laugh when my jaw dropped.

As if he knew we were talking about him, Simon started running toward me at full speed.

"Here he comes!" I braced myself.

At the last moment, his feet left the ground and his muddy paws went on me. Down we went. Standing over me, he licked my face then sat and wagged his tail, ever the Good Dog.

"You know, he never liked Reg." I told the chief as I scratched behind his ears in his favorite place.

"Dogs know more about people than people," said the chief. "Next time, maybe you should listen to what Simon says." The

Chief ambled down the parking lot to meet the ambulance, chuckling. "Simon Says."

I walked Simon back to the car and found his harness in shreds on the seat. Thank goodness for sharp puppy teeth. I put the convertible top up then hugged him again with a promise of favorite treats every day for life.

CHAPTER THIRTY-SEVEN

The secret to beautiful silver is care. Nothing more.
—"The Butler's Guide to Fine Silver" Mr. Hollister, 1898

We picked the perfect Indian summer weekend for Simon and me to return to Fair Winds. The air had a distinct chill to it but nothing a thick cable-knit sweater couldn't handle. The last five weeks since the accident at MEBA had been a whirlwind of tasks, decisions and emotions. I don't know where Lorraine found the strength to face friends and acquaintances. She accepted their condolences for what they believed was a tragic accident. In a matter of days, her lifelong best friend Evelyn and the man she'd raised as her nephew had been swept away from her. Theft and murder, greed and passion had hammered her again and again. She'd stood over the casket that held Reg's body as it was lowered into the grave next to his mother's grave that was still covered only with bare earth. She'd stood tall until it was done and then walked away, refusing the steadying, comforting assistance of others, struggling behind a mask to make sense of it all.

Only the police chief needed to know the truth about the revelations made on that little hill by the ship's propeller. He closed the case of Evelyn's murder without releasing the details. Of course, Lorraine and I knew what Reg had done. Rather than making us strangers, that knowledge had created a bond between us. Somehow, our connection was giving us the courage to accept the truth, deal with our grief and navigate the legal and financial details of closing out a life. She asked me to help the attorneys figure out the muddle that was our defunct software company. She offered me the opportunity to resume the work that had meant so much to me, but too much had happened for me to go back. Reg's friends set up a scholarship program at the University of Maryland as a memorial. It was easy to clear away his personal possessions from his apartment because Lorraine didn't want anything.

Now, it was time for us to turn toward the future and get on with our lives. As with so many other things since that awful day, we wanted to do it together.

That day, Simon and I found Lorraine sitting in the sunshine on the lawn at Fair Winds overlooking the Miles River. I settled into one of the white wicker chairs destined for storage during the winter months. Simon took off like a streak with Lorraine's dogs, his new best friends.

"Simon is growing up," said Lorraine. "He can keep up with the girls finally."

We both laughed as Simon stumbled over his own paws and rolled across the lawn.

Lorraine leaned back and closed her eyes. "I'm glad you could come down for the weekend. That sun feels good, warms up these old bones."

I frowned. "Old? Please! I may be younger than you are, but when we go someplace, I have trouble keeping up. It's embarrassing."

"Embarrassing?" She laughed, something she hadn't done much lately. "You're just trying to make me feel better." She laughed again. "And it's working."

"Here you are." Cook's voice boomed over the lawn as she

paraded towards us carrying a heavy tray like a trophy. "They're fresh out of the oven." The aroma of baked biscuits reached my nose and I gave her a big smile. She put the golden-brown morsels down on the table. "And Staci is brewing fresh coffee." Cook turned on me with her hands on her hips. "This time, Miss Abby, there'll be no running off somewhere leaving my little darlin's all alone to get cold."

"Yes, ma'am," I said obediently as I floated a lighter-than-air biscuit toward my mouth.

With our taste buds in heaven, Lorraine turned to me. "Have you given any thought to my proposition?"

"Mmmm," I said, licking the crumbs off my fingers.

"We need to approach this in a very logical, business-like way." She started counting the points on her fingers. "One, you have your aunt's silver inventory. Two, you are building a client base using eBay. Three, you're being thorough in your research so your reputation as a knowledgeable dealer is growing. Four, there is another major silver client who wants to hire you."

I was surprised and flattered that she wanted to hire me to sort through her vast sterling silver collection that included her mother's and aunt's silver, the Harrison family silver from her paternal grandmother, her in-law's silver given on the day of their wedding as well as her own Chantilly pattern. She confessed she had silver in safety deposit boxes as well as the pieces in the Fair Winds silver closet. She suspected there might be boxes in the attic as well. It was time to prepare an accurate inventory and do the research to identify each piece and give it a proper valuation. She wanted any missing pieces purchased and duplicates offered to the Baltimore Museum of Art for its extensive exhibit of Maryland silver.

She was very clear. Her offer was not charity. She expected me to do the work and would pay to have it done right. To make it easier for me to have access to everything, the offer included a small cottage on the grounds where Simon and I could live.

I'd made my decision.

"Lorraine, I want to thank you for your kind offer. It was so nice of you to think of me."

She looked at me. The area around her eyes that had felt the sting of so many tears lately started to crinkle in concern and disappointment.

I smiled. "I'd be a fool not to accept. I love the idea of coming here to live and work."

She jumped up and I met her halfway. When we hugged, Simon appeared out of nowhere and launched himself at us. Staggering to stay on our feet, I started to discipline him, again, but Lorraine took over. I had to laugh when he sat primly at Lorraine's feet, madly wagging his tail.

"I'll take care of the silver. You train Simon."

"Deal!" Lorraine smiled.

And Simon barked in agreement.

In the sparkling sunlit water beyond the lawns of Fair Winds, a white boat with its sails unfurled glided down the river. And I smiled.

Read the first chapter of the next book in the
St. Michaels Silver Mysteries Series

BUT FIRST...

Please take a moment and put a review of
Tarnished Silver
on Amazon or Goodreads

Word of mouth is an author's best friend
and is much appreciated.
Thank you!

SACRED SILVER

It is the Butler's responsibility to see that the table is set correctly for a formal dinner. Always select and position the silverware in the order it shall be used. Place it from the outside inward toward the plate in the center. Thus, the organization is guaranteed and a peaceful atmosphere is assured. If a guest is unsure about which piece to use, the hostess will provide the lead.

—"The Butler's Guide to Fine Silver" Mr. Hollister, 1898

"Simon, are you ready?"

My black Labrador retriever puppy went down on his front legs and thrust his madly wagging tail high in the air. Quivering with anticipation, he waited until I opened the front door to launch himself outside into the crisp December morning air. This was our morning ritual now that we'd moved to this little cottage on the Fair Winds estate on the Eastern Shore of the Chesapeake Bay. A pale mist hung over the waters of the river where a lone goose floated among the autumn leaves. Like him, I'd landed in a good place after I'd lost my dream job at a software company, inherited a mountain of sterling silver pieces and been used for target practice, all in only a few months.

But I'd landed in a safe place with river views, rolling lawns and a big white main house with high columns. Like the goose, I felt good floating along in this beautiful place without having to worry about anybody else. So often, my caring about other people ended in hurt and grief. Sometimes it was just life, but too often, people inflicted injury and betrayal on me intentionally. My heart was bruised and my mind was tired. I needed to heal. The best medicine for me was some alone time with Simon in this peaceful place. And of course, there was Lorraine, my employer and friend who made this all happen.

Suddenly, the goose shattered the early morning quiet with a plaintive call for his flock. In response, my loveable bundle of black fur shot across the grass and down to the water's edge. Though still a puppy, Simon was growing into a big dog. His wild barking caused the goose to thrash the water into white foam and take off as his flock responded in the distance. Simon stood on the shoreline wagging his tail. I didn't know what he'd do if he ever caught a goose and I didn't want to find out.

"Simon, come on," I called. "We have to go to work."

He retrieved his bright orange ball from under a bush, dropped it at my feet and sat primly with his tail wagging so hard, his whole body rippled. I threw the ball as far as I could and walked slowly toward the main house. I was looking forward to some quiet time over the holidays in this beautiful place. I hoped to tackle the stack of mysteries piling up on my nightstand, take afternoon naps or sit by the fire and not think for a change. That leisure time would only happen if I caught up on my work of cataloguing and organizing Lorraine's sterling silver collections. I also had to deal with the extensive inventory I'd inherited from my Aunt Agnes, a part-time antique silver dealer. But first, we had to get through the activities of the Christmas in St. Michaels Festival.

The morning chill and the aroma of something fresh-out-of-the-oven nudged me along the path to the main kitchen. "Come on, Simon! I've got a lot to do and there are goodies inside."

When I opened the door, the sounds of a busy kitchen overpowered the morning's tranquility. A whirring mixer, a beeping oven timer and a chorus of voices signaled that Mrs. Clark, an older woman with an ample tummy wrapped in a brilliant white apron, was orchestrating the organized chaos of making pastries, cookies and cakes for tomorrow night's Kick-Off party for the volunteers.

Simon ran on ahead in search of Lorraine's three large Chesapeake retrievers while I moved down the hall on the sly. Maybe I could grab some coffee, a delicious goodie and sneak into my office without anyone noticing.

No such luck.

"Here at last!" Lorraine announced right behind me as she slipped on her coat. She was medium height, trim and full of energy for a woman in her late fifties. Her shoulder-length brown hair was expertly trimmed and the highlights shone as she moved. "I thought you and Simon were going to sleep all morning."

"No, we just stopped to enjoy the view."

Lorraine smiled. "I know. Though I've lived here a long time, I never get tired of it." She ducked back into the breakfast room. "But we've no time for that. The police chief called requesting… insisting that our presence is required at First Presbyterian Church of Saint Michaels right away."

"Not me," I pleaded. "I have so much work to do and—"

"Oh, he asked for you specifically."

"What have I done wrong?" I asked, assuming I'd offended a villager or broken some regulation.

She smiled. "Nothing, I imagine. He wants our help with some silver. It'll be good to get away from all the cooking and decorating for a little while."

"Did someone say decorating?" inquired a singsong voice from the hall. A short-like-a-pixie middle-aged woman with long dark hair pulled back on one side with a feather barrette appeared in the doorway. "Kat Designs, at your service." She sniffed. "Oh, do I smell fresh coffee?"

"That you do. Since you're here, pour yourself a mug," said the cook as she raised her eyes to heaven. "But try to stay out of our way, please."

Kat, the interior decorator, was a little trying. Perky, eager and a little, she could be exhausting. Overwhelmed by the thought of getting the house ready for the holidays, Lorraine brought her in to deal with the tree, holly, garlands, tinsel, glass balls... everything. Kat gave us a detailed running commentary about every little thing, every day. But I had to admit that she was turning the rooms into magical places.

"Oh, sugar cookies!" Kat squealed as she snagged one. "My grandmother, a real Western Pennsylvania mountain woman, made the best." Cook stiffened as she was closing an oven door, her round face flushed by the heat, but Kat recovered nicely. "Yours are the finest I've had around here, Mrs. Clark. Besides, I should be partial to my Granny's cooking, right?" Kat took a bite and moaned in delight. Slowly, a smile spread over Cook's face, making her cheeks round like small apples. Everyone relaxed, especially Lorraine. She couldn't afford to offend the cook right in the middle of the party preparations.

I tried again as Lorraine gathered up her keys, purse and gloves. "I really need to stay here and work," I declared.

She stopped and gave me The Lorraine Look: she lowered her chin and tightened the area around her brown eyes that threatened to shoot daggers at my heart. "You really have to come with me." Confident that she'd had made her point, her face resumed its natural, lovely expression. "Do you want coffee to take with you? This might take a while."

"I have it right here for you, Miss Abigail." Dawkins, the new house manager, silently appeared behind me, almost scaring me to death. Though he was an American, he'd probably have done well in an important English house about a hundred years ago. He towered over both of us. His posture was almost painfully erect, commanding attention in a very quiet way. Carefully combed into place, his dark brown hair didn't dare move. Everything about Dawkins was all business, except his blue-gray eyes. They were soft and suggested a good soul… if you could get past his prim and proper attitude and the way he moved around silently.

I turned to him slowly. "I wish you wouldn't sneak up on me like that and I've told you to call me Abby."

With a hint of a smile on his angular face, he handed me a travel mug and glided away.

I turned to Lorraine. "The way he pops up really creeps me out."

Lorraine put on a red felt hat and cocked it at a stylish angle. "It's the job of a good butler or house manager to anticipate. Dawkins does it very well." She bustled past me and held open the door to the garage. "Come on, let's go. The sooner we get there, the sooner we'll find out what's going on."

The drive through the center of St. Michaels was slow thanks to the crush of cars and tourists dashing across the street. Christmas shopping was in full swing. The church was on the other side of town just beyond the basketball park and fortunately had its own parking lot. Built in the old Gothic style with stone and stained glass windows, Lorraine said it had been part of the community for more than a hundred years. We hurried up the brick walk and entered the peaceful quiet of the sanctuary. Bright red and soft white poinsettias were everywhere. A stately Christmas tree waiting to be trimmed rose toward the massive oak beams high above. We rushed forward to the altar where the Chief stood with an old man, as thin as a reed with wispy gray hair. His intense attitude along with his black suit, shirt and brilliant white collar suggested that this was his church. His sharp voice cut the silence to ribbons. "At last!"

His outburst didn't faze Lorraine. "And good morning to you, Pastor," she said as she bypassed him and shook hands with police chief "Lucky" Lucan. "Chief, we came as fast as we could. What's happened?"

"What's happened?" whispered the Pastor. "What's happened? We've been robbed!" His strident pronouncement boomed in the silent church. Then, he raised his hand to his chest and breathed, "The Gordon Communion Chalice is gone!" With a flourish, he waved a large piece of paper in our faces. "And this is what the thief left in place of the chalice." Words and pictures covered the sheet.

"That looks more like a children's puzzle than a ransom note," Lorraine said. "Somebody's playing a game with you."

"A game?" The Pastor's pale face was turning the color of blood. "This is no game."

"No," I added. "It looks like a treasure hunt."

ACKNOWLEDGEMENTS

I must thank my favorite librarians Misses Shauna, Shirley, Betty and Mr. Ted for their patience, resources and laughs as they dealt with my endless questions and interlibrary loan requests.

Thanks to Maria Johnson and Annie Roe-Rever who introduced me to the beauty and lore of sterling silver and nurtured my interest over the years.

Yes, the Harbour Inn and Spa exists as does the restaurant Harbour Lights. It is a wonderful place to enjoy great hospitality and great food. Jerry Lewis, the restaurant manager, was brilliant to recommend Louis XIII (*pronounced Louie Treize)* as the *insanely expensive cognac* that Reg enjoyed. The insight of Executive Chef David in the world behind our fine dining experiences was so helpful and his dinner selections were delicious, as always.

Many thanks to former police chief Miguel Dennis, for his time and attention to detail as we sat and talked murder. Any mistakes in procedure are mine.

Writing buddies are so important in the development of a good story and maintenance of some level of the writer's sanity. Jennifer, you're always there when I need you, thank goodness. You give the words *friend* and *writing buddy* new meaning. Bruce, thank you for all the hours of valuable *porch time* and *cabinet time.* Our conversations opened exciting streams of creative thought. And Sarah, your quirky sense of humor and keen insight added so much to the creative process.

My life changed so much while writing this book. I'm so thankful for my friends – like Cindy, Peggy and Norma – who got me through the tough times and filled this journey with laughter and hope.

To my family -- Matt, Barry, Erin and little Zoe – your love and support mean the world to me. You, as well as the family in Chicago, brighten my life.

And to the one who should have been here to see this story published, the dedication is yours as is my love. You will live in my heart always.

To the people of the Eastern Shore, especially those who live in Saint Michaels, thank you for everything you do to make this place a little bit of heaven.

Susan Reiss
Saint Michaels, Maryland

May 2013

Thank you for taking the time to read *Tarnished Silver*. If you enjoyed it, please consider telling your friends or posting a short review on Amazon or the retailer of your choice. Word of mouth is an author's best friend and is much appreciated.

Thank you,
Susan Reiss

St. Michaels Silver Mystery Series

SECOND BOOK

Sterling silver expert Abby Strickland wants to spend the holidays curled up with her books and her puppy, Simon. When an antique chalice disappears from a local church with a puzzle of clues left in its place, she is drawn into a dangerous treasure hunt. Along the way, she learns about things that people do for love… and some they shouldn't.

Can she navigate the maze of secret desires in time to save the spirit of the season…and a life?

St. Michaels Silver Mystery Series

THIRD BOOK

Accidental sleuth Abby Strickland goes to
the Plein Air Art Festival
where gifted artists compete for big prizes and fame.
Elite art collectors eagerly search for their next acquisitions.

Tension between rivals runs high as all are drawn
into a net of creative envy, greed… and murder.

It's a charming summer event… until somebody screams!

St. Michaels Silver Mystery Series

FOURTH BOOK

The discovery of an engraved bowl draws sterling silver expert Abby Strickland into a world where nothing is what it seems… where majestic sailboats, unique to the Chesapeake Bay, are called log canoes… *Hammered* doesn't mean drunk…and close friends become fierce competitors in the race for the coveted Governor's Cup Trophy.

Does the story of a century-old murder stay in the past or lead to blood and chaos in the water right in front of Abby's eyes?

Was it an accident or was it murder?

St. Michaels Silver Mystery Series

FIFTH BOOK

The murder happens right in front of her eyes, yet Abby Strickland, silver expert and amateur sleuth, can't believe it! Was her dear friend Lorraine driven by jealousy to fire the shot or was someone lurking in the shadows?

A storm of suspicion and fraud upends her world of elegance as Mother Nature sends a deadly storm toward the Shore and Abby discovers she is surrounded by killers.

NEW!

ST. MICHAELS HISTORICAL FICTION SERIES

There was a time on the Chesapeake Bay when oysters flourished and men braved wind and weather to pull their living from her salty waters. When family meant a lifelong bond of loyalty and love. It was a time when a man could make his dream come true. That's what one man did as he worked between Baltimore Harbor and his homeport of St. Michaels. Then one night, that dream disappeared in a flash of jealousy, madness and blood. And the accused began a daring shell game fueled by resentment and defiance. A game of murder he played to win.

A story of St. Michaels. Bold. Audacious. And ***TRUE.***

Made in the USA
Columbia, SC
27 December 2021

52844113R10178